Ot ...s b, **Malcolm Archiba**

www.malcolmarchibald.com

b, ...s, Islands and Villages of the Forth
(Lang Syne Press, 1990)
Scottish Battles
(Chambers, 1990)
Scottish Myths and Legends
(Chambers, 1992)
Scottish Animal and Bird Folklore
(St Andrew Press, 1996)
Sixpence for the Wind: A Knot of Nautical Folklore
(Whittles, 1999)
Across the Pond: Chapters from the Atlantic
(Whittles, 2001)
Soldier of the Queen
(Fledgling Press, 2003)
Whalehunters, Dundee and the Arctic Whalers
(Mercat, 2004)
Dundee Book Prize 2005: *Whales for the Wizard*
(Polygon Press 2005)
Horseman of the Veldt
(Fledgling Press, 2005)
Selkirk of the Fethan
(Fledgling Press, 2005)
Aspects of the Boer War
(Fledgling Press, 2005)
Mother Law: a parchment for Dundee
(Fledgling Press, 2006)
Pryde's Rock
(Severn House, 2007)

i

Stea vels

Malcolm Archibald

Cover by Martha Pooley

Picture of Crown Jewels:
©Crown copyright reproduced courtesy of Historic
Scotland

ISBN-13 978-1-905916-21-4

Printed by JBPrintSolutions

Note: **With the exception of historically recognisable
people, all the main characters in this book are purely
imaginary. Any resemblance to real people, living or dead
is coincidental. Some places are real, others in the
imagination of the author. Any errors are those of the
author.**

Fledgling Press 2008

Powerstone:

Stealing the Scottish crown jewels

by

Malcolm Archibald

For Cathy

Contents

Prelude

'Johnnie Armstrong was one of the greatest warriors Scotland ever produced,' John Armstrong said earnestly. 'He kept the border between Scotland and England safe and he was so powerful that nobody ever crossed him. They say that he had fifty men ready to ride at any time, day or night.'

Irene Armstrong listened to her father through the hammer of the North Carolina rain on their trailer roof. She had heard this tale so many times that she knew it off by heart, but enjoyed the feeling of family closeness and the sense of belonging to a long line of ancestors.

'Then the King came to call. He was James Stuart, King James V of Scotland and he envied the power that Johnnie Armstrong had. One day he rode down from his capital at Edinburgh to the Borderland and called Johnnie to him.'

Irene nodded, clinging to every word as she imagined the scene. She thought of the knights in their splendid armour, the Scottish king with his prancing horses and men at arms, and Johnnie Armstrong, bold and brave, coming to see his king.

'Of course, Johnnie had no idea that James was jealous. He rode happily to see the king whose border he had guarded for so long. When King James saw him, so proud and confident and well dressed, he turned to his men and growled: "what wants yon knave that a king should have."'

John Armstrong bent over his daughter. 'That means that our ancestor was as brave and bold and handsome as any king.'

'Yes, father,' Irene said dutifully.

'And then King James ordered that Johnnie should be taken away and hanged.' John Armstrong always paused after that, and Irene always cuddled closer to him for mutual support.

'Johnnie was astonished. He assured the king that he was a loyal man and that he had never robbed in Scotland but kept the border safe from English raids.

"Hang him," said the king.

'Johnnie offered his services and his men. He even offered to ride deep into England and capture any Englishman, of any rank and bring him to King James as a sign of his loyalty.

"Hang him," said the king.

'Eventually, Johnnie realised that he must die, so he faced the king bravely and gave his last words.

"I have asked grace at a graceless face, but there is nane for my men and me" he said, and added that if he had known the king's intentions he would have lived free on the Border, for no king could have caught him unless by treachery.

John Armstrong held his daughter tight for a long minute. 'So you see, Irene, our family were rich once, but we were betrayed by a tyrant king.'

'I hate that King James!' Irene shouted, breaking free.

'I have no doubt you do,' John Armstrong told her seriously, 'but hatred does not pay the bills. You must go to school and work hard and get yourself a better life than I ever gave you. You must strive to be as bold and brave and strong as Johnnie Armstrong was. Now,' he looked closely at his daughter. 'Do you promise me that?'

Irene smiled into his tired, defeated eyes. 'I promise, daddy,' she said. 'But I still hate James Stuart.'

Chapter One : New York, October

'Here we go, then.'

Irene tried to ease her tension with a deep breath and glanced sideways at her competitor. She was glad that he appeared equally nervous, shuffling his feet as he winked at her. The waiting period was always the worst and Irene felt her gaze drawn to the largest of the three empty chairs on the opposite side of the table. Standing between its neighbours, the seat and arms were of green leather, while the headrest was elaborately carved with the logo of the Manning Corporation.

She allowed her eyes to drop, aware that the television cameras were running and might even now be concentrating on her face, searching for arrogance or weakness or any other emotion that would raise the viewer ratings. The lights burned above, prickling the top of Irene's head.

'Not long now,' she whispered.

Kendrick nodded. 'Good luck.'

Irene took the hand that he offered. It was large and soft, with surprising strength. 'You too.'

A cameraman murmured in the background and somebody softly laughed. There was a hum of machinery and a faint cough from the invisible audience behind the screen. Paper rustled irritatingly. Both contestants stiffened as footsteps sounded to their left, but nobody appeared and they tried to relax, false smiles forcing away their nerves.

The table curved gently away from them, with the three empty chairs on the concave side seeming to symbolise an inner circle of acceptance. If she was successful tonight, Irene told herself, she would be a member of that inner circle. Drawing strength from the thought, she smoothed a hand over the highly polished mahogany. 'This is Ms Manning's own property,' she said, 'brought in especially for the show.'

Kendrick nodded. 'It once belonged to John Witherspoon,' he said softly. 'He is meant to have drafted the Declaration of Independence on it. Imagine that. The Declaration could have sat on this very piece of wood.' He was silent for a minute, and then grinned across to her. 'I wonder if we will ever meet again.'

'I hope so,' Irene said softly. 'You'd be a good employee.' She smiled toward him, allowing her eyes to crinkle.

Kendrick's bass chuckle was nearly as familiar as his grin. 'So would you,' he parried easily, 'as long as you remain under control.'

'Do you think Ms Manning is keeping us here to increase the tension?' Irene glanced at her watch. The minute hand seemed to have been hovering between eleven and twelve for at least a half hour.

'Undoubtedly. Watching us suffer makes for good viewing.'

Spotlights flared blindingly as a drum began to beat a staccato rhythm. Irene stiffened into attention. 'Here we go,' she whispered again as a door opened and three people walked in. Irene and Kendrick immediately stood as a gesture of respect. The men on the left and right exuded power and responsibility with their immaculate Giorgio Armani suits and their bulging leather briefcases, but they were inconsequential compared to the woman that walked between them.

The top of Rhondda Manning's head barely reached the shoulder of either man, but there was no doubting who was in charge. Every step she took snapped the grey skirt against her legs, while her simple jacket clung to a gym-trim figure. Even although Irene had studied every possible detail of Rhondda

Manning's life, she still found it difficult to believe that this small woman, who dressed with such simple style and spoke so quietly, could have built up one of the largest corporate empires in the world.

When the elder of the men pulled back the central seat, Ms Manning sat with a single fluid movement. She smiled across to both candidates as music sounded softly in the background and a camera rolled into position. Completely unscented by perfume, she looked across at Irene; her eyes grey and direct and startlingly clear.

Irene swallowed the sudden nervous lump that had risen in her throat. She could feel the heat generated by Kendrick's body, but was unable to detach her eyes from those of Ms Manning.

'Welcome to the last episode of *The Neophyte*,' Ms Manning said. Despite her wealth and success, her accent still contained the slow syllables of the Mid West. 'Within the next thirty minutes, you will both be walking out of this show for the last time. Thirty minutes to decide your destiny. Thirty minutes.' She allowed the words to hang as a promise and a threat as she looked at each in turn. Irene kept her expression neutral as she felt those grey eyes probing inside her.

Ms Manning continued, speaking slowly. 'By that time I will have made my decision. I will have chosen one of you to be groomed as my successor, and the other will be on the streets.'

Irene contained the nervous shudder. Her memory still held the words 'on the streets, on the streets,' that the audience was encouraged to chant every time one of the candidates was rejected. Then would followed the Walk of Pain, when the loser had to discard their Manning Corporation green jacket and pass through the audience as they left the studio. Nobody was permitted to leave by the back door, for the millions of television viewers loved to view the loser's anguish.

After enduring so much to reach the final, Irene could not bear the thought of undergoing that ritual humiliation. She must win.

'First we will review your progress,' the younger of the two men said. Laying his brief case on the table, he clicked it open and slid out a thick file of notes. 'Kendrick Dontell,' he smoothed out the syllables. 'You are a graduate of Harvard Business School and have worked in the New York Stock Exchange for three years. You have performed admirably in each task that you have been set, working honestly and diligently to overcome every difficulty.' He looked up, unexpectedly friendly. 'Harvard, eh? You will have stood underneath the Johnston Gate then?'

'Many times, sir,' Kendrick confirmed. The Johnston Gate, with its red brick columns and ironwork archway, was the first gate ever erected at Harvard and had been a popular meeting place for his class. He smiled as the man nodded.

'I have too, Kendrick. That's where I met my wife.'

Kendrick's smile broadened. 'So did I,' he said.

Irene glanced at Ms Manning, uncomfortable at this display of college bonding in which she could not participate.

Ms Manning may have caught her unease. 'Carry on, Peter,' she ordered, softly. 'The clock is ticking. Twenty eight minutes.'

Twenty-eight minutes; the words resonated through Irene's mind. In twenty-eight minutes she would know her future.

'You have been asked to perform a number of tasks, Kendrick, each one escalating in difficulty,' Peter continued. 'You managed a small shop, coped with a kindergarten school, which you found easy given your two children,' again the men

6

exchanged empathetic smiles, 'promoted a newly published book, organised a visit to the Manning Corporation from a foreign diplomat and finally created a new security system for the Manning Museum here in New York City.'

Irene hated the smug look that crept over Kendrick's face as he nodded to acknowledge each success.

'Indeed, you only have to successfully complete only one last task, Kendrick, and you will have proved yourself the perfect neophyte.' Peter closed the file and glanced toward Ms Manning.

'And now you, Irene.' Ms Manning nodded encouragement across the table. She raised an eyebrow to the older man on her right. 'Proceed, Charles.'

'Irene Armstrong, you have also proved yourself,' Charles spoke with an attractive Tennessee drawl. 'After a difficult childhood, you financed yourself into North Carolina State University, from where you successfully graduated. You entered the business world, rising to become head of department in a New York financial house. Since entering for *The Neophyte* you have taken charge of a busy travel agency, created a new web site for the Manning Corporation's Youth Programme, welcomed a French trade delegation to Houston's Manning Shopping Mall and tested the fire and security system in the Boston Manning Hotel.'

Far more aware of Ms Manning's scrutiny than of the cameras, Irene kept her face expressionless, acknowledging the applause with a nod.

'And you also have to prove yourself in our final task, Irene, before you can take your place as Ms Manning's neophyte,' Charles paused for a significant moment, 'or take a walk on the streets.'

'On the streets,' somebody from the unseen audience shouted, and others joined in, chanting the three-word mantra that would signify failure to one of the two remaining candidates.

Ms Manning waited until the noise faded before she spoke in her habitual low, soft voice, clearly enunciating each syllable. 'The last task we set was slightly different. It was also the most controversial of them all.' She raised the tension with a long pause. Unlike each previous episode of the show, no details of the hopeful neophyte's assignment had been released and everybody present waited to hear what would be said next.

'The task seemed quite simple,' Ms Manning said, 'you were to find out all that you could about your opponent, and tell me why that person should not be given the position as neophyte.'

There was a gasp from the audience as Irene and Kendrick looked at each other. Kendrick raised his eyebrows, but the smugness was back. Irene knew that Ms Manning had been fostering competition, setting the contenders against each other in a mini duplication of corporate life. Now she felt the hammering of her heart as she wondered what skeletons Kendrick had discovered. She saw Peter and Charles each produce a file from their respective brief case and hand it to Ms Manning. Both files were identical, with the white Manning Corporation logo embossed on a dark green background, except that one was thicker than the other.

To the brief rolling of a drum, Ms Manning opened the thinner file, lifted a printed sheet of paper from the top and scanned it briefly. 'This is a summary of Irene's investigation into Kendrick,' she explained. 'But before I begin, is there anything in your past that you wish to keep hidden, Kendrick?' The smile was deceitfully benign.

'Absolutely nothing,' Kendrick said. He glanced at Irene. 'Anybody is free to investigate my life.'

Ms Manning nodded. 'Let us see, Kendrick.' She scanned the summary with one flick of her eyes. 'Straight A grades at school, top of your year at Harvard and a prime performer at the Stock Exchange.'

That smug look was back on Kendrick's face as he nodded. Irene began to hate him anew, for the Ivy League Club was strong in the corporate world. Despite spending an entire two weeks probing Kendrick's life, she had found nothing untoward. She had hired a private investigator, had Kendrick followed, questioned his work colleagues and fellow students all the way back to infancy, with no success. The man seemed impenetrable, a veritable saint.

'You married Selia three years ago, Kendrick, and have two children, a boy named John and a girl named Ruth.' Ms Manning put down the paper and closed the file. 'You have never transgressed the laws of the United States in any particular, with not even a parking fine against you, and your teachers, lecturers, family and neighbours all acclaim you with great praise.' She smiled, 'Kendrick, you are a pillar of the community.'

Kendrick ducked his head modestly as Ms Manning lifted the second, thicker, file and turned her attention to Irene.

'A mixed bag at school, Irene, and a slight blemish when you took some unofficial time off, which is not surprising given your impoverished family background. You recovered commendably well, and attended North Carolina State University, which you financed by working long hours at Wal-Mart, among other places.'

Irene nodded. She felt the colour rise to her cheeks as there was a slight stir in the audience. She knew that it was part of the American Dream for a poor girl to work her way to success, but also knew that the United States could be as elite-conscious as any other nation in the world. She hoped that Kendrick had not been over efficient in checking all her previous work places.

'After an initial rocky period, you hit a run of top grades, and have worked in a number of positions since, usually rising to the top of whatever tree you chose to climb. Latterly you were head of department in a leading financial business. You are single, but have a partner named Patrick McKim. He is a fascinating man, but not the subject of this competition.' Miss Manning let the words hang as she shuffled the papers a little before she selected a single yellow sheet.

Irene leaned forward. She could nearly feel the triumph radiating from the man sitting next to her.

'Kendrick has unearthed some interesting facts about you, Irene. For instance, there was a job in Raleigh when you accumulated a number of parking fines.' Miss Manning raised both eyebrows as she stared into the camera, playing to the audience. 'And there was the night you seem to have spent in a police cell?'

Irene could hear the audible sigh from the audience as they sensed her chances slipping away. Kendrick shifted in his seat, not sure whether to be proud of his investigative success or embarrassed at this public denouncement of his rival. He looked across to her, as if to apologise. Aware that Ms Manning appreciated a fighter, Irene hit back.

'I was certainly in a police cell, Ms Manning, but only for shelter. I was returning home from the University and had run out of money. The police offered to help.'

Ms Manning allowed her eyebrows to drop. 'So I understand.' She replaced the yellow sheet of paper and closed the file. 'So now I have to make a decision. Now I have to choose one neophyte and order the unsuccessful candidate to go on the streets.'

The audience had been waiting expectantly for those words. 'On the streets!' they echoed, chanting in choreographed enjoyment.

Kendrick straightened in his seat. His glance at Irene might have included sympathy.

Ms Manning continued. 'I have watched you both over the last few months, I have viewed hundreds of hours of video tape, read your files and interviewed you personally, but now I must pronounce the final decision.' When she leaned back, Ms Manning's immaculately styled hair barely touched the carved logo on the headrest. She looked from one candidate to the other, pressed the tips of her fingers together and smiled.

'It's a big decision, choosing a successor. Who do I want? *What* do I want?' She sighed. 'I want somebody who is expert at business, so my Corporation does not go down the pan. Somebody who will fight for what *he*,' Ms Manning's eyes focussed on Kendrick, and then slid across to Irene, 'or *she*, believes. I want somebody who can identify a failing but potentially successful company, buy it and turn it around. I want somebody honest and incredibly hard working. I want a fighter.' She shook her head solemnly, 'I want somebody similar to me.'

The audience cheered, as Ms Manning had certainly intended. Irene felt herself smiling and knew that Kendrick was doing exactly the same. Ms Manning had that effect on people. She had the power of manipulation.

Ms Manning sat up straight and nodded into the nearest camera. There was a hush as the great screens rolled slowly back so that the appearance of a boardroom altered into the television studio that it in fact was. Now only a few yards of space and coils of television cable separated the contestants from the audience. Irene was suddenly conscious that hundreds of pairs of eyes were fixed on her back. The cameras had been intrusive but impersonal, machines rather than people, but now she fancied that she could hear the breathing of each individual among the crowd, she could nearly smell the cologne and after shave with which they had doused themselves.

'I have come to a decision.' Ms Manning leaned back in her chair, allowing her head to rest just beneath the Manning logo. Even then, Irene could admire the perfect set of her hair and the manicured nails that lay in line with the arm rests. The overhead lights gleamed on the ruby that was central to the single ring encircling her forefinger. There was a matching ruby on the antique necklace around her neck.

Irene could not look at Kendrick, although she was very aware of his suddenly shallow breathing. The audience had receded to unimportance.

'Within the next two minutes,' Miss Manning addressed the contestants, 'one of you will be my neophyte and the other will be on the streets.' This time the audience did not chant the programme slogan. 'How do you feel, Kendrick?'

There was a moment's hesitation before Kendrick replied. 'I feel good,' he said. 'I feel real good.'

Ms Manning nodded. 'And you, Irene?'

'Confident,' Irene lied. She nodded vigorously. 'Yes. I will be your neophyte.'

The hush deepened as Ms Manning stood, as she always did before imparting momentous decisions. Three cameras focussed on her, while one concentrated on each of the contestants.

'This contest has been close,' Ms Manning's accent became more pronounced as she came to the climax of the programme. 'And I am left with two excellent candidates. One has sailed through life on the crest of a wave of constant success; the other has struggled through adversity to achieve her present position. Both are examples of the American Dream, and the two are hard to separate.'

Irene heard the drums begin their insistent roll as Ms Manning stepped back, preparatory to sweeping her hand round in her trademark gesture that would destroy the dreams of one contestant and recreate the life of the other. The person Ms Manning selected would be virtually guaranteed wealth, power and success; the person she rejected would have to accept very public failure. Ms Manning was the human oxymoron between two extremes; her pronouncement was incontestable.

'So I have come to a provisional decision. In business it is sometimes better to hedge one's bets, to allow things to take their own course until muddied waters clear.' Her arm swung in a complete half circle until her forefinger pointed directly at Kendrick. The ruby gleamed like blood. 'In this instance I have decided that Kendrick shall be my neophyte, for an interim period of one year. If he makes a success of things in that time, which I have no doubt that he will, then he shall retain the position.'

The arm retracted then thrust out toward Irene. 'In the meantime, Irene, you must go *on the streets*!'

The finger dominated Irene's conscious vision. She could see the immaculate nail with the arc of the cuticle, and each individual crease around the knuckles. For one moment her entire life centred on that single digit, and then the audience began the chant that had become a catchphrase throughout America.

'On the streets! On the streets!'

Irene sat in disbelief, swamped by the baying. She could feel Kendrick standing beside her, could sense the triumph in his smile as he accepted the congratulations of Ms Manning and her senior managers before he turned to her, hand extended.

'On the streets! On the streets!'

Tears prickled in her eyes as Irene faced Ms Manning. She shook her head. She had planned and striven and had dedicated her entire life to winning this competition. Now she was a failure; the world would remember her not as the contestant who had nearly succeeded, but as the woman who had failed in front of millions.

'You fought well, Irene,' Kendrick's soft voice caressed her and his deep brown eyes held only sympathy. 'Shake now; show the world that you can lose as graciously as you win.' When she hesitated, he leaned closer, whispering 'if you don't, you'll regret it later.'

Recognising good advice, Irene blinked back the tears and took Kendrick's hand. She would have loved to squeeze hard, to make him wince, but there was a worldwide audience watching. 'Congratulations, Kendrick,' she said as brightly as she could. 'You will be a worthy neophyte. You will be just fine.'

'Well said!' Ms Manning had been watching closely, but now transferred her entire attention to Kendrick.

Irene suddenly realised that she was already pushed out of the picture. Technicians hustled past her as they wheeled cameras toward the successful neophyte. Two men guided her into a cluttered dressing room as Kendrick took his place on the table beside Ms Manning. She felt swift hands remove the green jacket from her shoulders, heard whispered words of sympathy as a camera focussed on her face. She forced a smile, as if indifferent that her chance of replacing one of the richest women in the world had just been replaced by a life branded by failure.

'You have to make the walk now,' a denim-clad technician whispered, and encouraged her with a gentle shove between the shoulder blades.

The audience continued to chant 'on the streets' as Irene followed the marked route, but she ignored the anonymity of faces, knowing that although some pitied her, most were gleeful, enjoying her discomfiture. The voices merged into a single bawl of derision, individual personalities into a crowd that cried failure, but she blinked away the burning tears and held her head high. Only when a doorman ushered her out of the studio did the noise abate. The corridor seemed to stretch into a bleak distance.

'You did great to get so far,' the doorman said, soothingly. He was middle aged and bald, with pouched eyes.

Irene shook her head. 'I failed,' she said.

'You'll be back,' the doorman said, adding earnest words of sympathy that were lost on her. Kendrick was the lion of the hour but she was only an also-ran, somebody to be moved quickly out of the vision of a society that worshipped only success.

Away from the cameras, Irene allowed the emotion to take control as she surveyed her aborted dreams. With one sentence Ms Manning had changed her life-plan from triumph to survival, from riches to unemployment. She was indeed on the streets. She felt the prickle of a tear that she was too late to prevent from coursing slowly down her cheek. God, but she hoped there were no cameras waiting for her outside. All she needed was for the world to remember her as the failed contestant with panda eyes and smudged mascara.

Keeping one hand on her arm, the doorman guided her along the corridor in which various people hurried, some giving her curious glances and others completely disregarding her. After weeks in the public eye, to be ignored was the deepest pain of all.

The studio was only one of a dozen within the huge communications building, but eventually Irene stumbled out into 48th Street and the bitter rain of a New York fall. There was a limousine waiting to take her home and a film crew asking more questions. She lifted her face, allowing the rain to take the blame for any inadequacies of her make up.

'How do you feel?'

'It sucks, I mean, truly sucks! I should have won!'

The camera moved closer, but the soundman shook his head, 'sorry, Irene, I did not get that. Could you repeat it, please?' He looked eager, aware that he had lost something sensational, but sense had returned to Irene.

'I said all congratulations to Kendrick. He is a worthy winner and I am sure he will do well.' She forced another smile, aware that her jaws were aching, reiterated her praise of Kendrick and said that she was proud to have come so far. She felt sick as the lights reflected on the wet streets of the city.

The questions continued.

'What will you do with your life?'

'Where will you go now?'

'Did you find the show a positive experience?'

Irene shook her head. 'Failure can never be a positive experience,' she said as the truth broke through her professional façade. 'And what will I do with my life? Does it matter? Anything else will be second best to this opportunity!'

The reporter drew back, alarmed at the venom in Irene's face.

'Let me out,' Irene demanded. 'I'll walk from here. Let me out!'

'But the interview?'

'Your interview sucks!' Thrusting open the door, she pushed past the camera crew, straightened her back and strode around the nearest corner. She did not know in which direction she was walking, only that she had to escape from the media. Only in constant movement could she find solace, and there was no better city in which to hide.

Chapter Two: New York and Mannadu: October

The bottles crowded the window ledge, each one an empty reminder of disgrace. Two had contained champagne, bought for celebration but drunk in disappointment. One had held Kentucky bourbon, its black label peeling now, and the remainder proclaimed themselves to be the king of beers. Lying amidst the tangled covers of her bed, Irene squinted through the array of curved glass at the distorted shape of the window. It was daylight outside, although she could not determine the time. She raised her head a little, swore at the pain that such effort caused and carefully sank back down on the pillow. Beside her, Patrick snored softly.

Failure. The word throbbed inside her head, reinforcing the thump of her hangover. Failure. She clenched her fists until her nails dug small semi-circular grooves in the palm of each hand. She had gambled everything on becoming Ms Manning's neophyte, but now she must start again. She had thrown up her job to concentrate on the competition, so she was back on the streets in reality, seeking employment, seeking a new life, hiding from humiliation.

Leaving Patrick lying diagonally across the bed with one arm thrown over the pillow and the other folded beneath him, Irene pushed herself upright. She slid off the mattress, winced and sat down, holding her head to compress the pain into manageable proportions. Only when she convinced herself that there was no alternative did she stagger to the bathroom, stripping off the silk pyjama shirt that was her only covering.

Setting the power shower to cold, Irene stepped into the cubicle, squealing as the fierce jets of water hammered at her. After a few minutes she was unable to bear any more and increased the temperature before she began to apply shower gel. Sinking into a corner, she allowed the water to rinse away the lather, and remained there until her headache began to dissolve and the churning in her stomach settled down.

Removing two painkillers from her emergency cupboard, Irene thrust them into her mouth and chewed, hating the taste. Losers did not deserve the luxury of a glass of water in which to dissolve them. Her stomach protested at this new assault, so she sat down quickly until the sensation eased.

So she had failed to win a game show. Irene shrugged as a new recklessness slithered over her. Well, she had done the very best that she could, but her early life had betrayed her, while Kendrick's money and influence had eased his path. Returning to the shower, she shampooed her hair vigorously and stepped under the nozzle. Streams of soapy water ran down her body, surging around her feet to drain away as if in imitation of her hopes. She had failed, but she would not give up on life. Who was she?

'I am Irene Armstrong,' she reminded herself. 'I am Irene Armstrong.' She spoke louder so her name echoed between the transparent plastic walls of the cubicle. 'I am Irene Armstrong, and there is nothing I can not do.' The phrase came from her childhood, a simple slogan that had helped her through some very bad times.

Steam from the shower filled the room as she cleaned a space on the mirror and brushed her teeth, allowing the toothpaste to foam and drop in frothy globules onto the sink. 'Damn you Kendrick, for beating me, and you, Ms Rhondda Manning, for choosing a lesser contender. I'll be back,' she deepened her voice and repeated the words in imitation of Arnold Schwarzenegger's famous catch phrase. 'I'll be back!'

Vigorously towelling her hair, Irene returned to the bedroom. Patrick lay exactly as she had left him, face down on the bed and mouth slightly open. Grinning, she flicked off the covers and allowed herself the pleasure of admiring his muscular back, with the small scar just beneath his left shoulder blade and the indentation of his spine that ran into his smoothly curving bottom. Her smile altered to a sudden frown when she focussed on the tattoo on his right buttock. Linda had been a previous girlfriend, in a different life, but Irene always resented that he had chosen somebody else before her. During their vigorous lovemaking she always raked her nails across that name, hoping to eradicate the written memory, and now she delivered a stinging slap to the same target. When he jerked forward she laughed, stepped back and slapped again, harder. She felt immense pleasure at Patrick's yelp.

'Up you get, lazy! I've got a life to rebuild and you're going to help.'

He rolled over onto his back and looked up, one hand clutching at the assaulted area. 'What the hell was that for?'

It was his eyes that had first attracted Irene, a brilliant blue that seemed to hold all the mysteries of the universe, but now they were shaded through over-indulgence in alcohol. He blinked, obviously suffering the same agonies that Irene had so recently endured.

'Just because it was asking for it. You've got two minutes,' Irene told him, with no sympathy at all. 'Then I'll take drastic measures.' She smiled sweetly, tied the towel around her head and walked to the kitchen to put on the coffee. A glance in the mirror reassured her that Patrick was watching the emphasised swing of her hips.

The knock at the door seemed to shake the entire house. 'Get that, Patrick, I've got nothing on.' Irene waited for a minute, as the knock sounded again, louder and more urgent than before. She looked into the bedroom, frowned as she saw Patrick once again recumbent amidst the sheets, and dragged on his dressing gown. It was many times too large, with sleeves that flapped loosely over her hands.

'Who is it?' Irene peered through the security glass and saw a tall man who she instantly recognised.

'Peter Madrid.' The man held up a card with his photograph on it and the unmistakable logo of the Manning Corporation. 'I wish to speak with you, if it is convenient.'

'Peter Madrid!' Irene stepped back, instinctively putting up a hand to the towel that covered her hair. Moving swiftly, she kicked shut the bedroom door to conceal both the unmade bed and its naked occupant, fastened the cord of the dressing gown tighter and unfastened the security chain. 'What can I do for you?' She eased open the front door, biting back her bitterness. This man had watched her answer a hundred questions over the last few weeks; he had overseen her on four different tasks and had reported on her suitability as a neophyte to Ms Manning. At that minute, Irene had no desire to ever speak to him, or anybody else from the Manning Corporation, ever again.

Peter stepped in, his suit as immaculate as ever but his eyes swivelling around the tiny apartment. 'Ms Manning sends her apologies for disturbing you,' he said quietly, 'and hopes that you have recovered from any disappointment that you may have experienced yesterday.'

Irene recommenced the assault on her hair with the towel as the twin sensations of defeat and failure returned. 'Yesterday is past,' she said, shrugging in an attempt to dismiss the heartbreak as unimportant. 'It was fun while it lasted.' She produced a bright smile. 'Come in to the living room and I'll make coffee.'

'You're not disappointed then?' Peter lowered himself into one of the two cream coloured armchairs and raised an inquisitive eye. He glanced at the framed poster that showed crossed Armalite rifles in front of an Irish flag and the word Noraid, before switching his attention to the broken television in the corner of the room. Irene followed the direction of his eyes. She had watched the videotape that Patrick had made of *The Neophyte*, until the sight of Kendrick's triumphant face had proved too much and she had thrown the remote control at the screen. It was too late now to hide the evidence.

'Disappointed?' Irene pursed her lips and shook her head. 'No. It was only a game show. If you wait for a minute I'll get the coffee. How do you like it?'

'Black and strong,' Peter told her.

'Like Kendrick,' Irene whispered sotto-voice, closing the door. She quickly squeezed into a pair of tight jeans and a white blouse, furiously brushed her hair and tied it back, checked her face in the mirror and groaned. The damp red hair contrasted badly with the blue shadows under her eyes. She looked exactly like a loser who had spent most of the night drinking.

Peter was sitting in the same seat when she returned with the coffee. He continued the conversation as if she had never been away. 'If those are your true feelings, then there is absolutely no reason for me to be here. But I do not believe that they are.' His eyes again strayed to the television set. 'I am sure that I would be sick, bitter and extremely angry, if I had gone to half the trouble that you did. Sit down.'

Irene obeyed.

'I'll ask you that question once more. Are you disappointed?'

The scalding coffee shocked Irene into speaking the truth. 'Let's see. I was on the verge of being offered probably the best job in the world, being trained to take charge of one of the biggest corporate businesses anywhere, with a virtually unlimited salary and unparalleled power. But I lost. And you ask me if I am disappointed.' She swallowed another mouthful of coffee, not caring that her voice was rising as quickly as her temper. 'Of course I am disappointed! What sort of damn fool question is that to ask? Do you want me to spell it out? I put everything I had into winning that show, and I lost. I failed, and I hate failure. So now, Peter Madrid, once you have finished your coffee, could you please stop gloating and leave my apartment? I have a life to rebuild and you are wasting my time.'

Peter shook his head. 'It seems that I am not.' He sipped delicately at his cup. 'Nice coffee; decaf? How would you like to rebuild your life within the Manning Corporation?'

Irene shook her head. 'Working for Kendrick? I would not even consider it. Either I'm at the top, or I'm out completely.'

'Good.' Peter nodded. 'That is the answer that Ms Manning hoped you would give. There is a limousine waiting on the street outside. It will leave at ten o' clock, either with you or without you.' He stood up and handed her the empty coffee cup. 'Ms Manning does not send limousines for losers.' He looked pointedly at the broken television set. 'Nor does she give people a second chance.'

Irene frowned. 'Is that an ultimatum?'

'It is a fact of life,' Peter said. He glanced at the clock that hung on the wall, its green digital figures counting away the seconds of the day. 'I will see myself out.'

For a minute Irene pondered what she should do. Would she be better to swallow her pride and enter the limousine, placing herself in the hands of the woman who had so publicly rejected her, or strike out alone from nothing? The clock clicked again as another figure slid into place. Irene looked up and flinched. 09:50. She had five minutes in which to decide, and then five minutes to reach the street. 09:51. There really was no decision to make; she knew that she would enter the limousine.

Rapidly changing into a neat dark business suit and low sling back shoes, Irene tore a hunk of bread from a slightly stale loaf and threw open the door just as the figures changed to 09:57.

'Irene? Who were you talking with? Where are you going?' Patrick appeared in the doorway of the bedroom, his body unclothed and his eyes still half closed.

'No time to explain,' Irene told him. 'I'll be in touch.'

'But my coffee?'

'You know where the kitchen is.' Irene crossed the corridor and madly pressed the button to summon the elevator.

'Where are you going?' Patrick padded after her.

The elevator seemed to take forever as it dropped the eight floors to street level, stopping once to let an elderly Jewish couple on, and again to allow them to leave. The foyer was quiet and the uniformed commissionaire smiled as he came toward her.

'Miss Armstrong! I saw you on the television last night. You looked good.' He hesitated for a second. 'I really think that you should have won, though.'

'Thank you, Mark,' Irene spared him the briefest of smiles, 'but I'm afraid that I am in a hurry.'

'Of course,' Mark opened the heavy glass doors and saluted as Irene bustled past. 'You businesswomen! Always rushing away to some meeting or other!'

The street was busy, with yellow cabs blaring their horns and commercial vehicles thundering past. Long and dark green, the limousine was parked exactly in front of the door, with a uniformed driver at the wheel. Even as Irene approached, the driver started its engine, the soft purr spurring her forward.

'Wait!' She heard the crack in her voice as she pulled open the door.

The driver turned around. 'Miss Irene Armstrong?' He was about forty, broad faced but not fat, with narrow eyes.

'That's right.'

'Please put your seat belt on, Miss Armstrong.'

'Irene!' Avoiding a despairing clutch by the commissionaire, a naked Patrick lunged toward the limousine. 'Where are you going?'

'I don't know!' Irene held the door open for a moment. 'Go and put some clothes on, Patrick, and I'll let you know as soon as I find out myself. Go on now.'

'It's ten o'clock, Miss Armstrong,' the chauffeur said. 'I must leave.'

'Drive,' Irene agreed. 'He'll keep.'

'Wait!' Patrick pressed against the window, but the driver eased into the traffic and rolled smoothly away. Unlike any other vehicle in which Irene had travelled, the limousine seemed to be able to split traffic like Moses parting the Red Sea. Signals altered to green at its approach, even the yellow cabs gave way and the road through the city was clearer than she had ever known.

Irene tapped on the glass partition that separated her from the driver. 'Where are we going?'

'LaGuardia,' the driver said, quietly, turning into Grand Central Parkway East. 'Sit back and enjoy the ride, Miss Armstrong. We should arrive in about twenty minutes.'

'LaGuardia?' Irene sat up straight. 'I thought you were taking me to meet Ms Manning.'

'I am following my instructions,' the driver said enigmatically.

It was an eight-mile journey, but the driver barely halted until he steered into a reserved slot in the parking garage for the Central Terminal. A man in the pressed grey trousers and green blazer of the Manning Corporation was waiting for their arrival, and gently ushered Irene through Terminal Building A, past the security guards and onto the tarmac.

'Onto the aircraft, ma'am,' he said, indicating the Cessna Citation Bravo that purred a few yards away. The tail carried the familiar Manning logo.

'Where am I going?' Irene asked, but the blazered man proved as politely unforthcoming as the chauffeur.

'I am following instructions, Miss Armstrong,' he said quietly, 'but I would not worry, Ms Manning takes care of her own.'

Irene had dreamed of being inside an executive jet, but the reality exceeded her expectations. The interior was the expected green-and-gold, but where the aircraft had originally been fitted for seven passengers in club class, the Manning Corporation had reduced the number of seats to four, ensuring more space for the lap-top computers and an even more relaxing flight.

'Please take a seat, Miss Armstrong, and fasten your seat belt.' The green blazered man had accompanied Irene on board. 'We will be airborne directly.'

'You don't allow me much time for contemplation, do you?' Irene did as she was ordered, only now aware that her headache was returning and she was beginning to feel the first pangs of hunger. Save for one mouthful of bread, she had not eaten since before the show yesterday evening, and the effects of the morning's coffee were beginning to wear off.

'Ms Manning likes efficiency,' the blazered man told her.

The Cessna taxied very briefly, and then took off in what seemed a nearly vertical climb that had Irene swallowing hard. A look out of the window showed her the vast spread of New York visibly diminishing beneath her, with the tall buildings of Manhattan already assuming Lilliputian proportions and the Hudson River a streak of blue.

After a few minutes the intercom hummed and a calm voice sounded. 'We are now flying at 7,620 metres and heading in a westerly direction. There is a gentle headwind but not enough to impede our speed or progress. We are approaching our cruising speed of 400 knots, or about 465 miles an hour, so sit back and enjoy the flight, Miss Armstrong. The steward will attend to any requests,'

There was fresh orange juice and a light meal of newly baked bread and cheese, followed by strong coffee, but Irene's repeated demands for further information from the blazered man were met only with a polite smile.

'I am only the steward, Miss Armstrong. I do what I am told.'

'Well, let me speak with the pilot then.'

The steward shook his head regretfully. 'I am truly sorry, Miss Armstrong, but Ms Manning's safety protocols are very strict. The cockpit is fully secured and separate from us. We cannot approach the pilot when we are airborne.'

America seemed to crawl below them as the Cessna powered westward and Irene drank a never-ending succession of cups of coffee. She forced herself to sit quietly, either staring at the clouds that wafted below them or perusing the magazines that had been provided.

Leafing through the in-house magazine for the Manning Corporation, Irene refreshed herself with the sheer scale of the company. She read how Ms Manning had pushed herself through college and had begun in electronics in a very small scale. By sheer hard work and brilliance, she had steered her own company to be one of the main players in America, and then had branched out into other fields. Now the Manning Corporation was involved in real estate and hospitality, clothing and drink, transport and pharmaceuticals, as well as the original electronics.

Irene shook her head. The corporation was so vast it was astonishing that one woman could keep her finger on everything. Ms Manning truly was an impressive woman.

After the first couple of hours Irene had given up attempting to judge where they were and tried to sleep, but her active mind forced her awake, to think about the forthcoming interview. It was early afternoon before the Cessna touched down, and the steward was smiling as he approached.

'We have reached our destination, Miss Armstrong. On behalf of Ms Manning, I would like to thank you for your patience and hope that you have had a pleasant flight.'

Irene stretched her legs and straightened her back as she stepped outside. However luxurious the cabin had been, the headroom had been less than generous to a woman of her height. She looked around, shivering in a wind that hissed straight from the Arctic. The aerodrome seemed to consist of a single long strip of tarmac beside a building of compact concrete, from whose squat tower rose a mass of complex communications equipment. A bleak, green-and-grey plain stretched to low hills that struggled above the distant horizon. 'Where are we?'

'Our destination,' the steward repeated. 'Within the continental United States, but I am afraid that I am not at liberty to divulge any more than that.'

'Why the hell not?' Irene demanded, but the steward merely smiled and ushered her toward another vehicle. The Ford Expedition King Ranch waited with its engine throbbing and the expected Manning logo shining on its doors.

'The driver will take you further. It may be a bit wild out here, Miss Armstrong, but Ms Manning will ensure that you can rough it in comfort.'

Irene sighed, hoping that whatever Ms Manning wanted, it had better be worth all this trouble. She slid inside the air-conditioned interior and did not trouble the driver with questions. Stretching out on the comfortable leather seat, Irene nursed her head that still retained the memory of a hangover and wondered where she would be today if she had won *The Neophyte* competition. Probably already hard at work in some Manning Corporation office, she told herself.

The driver negotiated the rough track that led north and west toward the hills, saying nothing, but on one occasion pointing to a herd of buffalo that moved slowly to their right. Irene looked without curiosity; wildlife did not interest her as much as her future career.

Twice Irene saw smaller four-by-four vehicles driving alongside them but at a discreet distance, and once a Ford pickup crossed their track, with the unmistakable form of armed men sitting in the rear. Her driver drove straight on, unheeding, into a vast space beneath a sky that extended into infinity.

After an hour, Irene realised that they were heading toward a high, white building. Perched on a smooth knoll, castellated round towers protruded above tall, windowless walls of whitewashed stone. Irene shook her head; this building belonged to Europe, or at least Hollywood, rather than the reality of the United States. She half expected to see the Sheriff of Nottingham ride out on a prancing charger.

'What the hell is that place?'

The driver did not turn around. He stopped a hundred yards from the arched doorway that seemed the only entrance and spoke a few words into a radio. After a few minutes the iron-studded door opened, and he manoeuvred through the entrance and into another world.

Surrounded on three sides by a high white wall, the courtyard was filled with the patter of the fountain that acted as centrepiece to a formal garden. While bronze mermaids disported with dolphins around an oval pool of clear water, shaded bowers sheltered carved wooden seats, and winding paths joined at an inner doorway that led into the main castle. Three towers soared to the empty sky, dominating yet not threatening any occupants of the courtyard garden.

Irene stared around her, she had been wrong; this place was no Nottingham, rather it came from some Persian pleasure palace.

Halting the King Ranch in one of the seven parking bays, the driver opened the door for Irene. She eased herself out, wondering what surprise next awaited her. Her period of uncertainty was brief.

'Five minutes early, I see.' Dressed in hip-hugging blue jeans and a check shirt, Ms Manning had pulled the peak of her green baseball cap low over her eyes. She looked relaxed, but had not lost her aura of easy authority as she held out her hand. 'Come in, Irene. Welcome to Mannadu. Perhaps not Xanadu, but we do our best.'

Irene hesitated only a second before accepting the hand, and was immediately aware of Ms Manning's close scrutiny.

'Well done, Irene. It must have been hard to come here after yesterday's rejection.'

Irene forced a smile. 'Why have you brought me?'

'Come with me and I'll show you.'

Feeling like the fly accepting the invitation of a very predatory spider, Irene followed.

Chapter Three: Mannadu & New York October

The inner doorway opened into a great hallway with an echoing marble floor and tall Ionic pillars that descended from a domed ceiling. It should have looked formal, but instead was relaxingly cool, with a smaller version of the outer fountain playing in the centre. An arched doorway led to a smaller hall, from where half a dozen exits invited investigation. Ms Manning chose the most central, leading Irene into an oval room with polished oak panelled walls and an ornately corniced ceiling.

Irene breathed deeply of the scent of fresh coffee.

'You'll be hungry,' Ms Manning gestured to one of the two chairs that were arranged around a circular table. The green-and-gold rims of the plates seemed to peep furtively from under a pile of food. 'Eat.'

There was a half-inch thick steak that could only have originated in Iowa, potatoes that melted in Irene's mouth, enough coffee to float a small fleet and bread so fresh it must have come straight from the oven.

'Good.' Ms Manning joined her, matching her bite for bite and swallow for swallow. 'I like to see a woman with an appetite. I've no time for those half people who live on grass and water. Food is for eating, and exercise removes the excess. Don't you agree?'

Until that moment, Irene had never considered the question. She looked up, suddenly aware that she was alone in the company of one of the richest people in the world, the same woman who had callously discarded her the previous evening. She patted her lips with a napkin of crisp linen and repeated, 'why have you brought me here?'

'To speak with you,' Ms Manning told her. 'Are you tired?'

Irene shook her head.

'Good. Walk with me then.' Ms Manning was upright on the last word and strode from the room, with Irene following like a small dog.

'You would have been surprised at my invitation, after my decision of last night.' Ms Manning allowed Irene to walk at her side as they strode along a long corridor, their feet sinking into a deep pile carpet. Wall lights gleamed on polished oak, with doors inset at regular intervals.

'I was,' Irene agreed. 'I had expected to be on the streets today.'

'You may yet be,' Ms Manning warned, 'but only if you fail me.'

Irene hesitated. 'I thought that I had already done that. You chose Kendrick.'

'He was a worthy winner,' Ms Manning's voice contained neither sympathy nor understanding. 'But remember on what terms.' When she looked upward into Irene's face and raised her eyebrows, Irene involuntarily flinched. Ms Manning always used that expression as a rebuke to point out something that should have been obvious. She continued before Irene had time to think. 'How did you feel when I announced that choice?'

Irene's answer was spontaneous. 'Sick. I thought that your decision sucked.'

Ms Manning stopped and looked upward again. 'Point one: I appreciate your honesty. Point two: when dealing with business matters; you will drop the teenage slang. This is the Manning Corporation and we work and speak in a professional manner. Point three: that is precisely the reaction that I hoped you would have. If you had shown a lack of concern, I would have terminated this meeting immediately. Follow.' Pushing open an arched door, Ms Manning watched as Irene stepped forward.

Irene stopped in astonishment. They had entered a room of gleaming marble, with an oval swimming pool stretching before them. Sculptures from classical antiquity guarded the edge of the pool, with Achilles admiring Poseidon's trident while Hercules flaunted his muscles to a bow wielding Apollo.

'You look surprised,' Ms Manning said.

'A little,' Irene tried to hide her astonishment.

'Why?' Ms Manning stepped toward the nearest sculpture, a white marble David with the face of an angel and the body of an athlete. She touched its gleaming arm. 'It is no secret that I am a connoisseur of the arts; the Manning Corporation contributes millions of dollars to museums throughout the United States, so why should I not have my own collection?' She smiled and stepped away. 'These are originals, created by the finest contemporary sculptors in the world. I like to admire them as I swim. Join me.' It was as much a command as any business order, but Irene could not hide her surprise when Ms Manning peeled off her clothes and stepped naked into the pool. 'Come on, Irene, or do you have something to hide from me?'

The question was mocking, but Ms Manning's eyes were acute.

'I think you know all there is to know about me,' Irene told her. Very aware of the intensity of that gaze, she fumbled over her buttons, determined to show no emotion as she kicked off the last skimpy vestige of her underclothing. She looked straight into Ms Manning's face, smiled brightly and descended seven steps into water that lapped warmly around her waist.

'Well done,' Ms Manning approved. 'That took as much courage as appearing before the cameras. And more trust. Good. Another point though; I know a lot about you, but not everything. Not yet. There is one important factor left that I will find out today. Now follow me, but don't drink the water.'

Diving beneath the surface, Ms Manning propelled herself forward to the opposite end of the pool, with Irene keeping pace with her. They surfaced together, with their hair plastered onto their heads and faces streaming. 'Do you like my sculptures?'

Irene again surveyed the array of marble figures. 'Very nice,' she approved. 'You have a fine collection of naked men.'

'And so obedient,' Ms Manning's grin was suddenly child like. 'Just like men should be, don't you think?'

Irene laughed and was about to agree when she saw the raised eyebrow. 'Perhaps all men should be obedient,' she said, thinking rapidly, 'when they are your employees.'

'Exactly,' the eyebrow fell. Ms Manning dipped below the surface again and powered back along the pool. She surfaced in a small explosion of water and shook the excess from her hair. 'And when he is not an employee? What sort of man would you seek in a partner, Irene? What sort of man is Patrick McKim?'

Irene had anticipated the question. She wondered if Ms Manning had chosen Kendrick because he was married to a supportive wife, while she had enjoyed a succession of partners of whom Patrick was only the latest. 'Rough and ready, a bit wayward with no dress sense, but I like him and he is loyal.'

'How loyal, Irene?' The stare was as intense as Irene had ever seen it. 'Would he be loyal enough to remain at your side if you climbed higher than he could ever dream? And how much do you like him? Do you like him enough to drag him with you? Or would you discard him and fly alone? It's a tough life at the top, Irene, and sometimes there is no place for a partner.'

'Kendrick has a wife,' Irene responded, 'but you chose him.'

'That's better!' Ms Manning nodded. She stood up straight so her small breasts just broke the surface of the water. Irene knew that she was forty-three years old, yet she had the body of somebody fifteen years younger, with clear skin and fine muscular definition. Her midriff was free of excess fat, while her hips flared elegantly from a trim waist. 'Tell me what you really think, Irene, not what you believe I want to hear.' She stepped closer, leaning back with her eyes firmly on Irene's face. 'You're on the streets anyway, so you've nothing to lose. We're alone here, Irene, woman to woman with no witnesses and nothing at all between us.' Her smile was as mischievous as any teenager's but as unrelenting as time, 'literally.'

Irene allowed her frustration to take control. 'I think that you chose wrong, Ms Manning. You chose the man who had started with every advantage, the man who was cushioned by wealth, rather than choosing me, who had to fight for everything.'

Ms Manning held up a hand. 'So fight, Irene. Have you given up so easily? As I have already said, remember on what terms I accepted Kendrick?'

'You said that I was on the streets and he was the neophyte for a provisional period of one year.' Irene glared into Ms Manning's eyes, no longer conscious of their social standing or their nakedness, determined only to put her anger across.

'Exactly.' Ms Manning nodded calmly. 'He has one year to foul up, and you have one year in which to prove yourself.'

'I don't understand,' Irene's anger dissipated immediately. 'Do you mean that I still have a chance to become your neophyte?'

'Why do you think I brought you here?' Ms Manning raised her eyebrows again. 'Kendrick was the obvious choice on the show. He has all the attributes that society expects from a successful corporate businessman. He has the education, the background, and the commercial experience. He has an attractive wife and a smart suit. He *had* to win on the day, but Irene, remember that I also lacked Kendrick's advantages. I had no elevator to reach the top. I had to claw my way up, as do you; it takes a long ladder to stretch from a trailer to the topmost tower of Mannadu!'

Ms Manning's eyes drifted from Irene's face to the sculptured male bodies standing in magnificent compliance around the pool. 'Kendrick will make an excellent employee, but I want a leader, not a follower. Kendrick is a man who obeys the rules, but I have had to make my own rules, and so will my replacement.'

Ducking beneath the water for the third time, Ms Manning swam back to the far side, with Irene following, her mind racing with new ideas.

They surfaced together, with Ms Manning looking quizzically at Irene. 'Now that I have you thinking, Irene, you can come with me. This way.'

The changing room opened from the side of the pool, with gentle towels, warm air and surprisingly inexpensive plastic combs. There was silk underwear to slide on beneath crisp cotton jeans and tee shirts, while soft-soled slippers fitted Irene's feet. 'That water was disinfected,' Ms Manning said quietly, 'and these clothes are sterile. You will note that they are natural white, with no artificial colouring. You will only wear them once, and then they will be discarded.'

'Why?' Irene luxuriated in the sensation of silk against her body. Her mind was buzzing with the possibility that she could still be Ms Manning's neophyte.

'You'll see. Follow.' Although Ms Manning's grin contained pure mischief, there was an uncharacteristic shadow of doubt in her eyes as she scanned Irene. As if coming to a difficult decision, she nodded, pressed a hidden button and a section of the wall eased open. Ms Manning stepped through the door into a long, high ceilinged room. The floor was of polished wood, while hidden lighting cast a subdued, nearly natural glow on a row of paintings that stretched some fifty metres to the opposite wall.

'The temperature is automatically adjusted and controlled,' Ms Manning spoke reverently, as if in religious awe, 'so that no possible damage can come to the exhibits.' She touched her white top. 'Now you understand the antiseptic bath and the sterile clothing? We are as clean as possible and this is a germ-free environment. Look…' Ms Manning's voice rose slightly as she pointed to the first work of art, an impressionist depiction of a curved wooden bridge, its reflection caught in limpid waters overhung by the branches of a tree. 'That is Claude Monet's *Garden*. It's one of his later works.'

As she obviously waited for a reaction, Irene shook her head. 'Is it genuine?'

'Of course,' there was pride in Ms Manning's smile. 'Everything is genuine.' She swept her hand in an arc that indicated every picture that hung on the wall.

'It's magnificent,' Irene said.

'It is,' Ms Manning agreed happily. 'And so are the others.' Again the hand gestured toward her collection.' Salvador Dali,

Vincent Van Gogh, Picasso, Andy Warhol, Fransisco de Goya, Paul Cézanne, and the British ones, John Constable, William Turner, Alexander Nasmyth, Henry Raeburn, Horatio McCulloch.'

Ms Manning repeated each name with veneration, pronouncing every syllable as she pointed to a painting. She walked slowly along the walls of the gallery, pausing before selected pictures as she highlighted the style and history of the artist.

'You see, Irene, I do not believe that business is only about personal financial security. It is not only about providing employment for tens of thousands and ensuring the prosperity of the nation. It is certainly not about power and the trappings of wealth. This is the real joy of success; the ability to preserve the artistic treasures of the world.'

As a child, Irene had visited the North Carolina Museum of Art in Raleigh but she had been too young to appreciate the experience, and had been glad to escape to less cultural environments. Maturity, however, had brought appreciation and Ms Manning's enthusiasm was contagious. She stared at each work of genius, actively enjoying the tour.

'Because I am not attached to any man, Irene, there have been many rumours about me. I am sure that you are aware of them.' Ms Manning paused at another door, her grey eyes steady. Irene felt the sudden surge of her heart, wondering if Ms Manning was about to proposition her, and how best to react. The naked swim suddenly became more sinister. Perhaps acceptance was the price of ultimate success in *The Neophyte* competition.

Ms Manning's smile was reassuring. 'The rumours are false. I am like everybody else in my emotional needs, but rather than find them with another person, I find them in art; great art, the best in the world.'

Irene felt herself relax. 'It's awesome,' she said softly. She looked back at the gallery, allowing her eyes to scan backward, unconsciously assessing the value of each masterpiece that hung on the wall. 'What is this room worth?'

'It could not be bought,' Ms Manning said, 'but its real value is not in dollars, but in art. Follow.'

The door was of plain wood, varnished to a soft sheen, and led to another room of spectacular sculptures. Three Assyrian warriors strode across a stone plateau, their beards plaited and swords displayed. Behind them stretched a screen of brilliant mosaic. 'These pieces all come from Asia,' Ms Manning said. 'Do you recall the fall of Baghdad, when the museums were looted? And the destruction wrought by the Taliban in Afghanistan? I had my people working there to salvage what I could, and this is the best of the results.' Her smile was a little wistful. 'You may think it wrong to keep looted art, but it is safer here than anywhere else.'

Irene met the smile, aware that Ms Manning was challenging her, possibly in an attempt to shock, or probing for a conscience.

'You see, Miss Armstrong, we live in a disrupted world and nobody knows how long it will last.' Ms Manning's voice had altered, and Irene knew that she was speaking about something close to her heart. 'Our world is crumbling; we live faster and more disrupted lives, families are splintering and the hegemony of western civilisation is threatened. These are facts, not opinions.'

Irene nodded. Nobody could deny that the present frantic pace of the world could not continue.

'The barbarians are at the gates of Rome,' Ms Manning was no longer smiling. 'Al-Qaeda is only one threat; China is rapidly replacing the United States as the world's superpower, India may be next, and who knows what new thing will come out of Africa?'

Irene listened, aware that Ms Manning was revealing another side of her character. This was not the hard-nosed businesswoman talking, but a concerned, even a scared woman. 'And when this world ends, Miss Armstrong, what will we have to show for millennia of civilisation?'

Realising that the question was rhetorical, Irene waited for an answer. 'Art. We will have art, but only if we collect it *now* and preserve it somewhere safe. Somewhere like this.' She smiled again in a lightning change of mood that Irene found immediately suspect.

'Follow.' Ms Manning pushed open another door.

There were more rooms of sculpture, one for each continent, and chambers of silverware and jewellery, ancient parchments and mediaeval books, carved stones from Europe and treasures from Mayans and Aztecs, Maori figurines from New Zealand and magnificent jade artefacts from China, multi-armed Hindu gods from India and intricate gold work from West Africa.

'This is amazing,' Irene repeated as she walked from treasure to treasure, from priceless Indian silk to pottery that had been looted from the Summer Palace of the Chinese Emperor, from a hand painted Bible that the monks of Iona had hidden from the Vikings to a Persian chess set and a jewelled horse from Mongolia.

'It is,' Ms Manning agreed. 'And you could be the heir of all of this, if you successfully complete the final task.'

They stood before the throne of a Chinese Emperor, under the shadow of a pot-bellied Buddha. Soft lights highlighted Ms Manning's cheekbones and accentuated the clarity of her eyes.

'Heir?' Irene played for time, allowing the atmosphere of this secret museum to percolate through her. 'As neophyte?'

'As my successor; my *sole* successor.'

The connotations were obvious. 'So I must dump Patrick.'

'Do you think he is a fitting partner for you? Do you think that he would appreciate these artefacts, care for them and secure them for the benefit of future generations? Do you honestly think that Patrick McKim is the most fitting person to entrust with some of the finest treasures that humanity has produced?'

Irene did not have to think hard. She knew that Patrick had many good qualities, but art appreciation was not among them. 'Perhaps not.'

'Then he is not the man for you. Or you are not the woman to replace me.' It was a direct challenge. Ms Manning's eyebrows rose again.

'Suck an elf!' Irene looked around her. She was being offered the world, but the price was high. She had to decide what was more important, a continuing relationship with Patrick, or to become one of the richest women in existence. She shrugged; there really was no contest. 'So it's goodbye to Patrick then.'

'Good choice,' Ms Manning said.

'And the final task?'

Ms Manning made another of her sweeping gestures, encompassing the entire collection. 'Your final task is something that Kendrick could not do by keeping to the rules.' She held her eyes. 'I have told you my fears for this world, and how I am attempting to save what I can before it is too late.'

Irene nodded. 'You have,' she agreed.

'Well then, I want you to add something unique to Mannadu. I want you to bring something priceless and irreplaceable. And something that is not already held in the United States.'

During the last few months, Irene had learned to expect the unexpected, but this final assignment stunned her. 'But how?' Irene failed to hide her consternation. 'I cannot afford even a decent print, yet alone a piece of original sculpture.'

'Use your imagination,' Ms Manning told her. 'Remember I said that Kendrick, who lives by the rules, could not complete this task. I'm sure that you realise that I did not purchase most of this material over the counter.'

'You mean I must steal something?' Irene could not keep the shock from her voice.

'I also said that a business leader must create her own rules. Use any method you think best, and I will allow you a budget of one million dollars and a time limit of one year. From today.'

'Jesus.' Irene shook her head. If Ms Manning was investing a million dollars, she must be expecting a return worth considerably more. She had never suspected that Ms Manning would countenance any criminal activity, yet alone encourage major theft; Irene's estimation of her host altered rapidly. Once she adapted to the initial surprise, she realised that she actually admired Ms Manning all the more. 'And if I succeed?'

'If you succeed, you will replace Kendrick, permanently. If you fail, you must take the consequences of your own actions. You and I will have no more contact, and the Manning Corporation will never employ you, in any capacity. You may be in jail, or you may be on the streets.'

'On the streets,' Irene echoed, and looked around the room. The green Buddha stared down at her, implacable and unemotional.

* * *

'Can't we just keep the million and run? Patrick asked.

Irene shook her head emphatically, denying her own temptation. 'Not ever, baby. I want that position more than anything on earth.' She had not mentioned the minor detail that he would not be with her.

They sat side by side on the couch in the lounge, with their legs and shoulders comfortably touching and the *Book of World Art Treasures* at their feet. 'It's a bit of a conundrum,' Irene said, 'much more difficult than any of the other tasks that she set.' She stood up and walked to the kitchen.

'It is exactly what Ms Manning intends it to be, it is the final and defining obstacle between you and your dreams.' Patrick lifted the remote control and flicked on the new television that dominated one corner of the room. 'You have to steal some great art treasure that will add to the collection of one of the richest people in America. Sounds like quite a challenge, Irene.'

'The million dollars might help,' Irene made two mugs of coffee and returned to Patrick's side. 'But I don't know anything about art theft. You have some shady friends; ask them where I start.'

Patrick sipped the coffee. 'I have no shady friends,' he denied, 'I only have friends who are sometimes forced to do shady things.' He gave her the charming grin that highlighted his eyes, and she snuggled closer.

'My apologies. So ask your oh-so-respectable friends where I should start.'

'No need. I will answer for them.' Patrick pulled her even closer. 'We start by selecting something to steal,' he decided. 'Then we work out how to do it.'

'We?' Irene's conscience quailed slightly. 'You don't have to get involved. If I fail, they'll throw me in jail and bury the key.'

'And if we succeed, I'll be with the richest woman in America.' Patrick's blue eyes creased as he grinned to her. 'So what will we go for? The *Mona Lisa*?'

Irene killed her scruples; she had to make her own rules. 'That's been done before.'

'*The Scream*?'

'Stolen a few years ago. The Norwegians will be more careful next time.'

'Michelangelo's *David*?'

'Too difficult to transport. No, no,' Irene shook her head. 'I'll have to think of something even more spectacular. I'll have to think of something that has never been thought of before; something that nobody would ever dream of stealing because it's too valuable. Something that makes the whole world sit up and take notice, so that even Ms Manning is impressed.'

Patrick put aside the remote control. 'Like robbing Fort Knox?'

'Yes, except the Fort Knox of art treasures.'

'Let's check the internet,' Patrick said, rising on the last word. He had hardly glanced at the book.

Irene looked over his shoulder as he typed in *World Art Treasures*. 'Seven million and sixty sites,' she said. 'Plenty choice then. Where do I start?'

'At the beginning,' Patrick said, quietly. 'Get a pen and paper, Irene, and start to take notes of site addresses. We'll pick the most valuable.'

'And the most portable,' Irene added. 'There's no point trying to wrestle a forty foot slab of Aztec gold over the Rio Grande; the Border Guards might just notice.'

Patrick nodded and began to scroll down the first page. 'The Pyramid of Cheops, I don't think so. Temple of Anada? That's bigger than Central Park. How about a nice Chinese head?'

'No,' Irene said, 'it's held in the New York Metropolitan. Ms Manning was very specific that it had to be from abroad.'

'Jesus,' Patrick checked the next ten entries. 'About half of these are held in the States. She makes things difficult, doesn't she?' He spent a few more minutes scrolling down the list. 'Here's a nice site. The Melbourne Museum. That's in Australia, so it's all right if we rob it. How about some Aboriginal Art? Or here are the Ashes: that's some sort of sporting remains that the Australians and Limeys play for.'

'I agree that they are valuable,' Irene said as diplomatically as she could, 'and very portable, but I don't think it's what Ms Manning wants. I don't think that the ashes of a cricket stump can be called art.'

'Man, you're hard to please!' Patrick stood up. 'You find something then. I'll see if there's any football on. The Jets are playing Buffalo.'

'Go the Buffalo Bills!' Irritated that Patrick had lost interest so quickly, Irene cheered for the team that opposed his Jets. 'I could try Venice,' she said, 'and bring back some priceless glass.'

'You'd probably drop it,' Patrick retaliated for the Bills quip, but Irene ignored him.

'Here's a cool one: Titian's *Danae* in the Capidimonte Museum in Naples. It's got an interesting history too, because Hermann Goering stole it during World War Two and it was recovered from a salt mine in Austria.'

'Is that so?' Patrick half rose from his seat as the Jets powered forward, and then swore as somebody called a time-out and a commercial for Budweiser took control of the television screen. 'A salt mine, eh? Now that is cool; did the salt not damage it?' With the football temporarily suspended he could spare some attention for Irene.

She treated him to one of the frowns that regularly subdued her underlings. 'And here's more. During the war the British carried all London's art treasures to underground quarries to protect them from German bombers.'

'Hitler should have nuked them. The Brits drove my ancestors out of Ireland.' Patrick returned to the television, switching channels as the commercial break seemed to last longer than the game. He swore again, 'talking of the Brits, here they are now, Queen Elizabeth in all her pomp and glitter.'

Irene studied the screen, consciously comparing the British queen with Ms Manning and wondering who was the wealthier. 'That's the queen eh? She thinks she's real special, with all these horsemen around her.'

'Toy soldiers,' Patrick gave his opinion. 'A squad of US Marines would wipe out the lot of them.'

'Nice jewellery she's wearing,' Irene commented. 'I could see me wearing that tiara when I next go shopping in Macy's.'

'That would be worth stealing for Ms Manning.' Patrick held Irene's eyes. The smile began slowly but spread until his whole face altered. He reminded Irene of a mischievous small

47

boy in an adult's body. 'Think of that as a blow for old Ireland. Steal the crown jewels of England and bring them to America.'

'They're certainly valuable,' Irene agreed.

'And portable,' Patrick continued.

'And spectacularly impressive.' Irene was also smiling. 'What a coup that would be!' She returned to the computer and typed in 'Crown Jewels of England.' Paraphrasing the words, she read out the various entries.

'The Crown jewels are more than just a crown; the collection also contains sceptres, orbs, swords, gold and silver plate and other regalia. The plate was refashioned in 1661 after Cromwell had ordered the originals melted down.'

'Well done, Cromwell,' Patrick approved. 'I'll bet he was an Irishman.'

Ignoring him, Irene continued, 'The Imperial State Crown was worn at the coronation. Its jewels are so ancient that Edward the Confessor is believed to have worn the sapphire as a ring.'

'Edward the who?' Patrick asked.

'Confessor. Listen. The Imperial State Crown holds over 3000 diamonds and pearls, including the incomparable Cullinan diamond. The Queen Mother's Crown has the Koh-I-Noor diamond, the Mountain of Light which carries a curse for male owners, but any woman who owns it will rule the world.'

'Sounds just Ms Manning's sort,' Patrick moved closer. Let's get them.'

'There's just one problem,' Irene read on. 'The English crown jewels are housed in an underground Jewel House beneath the Waterloo Barracks.' She looked up. 'Barracks. Get it? That means soldiers.'

'Toy soldiers, though. Brits.'

'Soldiers with guns.' Irene stepped back from the screen. 'Museum guards I can cope with, soldiers with guns are scary. Even a Brit can shoot somebody; all he has to do is point and click.'

Patrick had replaced her at the computer. 'You give up too easily.' He continued the search and laughed out loud. 'We can still get at the Brits though, and without burrowing under a barracks. Look: they've got more than one set of crown jewels. The Queen has a spare set in Scotland. The Scottish crown jewels.'

Irene leaned over his shoulder as childhood memories stimulated her interest. 'The Scottish crown jewels? I did not know that they had any.'

'Well, they have, and I bet that a tin-pot little country won't guard them as well as the English,' Patrick cracked his fingers in a gesture that Irene always found intensely irritating. 'That's our target, so let's get to work.' He grinned across to her. 'They might have soldiers with guns in London, but in Scotland even the soldiers wear skirts. This should be easy.'

Irene looked at him, aware that the decision had been made. She was going to steal the crown jewels from the Queen of Britain. She was going to steal the crown of James Stuart. In her mind she could nearly hear the approval of Johnnie Armstrong.

Chapter Four: Edinburgh: December

The view from the hotel window was spectacular. Directly opposite her window, Edinburgh Castle glowered from its volcanic rock onto a swathe of gardens and the bustling artery that was Princes Street. A long row of double-decked buses chuntered along the street, while pedestrians ignored every traffic signal as they dashed over the road as the fancy took them.

'Don't they have rules of the road here?' Patrick slid a hand around Irene's waist.

'Apparently not. That's the castle over there.' She indicated the massive stone structure with its towers and walls. 'I've never seen a real castle before. It's different to what I imagined.'

'Bigger.' Patrick gave his opinion. 'But just as old fashioned.' He lifted the binoculars from the highly polished table and scanned the castle. 'It looks quite solid, though, but there are lots of windows to break into.'

'Are there any guards?' Irene lifted her own binoculars and stood beside him at the window.

'According to the guidebook, there are uniformed stewards in the castle for the benefit of the tourists. They speak different languages.' Patrick grinned to her. 'It doesn't say that they carry guns.'

'Nobody carries guns over here,' Irene retorted. 'The walls look thick though, and that rock is steep.' She allowed her binoculars to sweep over the volcanic plug, slowly searching for an easy way up.

'That doesn't matter. We won't be climbing any cliffs and I don't think that we'll be tunnelling through the castle walls.' Placing his binoculars on the window ledge, Patrick leafed through the booklet that he had bought at the airport. 'They call the jewels the Honours of Scotland,' he said, 'and they are on exhibition inside the castle.'

'We'll go there right after breakfast,' Irene smiled brightly, 'how good of them to show us everything.' Raising her binoculars again, she examined the battlements of the castle. A score of heads bobbed above the walls as, despite the winter chill, tourists gaped over the view of Scotland's capital. There were stone walls and colourful winter clothing, grilled windows and laughing children: a composition of opposites. 'Imagine if the States allowed tourists to wander around Fort Knox,' Irene said. 'I mean; it's as if they're asking to be robbed.' She slapped his leg smartly, 'how do we get in, Patrick?'

'Through the front door,' he replied. 'It tells us here: the Castle of Edinburgh rears from its volcanic rock right in the centre of the city. With public gardens to the north, and busy streets on the other three sides, the only public entrance is on the east, where a gateway glowers down the length of the Royal Mile, once Edinburgh's main thoroughfare.'

Irene dragged Patrick up the steeply curving Mound, before passing the ancient tenements that led to the Esplanade in front of the castle. Two young soldiers stood sentinel, modern reflections of the statues of Robert Bruce and William Wallace, the mediaeval guardians of the realm who stared sightlessly over an international collection of visitors.

'Military. That's not good,' Patrick commented. He eyed the nearest soldier with distaste. The sentry stared ahead, his pressed uniform and bayoneted SA80 rifle somehow out of place against the dark stone of the castle.

'He's not wearing a kilt,' Irene said. 'I wanted to see a soldier wearing a kilt.' She stopped to take a photograph before crossing the bridged moat and passing through the main doorway. The castle closed in on them, wearing its history like a sombre shroud. A squad of soldiers marched down the precipitous road from the castle's interior, their boots echoing on the granite setts as they exchanged jokes. A sergeant winked to Irene, his back straight, eyes mobile.

'Lots of military.' Patrick sounded gloomy.

'Let's get an idea of the place first,' Irene suggested, photographing the portcullis whose spikes threatened from above. The walls rose before them, formidable as ancient cliffs, while each doorway led into cavern-like rooms, shadowy, strong and enigmatic. Irene thrilled at the dark blood of history as tourists exclaimed at the eighteenth century cannon and stared over the battlements, eating hamburgers where once besieged men despaired of their lives.

'This is a place of stone,' Irene said, tapping her toe on a basaltic outcrop of rock. 'Stone ground, stone walls, stone floors and stone roofs.' She shivered in the keen wind. 'Maybe we should find something else?'

'Enough of this,' Patrick shoved past a crowd of people who listened to the tales woven by a green-uniformed steward. 'Come on Irene; let's find the Crown Jewels.'

There was a courtyard in the heart of the castle, with Scotland's National War Memorial on one side and the much older Royal Apartments on the other. A slender central tower thrust toward a sky of grey.

'Here we go,' Irene could not contain her rising excitement as she squeezed through the entrance, immediately aware of the aura of age.

Irene was unsure what she had expected, but, refusing the sombre allure of the great hall, she moved straight to the rooms in which the story of the Crown Jewels was told. Unobtrusive wardens stood quietly in the rear, watching everybody and smiling as they answered the occasional enquiry. Irene took copious notes from the cards. 'These Honours are old,' she said quietly. 'Older than the English crown.' She pointed to the words. 'It says here that these are one of the oldest sets of crown jewellery in Christendom.'

'That's cool.' Patrick nodded 'Where's Christendom?'

'The Christian west, you ass hole! Europe!' Irene landed a playful punch on his arm.

Patrick rubbed his arm. 'Does it say how valuable they are?'

'No. But Pope Julius II gave the sword to King James in 1507, and Pope Alexander gave him the sceptre in 1494. That's just two years after Columbus discovered America.' Irene shook her head. 'It says that the crown was refashioned for King James V in 1540. That means it was made from an even older crown.' The mention of that king brought an image of her ancestor hanging from a tree and she frowned. She must keep this impersonal, but she wanted James Stuart's crown.

'Yes, but is it valuable?'

'It's made of Scottish gold and Scottish pearls, with other precious stones and as much history as you can get.' Irene nodded. 'Yes Patrick, these Honours are valuable, or rather invaluable. Irreplaceable. You could not buy them or make them.'

'Will they do for Ms Manning?'

'Oh yes.' Irene looked forward, into the brightly lit room that held the Honours of Scotland. She shivered with apprehension, for these jewels were not just a means to her end of becoming Ms Manning's neophyte; they held an extra significance in her life. 'The oldest crown jewels in Britain, one of the oldest in Europe, worn by James IV, James V and

Mary Queen of Scots. They are a unique set of royal jewellery unmatched anywhere in America.' She nodded, 'oh yes, Patrick, they'll do for Ms Manning.'

'Let's see them then.' With uncharacteristic chivalry, Patrick stepped back to allow Irene first access to the Crown Room. She bobbed in a whimsical curtsey and negotiated the curving stair.

Tapping the massive entrance door, Irene pulled a face. Raised on Hollywood movies where muscular heroes kicked their way into apartments, she could not imagine even Arnold Schwarzenegger bursting through four-inch thick steel. She stepped into the darkened Crown Room and stopped.

Ms Manning's personal collection had been magnificent, beautiful but clinical; a collection without a soul, but the sheer splendour of the Scottish Honours twisted something deep inside her. Irene drew in her breath, aware of the rapid increase in her heartbeat.

The crown was central to the display, its circlet of gold mined from Crawford Moor in the heart of the Scottish Lowlands. The metal glowed with a soft sheen, made more valuable by the knowledge that it had adorned the heads of royalty. Augmenting the gold, twenty precious stones and twenty-two gemstones glinted under the subdued lighting.

Irene pressed her nose against the glass, striving to see everything that she could, as if she could hold the object with her mind and mentally transport it to New York.

'What do you think?' Patrick squeezed against her, whispering in the restrained atmosphere of the room.

'It's beautiful,' Irene tried to hide the awe from her voice. She closed her eyes momentarily, seeking some objectivity. She was not here to admire these objects, only to use them. 'Ms Manning will approve.'

Patrick nodded to the crown. 'I've been counting the stones. I make it eight diamonds and over seventy pearls, plus a bunch of semi-precious stones, and a whole lot of gold.'

Irene could nearly see the dollar signs in his eyes. 'I believe you,' she said. 'But it's not the intrinsic value of the thing that's important; it's the historical association and the symbolism. Imagine, kings and queens have worn that crown.'

'Have they used that too?' Patrick gestured to the sword. 'It must be five feet long! How many heads has that cut off, eh? I can see old Braveheart carrying that into battle. No wonder he won.'

Irene's eyes caressed the long blade of the sword. 'What more would Ms Manning want that a present from a pope to a king? Look at the workmanship; it's magnificent. And the Scots hid it from Cromwell, and again from Hitler.'

'Yeah.' Patrick turned his attention from the sword to the rectangular lump of sandstone that was also displayed. 'What the hell's that?'

Irene squinted to read the description. 'The Stone of Destiny,' she intoned, making the words sound very solemn. 'It says that the kings and queens of Scotland sat on it to be crowned. It's an ancient seat of power.'

'Well imagine that. The kings sat on an old rock.' Patrick shook his head. 'It's time that somebody dragged this country into the twenty-first century. 'Do you think they've heard of television yet?'

'They invented it,' Irene said absently. She stared at the Stone, wondering at its story, at the generations of kings that had perched on its rugged surface, and what had happened to them. 'It's amazing really.'

'Yeah, really amazing that people who keep a stone all locked up could invent a television. But what's that?' Patrick nodded to the sceptre that lay at the side of the Stone. 'That looks better. Did the Pope give the king that too? What was it – a royal truncheon to crack skulls?'

'It's a symbol of power,' Irene corrected. 'Did you not read any of the stuff back there?'

'Another symbol. Everything's symbolic; nothing's for real. Is it gold though?'

'Gilded silver.'

Patrick grunted his disappointment. 'Hey, though, is that a diamond on top?'

'No.' Irene shook her head. 'Rock crystal, the same as fortune tellers use in fairgrounds.'

'Jesus. That good eh?' Patrick stood up. 'We should have stayed with the *real* crown jewels. We've flown all this way to look at a fairground trinket.'

'That fairground trinket is worth countless millions,' Irene said quietly, 'and it carries the soul of a nation. We'd be making Ms Manning a royal gift.'

'And she'd be giving you her queendom.' Patrick suddenly grinned. 'Where did all this poetry come from, Irene? Hey there, we've seen the damned things, let's go away and plan.'

'Edinburgh is a city of many layers. Surrounding the castle, the mediaeval Old Town of narrow streets, wynds and closes has a history of riot, secret vice and blood soaked into its weary stones. Beyond the Old Town is the New, a masterpiece of Georgian and Regency planning, a place of Classical architecture, of crescents and terraces, of formal gardens and sophistication. Beyond that again spreads the Victorian city of tenements and tall-spired churches, dominated by students, artisans and clerks, and yet further out is a peripheral ring of trim bungalows and municipal housing schemes interspersed with some of the most expensive dwellings in Scotland.'

Putting down the guidebook, Irene sighed. She had no intention of venturing beyond the town centre, and had found sanctuary from the chill in a small and busy pub a musket shot from the castle. The interior was dark but cosy and she smiled her way to the bar to order pie and chips and two pints of Scottish beer.

Patrick screwed up his face at the taste and colour. 'Don't they have American beer, here? This stuff is dark.'

'Drink up and don't draw any more attention to yourself.' Irene opened up the notes that she had made. 'We have a lot of work ahead of us. First we have to decide exactly what we want, then how to get it.'

'We want the crown,' Patrick said at once. 'The rest is just garbage. Big swords, hunks of rock and gilt sticks with crystal balls.'

'We want the full Honours,' Irene said, ignoring his outburst, 'but not the Stone of Destiny.' Some instinct told her not to touch the Stone; while the Queen claimed the Honours, she guessed that the people placed more value on that undistinguished chunk of sandstone. It would be better not to disturb tranquil waters, for who knew what Caledonian monster lurked beneath. Besides, King James V had worn that crown, and she wanted it badly. 'We want the full honours,' she repeated.

'Why?'

'A full set is always worth more than the sum of its parts,' Irene said. 'Don't argue.' Her smile was intended to remove any sting from the rebuke.

Patrick did not argue. 'If that's what you want.' He took a sip of his beer and screwed up his face.

Irene looked around her. Dominating the back wall of the pub, a large painting showed a scene from the Battle of

Waterloo, where British cavalrymen hacked at a mob of French soldiers. One of the British also held a tricolour standard. 'They like their history, don't they?'

'It's all they've got,' Patrick said. He drank some more of his beer. 'We have four problems then. We have to break into a castle, remove the stuff, get away again and carry everything into the States.'

'We'll take them one at a time,' Irene decided. 'One: breaking in. We don't have to. The castle doors are open, so we go in as ordinary tourists, just as we did today. There must be somewhere that we can hide in a place that size. That's been done before; I've seen it in loads of movies.'

'That plan's so simple it must work,' Patrick grinned. 'Imagine allowing unarmed stewards to guard a queen's treasure in a place full of dark corners. So we'll do as you say. Breaking the stuff out might be more difficult.'

'I agree.' Irene looked at him across the littered table. 'The only way into that room is up a narrow curving staircase and through the steel door. There are no windows in the Crown Room, the walls are at least two feet thick and it's up three flights of stairs; I saw electronic surveillance equipment too. I hoped you could think of something.'

Patrick shook his head slowly. 'Maybe we can't sneak in and lift the crown then. Listen, the stewards don't carry guns, so how about we do it the old fashioned way. You've got a million dollars to play with. Hire a few hit men from the States and hold the place up. Smash the glass and run. Sure there'll be alarms ringing, but the limeys won't know what to do; they live in the past.'

'And you live in Hollywood.' Irene glanced up. A party of soldiers had entered the pub, led by the sergeant who had winked at her in the castle. Each man armed himself with a pint of beer before filing to a table that miraculously emptied at their advance. The sergeant grinned to Irene.

'Hello there,' he said, 'did you enjoy your visit to the castle?' His accent was very Scottish.

'It was very interesting,' Irene told him. The sergeant was not tall, perhaps an inch shorter than her five eight, but he was broad shouldered and fit. Multicoloured medal ribbons decorated his breast.

'You spent a lot of time in the Crown Room,' the sergeant observed. He nodded to Patrick, eyes narrow, sizing him up. 'American are you?'

'New York City,' Irene said proudly.

'The Big Apple eh? Nice place.' The sergeant approved. Light gleamed on the badge on his Glengarry. 'My wife goes shopping there sometimes. She flies over for the weekend,' he glanced across to his men, who were talking forcibly about football. 'Well, enjoy your stay in Scotland.'

'We will,' Irene said, and then on an impulse, she leaned closer. 'Tell me, are you based permanently in the castle? Like a sort of guard? Or do you get out to other places?'

The sergeant crouched down at her side, obviously willing to talk. 'We get around,' he said. 'The redcaps, that's the Royal Military Police, are always in the castle, but you don't want to see them.' He shook his head. 'But they'll see you all right. Eyes in their arse, these boys. The headquarters of 52 Infantry brigade is also in the castle, the clerks and staff and so on.' He shrugged, 'we're only there temporarily. We're just back from a tour of Iraq, so it's good to get some peace.' He sank about half his pint in a single draught. 'Why do you ask? Are you from a military background?' He glanced at Patrick, eyes still challenging, 'or do you want to change your boyfriend for a squaddie?'

Irene gave the crinkle-eyed laugh that men always loved. She leaned closer to Patrick and patted his arm reassuringly. 'Not at all, I'll keep him for a bit longer. No, sergeant, I just wondered how much of the castle is for real and how much for tourists like me.'

Stepping across to his men, the sergeant requisitioned a chair from a disgruntled private soldier and dragged it across. 'About half and half,' he said. 'It's still a working military base.'

Releasing Patrick, Irene smiled into the sergeant's eyes. 'With all the terrorist threats, should you really be telling me all this military information?'

'If it was a secret,' the sergeant said, grinning, 'I would never get to know about it.' He glanced over to his men before returning his attention to her. 'Anyway, it's all on the Internet, if you can be bothered to search. Is it Edinburgh Castle you are interested in, or just castles in general? Scotland's got plenty to choose from.'

'Only Edinburgh.' Irene's smile had charmed scores of men in her career, but the sergeant seemed immune. She got the disturbing impression that he was assessing her even as she asked the questions. 'We really loved your crown jewels,' she said breathlessly, 'does the Queen wear them when she comes to Scotland?'

'Not any more,' the sergeant said. His smile seemed to have disappeared as he moved his attention from Irene to Patrick. 'She likes them to stay in the castle so that everybody can see how rich she is.'

'Come on, Sarge!' one of the privates shouted across the room. 'Stop chatting up that woman before I tell your wife.' There was a series of catcalls and whistles that caught the attention of the barmen. 'Bring her over here instead!'

The smile was back on the sergeant's face. 'You're in demand. Come on over and meet the Jocks.'

'The what?' Patrick looked confused, until Irene nudged him hard in the ribs. 'The soldiers,' she explained, fiercely. She nodded to the sergeant. 'Glad to,' she said. An opportunity to talk to members of the garrison was potentially invaluable. If she could ply them with drink, they might speak about the security arrangements for the Honours. 'Come on Patrick. You should feel quite at home.' She gave her most seductive smile to the sergeant. 'He was in the Marines.'

The sergeant nodded, understanding softening his eyes. 'I thought there was something, but we won't hold it against him,' he dragged their chairs across the room, with the patrons of the pub clearing before them.

The soldiers were younger than Irene had thought; boys barely out of their teens with thin faces and strain in their laughing eyes. They welcomed her like a sister, nodded to Patrick and began an exchange of quick-fire repartee that left her floundering. Leaning back in her seat, Irene waited for a gap in the conversation before she attempted flattery.

'So what are you? Special Forces?'

The laugh was predictable as the soldiers glanced at each other. The youngest spoke. 'No, we're real soldiers. The government calls us the Royal Scots Borderers, first battalion of the Royal Regiment of Scotland, but everyone else knows that we're the Royal Scots.'

Irene saw the sergeant hide a smile and guessed that there was some dispute between the British government and the serving soldiers. She put the information aside in case she could use it later.

'Royal Scots? That sounds impressive. I bet you're all combat veterans.'

'Up the Royals!' A red haired private shouted, causing a few heads in the pub to turn. Seeing the reaction, the other two privates joined in.

'Up the Royals! Up Pontius Pilate's Bodyguard!' There was slight bitterness in the laughter.

'Pontius Pilate's Bodyguard?' The significance was lost on Irene.

'It's an old joke,' the sergeant explained. 'There was an argument once, about 1640, when the Royals were serving with the French. We claimed precedence over one of the senior regiments of the French Army, and they objected.' He grinned. 'I'd like to have seen that. Anyway, one of the French officers said that the Royals had been asleep at their posts, and said that if we even predated them, we must be Pontius Pilate's Bodyguard. Our lot just laughed, and said that if we had been, Christ's body would never have left the sepulchre. So we've been Pontius Pilate's Bodyguard ever since.' His smile was suddenly sour. 'Until the government decided to destroy centuries of tradition with a pen.' He disappeared for a minute, returning with a tray on which were six pints of beer. 'Come on lads, I'll be leaving soon.'

'Leaving?'

'Back to work.' The sergeant passed around the drinks. 'Do you like Scotland, then?'

'Love it,' Irene enthused as the young Royals gathered around her. She was well aware that they were ogling, but enjoyed the attention. These joking warriors were a change from the corporate suits and sycophants with whom she normally spent time.

'Even in winter?' The red headed private seemed doubtful.

'We have winter in the States too,' Irene told him, 'and it's about the only time we could both get off work.'

'Your crown jewels were awesome,' Patrick said, 'but it's amazing that they've never been stolen.'

'How?' The redheaded private asked, his eyes shrewd. 'How's it amazing?'

'How?' When Patrick looked blank, Irene realised that the Scots often substituted the word 'how' for 'why'. 'Well, they're so valuable. Somebody must have tried to steal them.'

'Maybe.' Another of the privates, a man with a sombre complexion and a scarred lip said, 'but how're they going to get them oot? What with the redcaps and us and all the cameras and that.' He shrugged. 'Anyhow, we'd kill the bastards.'

Irene exchanged a glance with Patrick, who was suddenly very quiet. 'Kill them? For stealing?'

The privates nodded. 'Aye. How no'? That's what we're paid for.' The scarred man stared at Patrick without a trace of humour. 'You ken that. The American Marines would dae the same.'

Irene recognised the words as a challenge, although she was not sure how. She laughed to defuse the tension. 'Quite right too,' she said. 'That's the Queen's crown after all.'

'Aye so it is,' the red head said, 'but she doesnae wear it.'

The sergeant glanced at his watch. 'All right lads. Back on duty in ten minutes.' He downed his pint in a single vast swallow, stood up and adjusted his uniform. 'Have a good holiday in Scotland, miss, and you too, marine.' He smiled to Irene, but when he looked at Patrick the humour dropped from his eyes and just for a second Irene saw something of the steel within. The trio of ribbons on his chest took on a new significance.

'She's wanting it this year though,' the red head continued as though the sergeant had not spoken.

'Wanting it?' Irene found it difficult to keep up with the speed of the conversation.

'She's wanting the croon,' the redhead explained, shaking his head at her inability to comprehend.

'How's that?' Irene slipped into Scottish vernacular. 'Is she coming to Edinburgh?'

All the three soldiers began talking at once, obviously eager to impart their information. After a few minutes Irene held up her hands, laughing. 'One at a time, please, gentlemen.'

The soldiers grinned and subsided into quiet until the scarred man spoke. 'The Queen comes up to Scotland every summer for a wee holiday and to remind us that she exists. This year her visit is at the same time as some European political meeting, so she's doing the whole pageantry thing, with the Crown Jewels carried doon the High Street under a guard of honour. The whole works.'

Irene nodded. Suddenly everything seemed very simple. 'Will you be there?'

'Naw.' The soldier shook his head. 'We're away tae Helmand. Some other lot will be the escort.'

Irene nodded. Lifting her camera, she took a couple of quick photographs, for which the soldiers posed quite happily. She could feel her heart beginning a rapid tattoo as ideas were forming. Not yet complete, they formed a series of unrelated images in her mind, and she knew she must have peace in which to create an ordered tableau. 'Your sergeant will be waiting for you,' she said, and was surprised at the speed with which the three soldiers finished their beer before leaving the pub. She looked at Patrick.

'Let's go for a walk.'

Irene liked to walk. She found that the regular physical motion helped clear her mind of all non essentials and enabled her to view her problems one at a time. Walking also created a personal space into which people were reluctant to intrude. Normally she paced the lawns and bowers of Central Park, but today Edinburgh would have to do.

She headed downhill, following the line of Edinburgh's historic Royal Mile to Holyrood Palace, past the Scottish Parliament building and into the green oasis of Holyrood Park.

'This is Edinburgh's answer to Central Park,' she said, looking up at the impressively unadorned heights of Arthur's Seat. Snakes of mist smeared the summit. 'According to the guide book, this used to be a Royal Hunting park, but now anybody can walk in it.'

Patrick grunted. He knew her well enough not to break into her thoughts.

'So let's walk, then,' Irene commanded.

She expected the images that came unbidden, each one inspiring the next so they crowded her mind, jostling for attention in an overlapping conglomeration of ideas. Some she accepted and slotted into place, others she rejected without remorse. Very gradually, she formed a comprehensive picture, chipping at the anomalies until it was as near perfection as possible.

With Patrick a silent shadow at her side, Irene followed the line of the Radical Road, panting as she forced herself up the steep path that cut under the Salisbury Crags, the great red cliff that overlooked the Royal Mile, until she stopped at the top and waited for Patrick to catch up. The Edinburgh wind carried a chilling dampness, so she pulled her coat tighter around her and wished that she had brought a scarf.

'This is a city of history and views,' Patrick said when he had recovered his breath.

'And our springboard to success,' Irene added. She stood on the edge of the path with the hundred-foot drop beneath her and the spires and turrets of the Auld Town a jagged skyline in front. 'There's the castle up there, and Holyrood Palace down there,' she indicated each building with an expansive gesture from her right arm. 'And there,' she pointed to a spreading collection of modern roofs, 'is the Parliament building.'

'So I see,' Patrick shivered. He also had not brought sufficient clothing for a Scottish winter.

'So when the Honours of Scotland are brought from the castle, they must pass down the Royal Mile, take a right in front of the palace, and enter the Parliament.' She turned to face him, controlling the excitement that continued to grow inside her. 'We'll take the Honours on the journey, Patrick, not in the Castle. The security there is impossible, but when the Honours are on the road, they are far more vulnerable.'

'Limey bastards,' Patrick agreed. He shivered as a blast of cold air whistled through the nick in the Crags behind him. 'Come on; let's get back to the hotel.'

'Not yet.' Irene looked over the skyline, surveying the castle and the church spires, the steep rooftops and the crow-stepped gables, the small windows and walls of solid stone. 'Don't you find this all romantic? Knowing that kings and queens have passed over here?'

Patrick shook his head. 'No. It was kings and queens that sucked the soul from Ireland.'

Irene shook her head. 'Can't you let up, for once? Mary Queen of Scots might have stood on this very spot, and Robert the Bruce could have hunted just here.' She stamped her foot on the pebbled path. 'Come on Patrick, do something romantic. Do something that we can remember for ever.'

'We're not here for romantic,' Patrick reminded her. 'We're here to steal the Crown Jewels. What happened to that hard-assed New York businesswoman?'

Irene looked at him for a second, the animation fading from her face. 'You're right of course; we don't have time.' She remembered Ms Manning's words; she had to travel alone if she was to become a corporate success. Once they had stolen the Honours, she would lose Patrick. He had just proved his expendability. 'Now, you tell me about these useful friends of yours.'

Chapter Five : New York: March

Irene presided over the gathering, sitting slightly nervously in the centre with Patrick directly opposite and the five others in a loose circle around them. There was a half empty bottle of Jack Daniels in the middle of the table with a coffee pot at its side, while cigar smoke hazed the room.

'Thank you all for coming,' Irene stood to speak, as she had done in a score of board meetings in her previous job, but then she had been practically certain that the committee members were not responsible for an unknown number of murders. 'My colleague, Patrick McKim has brought you all here, but until now you are not aware why.'

The faces stared at her, some unemotional, others questioning. Allowing the ash to fall from her cigar, the only other woman lifted the bourbon bottle and poured herself a drink.

'I have been contracted by an influential client to steal the Scottish Crown Jewels. I need help to do this. That is why you are here.'

'Steal the what?' The woman looked over the rim of her glass. Although only in her mid-thirties, bitter lines were already forming around her mouth.

'Let me explain,' Irene said. Taking a couple of steps, she closed the dark blinds that covered the windows and pushed a button. The computer at her back clicked into a PowerPoint demonstration. 'Let's start from the beginning; this is a map of the United Kingdom,' and she waited until their eyes had adjusted to the bright screen, before pointing to the northern third. She clicked again. 'And this is Scotland. Until 1603 Scotland and England had separate kings, with separate crowns and separate crown jewels. Until 1707 they were separate countries with different parliaments.'

The woman poured herself another drink and stared pointedly at Patrick. 'Do we have to listen to this?'

Irene sensed that others in her audience shared the woman's impatience and rushed things along a little. 'In 1707 the parliaments were united into what is now the British parliament in Westminster.'

'Jesus, do we really care?' The nearest and smallest of the men was staring at the ceiling.

Controlling her nerves, Irene patted his arm. 'If you listen, Desmond, you might learn to care,' she allowed her smile to wash over him. 'One of the conditions of that Union was that the Scottish crown jewels, known as the Honours of Scotland, were never to leave the country. The Scots stuffed them in a wooden box and forgot them for over a century, but then a man named Walter Scott brought them out and put them on public display.'

'Get down to facts. How valuable are they?' The burliest of the listeners spoke with a thick Eastern European accent. He was tall, with a shock of blonde hair but eyes that were so intense that Irene struggled to hold them.

'Invaluable,' Irene said, 'they could not be bought. But my client wants them.'

The man slunk back into his chair, his eyes never straying from Irene's face. 'What will he do with them? Wear the crown when he's on the can?'

The crude comment raised a grunt of laughter, as Irene's feminist side registered the automatic acceptance that her client was a man.

'What happens to the Honours after they are stolen is not our concern,' said Irene deliberately choosing gender-neutral terminology. Let these creatures believe what they wanted; she would use them as required and discard them when necessary.

'Patrick and I have checked out the Honours in the castle, but there's no way they can be taken from there. They are held in a small room at the top of a flight of steep stairs. The only entrance is through a steel door with a score of electronic security devices, and the building itself is in the middle of an army barracks.' Irene clicked again, showing various views of the castle and the Crown Room. For good measure she had added the shots of the Royal Scots that she had taken. 'These are not National Guardsmen either, but front line infantry, veterans of Iraq.'

'If the place is so strong, then why show us?' The woman was wiry, with short dark hair and stern eyes. She might have been pretty a few years back, but now it looked as if life had worn her down. Pushing aside her glass, she poured herself some coffee.

Irene allowed the PowerPoint to stop at an image of the crown. She had taken especial care in selecting a shot that combined the maximum amount of gold with the minimum of velvet, and now applauded her choice as her audience craned forward. She could nearly taste their avarice. 'I am showing you the present home of the Honours partly to explain how much the Brits value them, and partly to show how fortunate we are.'

The burly man held his glass as if it were an enemy. 'Fortunate?' His eyes were venomous.

'Indeed,' Irene knew that she was in command of the situation, 'because we are not going to take the Honours from the Castle. The Queen is visiting Scotland in July, when there's an international conference at the Scottish Parliament. The Honours are being driven down the Royal Mile,' Irene clicked again, to show a map of central Edinburgh. She felt renewed interest among her audience as she pointed to the street that ran between the castle and the palace.

'So that's when we hit them?' The second man spoke with a Boston accent. Tall and dark headed, he wore a harp pendant around his neck.

'Yes, Bryan,' Irene confirmed. 'That's when we hit them.'

Placing both hands on the table, Desmond looked directly at Irene and spoke in a surprisingly deep voice. 'We hit them, but if your client gets the crown, what do we get out of it?' He looked around the table. 'I know Bryan, and everybody knows Mary,' he nodded to the second woman. 'As America's leading female rally driver, it would be a sin not to know her.' Mary smiled at the professional recognition. 'But I don't know *him*,' he stared at the blonde man.

'Of course. I should have introduced you all,' Irene stood up. She had made her point. Now everybody knew that she was in charge; she had the information and she had brought everybody together. Now she could begin to mould them into her team. 'You have all met me, and you know Patrick McKim, ex-marine and my partner. You should know Mary O'Neill; rally driver and member of the Irish Daughters of America. Then we have Stefan Gregovich, one of our leading Ukrainian citizens.' The blonde man raised a surly hand as the others nodded to him.

'And lastly we have Bryan Kelly and Desmond Nolan, both well known in the Irish American community.' Irene finished the introductions with a flourish.

'All very cosy, but you have not answered my question,' Desmond said. 'If there's nothing in this for us, I'm wasting my time.'

Irene took a quick sip of her coffee to combat the rapid drying of her mouth. The caffeine hit was essential, for she was unsure how these people would react. They might invite her to an Irish pub, or blow off her kneecaps, as the whim took them.

'It's an opportunity to prove that Irish patriotism of which you're so proud,' she said simply. 'And a chance to hit back at England.' Although she injected passion into her voice, Irene could not understand the intense nationalism of these people. Why did they constantly relive past events? Their ancestors had chosen to immigrate to the USA; well then, they should adopt the values of their new nation and forget the 'old country.' If Ireland had been that good, then nobody would have left in the first damn place. However, if Desmond was happy to allow centuries-old injuries to dominate his life, then she would exploit his hatred, as others had done before her.

Irene gave another of her captivating smiles, feeling her mouth ache with the strain. 'Patrick and I will do all the legwork and make all the arrangements. Apart from your various specialities, all you have to do is turn up for a couple of days before the job, perform the actual task and get home afterwards. Three days work, or four at most.'

'Various specialities? That's a bit open ended, is it not?' Desmond stood and took a step for the door, until Bryan extended a lazy hand to push him back.

'Don't be so hasty, Desmond. Listen to what the lady has to say. She has not called us all here for nothing, now.' He accentuated the Irish in his voice.

'Save for Stefan, you are all sons and daughters of Ireland,' Irene played her ace. 'Patrick hand-picked you as members of Irish organisations dedicated to uniting the Irish nation.'

'As our fathers and grandfathers were before us,' Bryan agreed. He eyed Irene warily.

'So what better opportunity could you have of striking a blow against the English than by stealing the crown jewels? Imagine the reaction as the Irish manage to remove one of the Queen's personal treasures from right under her nose?' Irene saw interest bleed into the eyes of Mary and Bryan, but Desmond was not so easily convinced.

'You said this was the Scottish crown jewels. Not the English.' Desmond stood up again.

'Yes, but it's the same queen.' Irene leaned forward to emphasise her point. She had spent the last week intensively researching British history and now ruthlessly applied her knowledge. 'This queen calls herself Elizabeth the Second – not Elizabeth the First, even although there has never been a previous Elizabeth on the Scottish throne. She considers Scotland as just another conquered country, an appendage of England.'

'So?' Desmond shrugged.

'So in her eyes Scotland as a country does not exist, any more than Ireland did.' She would like to confront Mary, but first must destroy Desmond's scepticism. One doubting member would compromise the effectiveness of her entire team. Another sip of coffee strengthened her for a renewed attack.

'There is an even more compelling reason. As I have already explained, in 1707 a Treaty of Union combined the Scottish and English parliaments. That treaty contained a clause that banned the Honours from being removed from Scotland.' Irene controlled her nerves as Desmond's glare remained uncompromisingly hostile. 'So if we succeed, or rather *when* we succeed, we will remove the Honours from Scotland, and thereby effectively nullify the treaty. We will be hastening the break up of the union, which means that Scotland

73

will not be bound to England, and Northern Ireland will be in limbo.'

Desmond sat down at last. 'No Scottish Union? So no Great Britain, and no reason for Northern Ireland?'

Irene nodded, wondering if Desmond really believed all this nonsense, or if he was merely trying to save face before his colleagues. 'We will be striking a greater blow for a united Ireland than has been struck since 1922, and without using terrorism, so the world will support us.' She held his gaze until he nodded again, then she sat down, trembling with the mental effort of persuasion.

'And me?' Stefan asked thickly. 'I do not care about Ireland or Scotland or any other land. Why should I take part in this robbery?'

'For the money, of course,' Irene was much happier away from ancient politics; she felt secure when dealing with honest greed. 'You work for three days and I pay you half a million dollars, plus whatever other jewellery you can keep. The crown, sword and sceptre are reserved for my client, but anything else that you can lift is yours.'

Stefan grunted and settled back down. 'A million dollars,' he said. 'Nothing less.'

Irene barely glanced at Patrick before shaking her head. 'Too much. 750,000, and that's final.'

The nearly reptilian eyes surveyed Irene before Stefan shrugged. 'All right.' He glowered at the others, as if gloating that he had upped his reward.

'Then let's get down to business,' Irene gave her brilliant smile to signal that the meeting had come to an agreement. 'Desmond, you are a document man. You job is to produce false passports for us. Bryan, you're the munitions expert. I want explosives. You, Stefan, know more about hits than the rest of us put together, so you work out details for the actual attack.' Dropping her smile, Irene faced Mary last, allowing a full ten seconds of silence before she spoke. 'We all know Mary's expertise.'

Mary's expression did not alter as she held Irene's gaze. She said nothing.

'So if you could brush up on the British rules of the road, we'll know that we are in safe hands.' Irene could not explain why she felt uneasy in Mary's presence. Perhaps it was because they had both smashed the glass ceiling, and any other barrier that got in their way, to achieve success, but while she had failed at *The Neophyte*, Mary had triumphed in a theatre traditionally dominated by men.

Mary stood up, gave a curt nod and walked out of the room. 'I'll think about it,' she said.

Patrick raised a hand. 'She'll come around. I'll make sure of that.'

Aware that everyone was watching her, Irene clapped her hands, 'Let's do this, people!' But even to her, the words sounded hollow. Recruiting another woman had been a mistake. There could be only one top bitch in any operation.

Chapter Six: St Andrews: April

The Swilkin Burn ran slow and dark beneath the bridge as Alexander Meigle placed the ball on the tee. When he looked up, weak sunlight highlighted the insignia of two crossed golf clubs that was emblazoned on his shirt. 'Three hundred and seventy-six yards,' he eyed the distance to the First Green, 'and a par four.'

'I have played the course before,' Colonel Drummond looked skyward, measuring the wind. He pulled his driver from the golf cart and took a practice swing. 'Hickory shafted,' he said, 'by Auchterlonies.'

'Your choice,' Meigle placed the face of his club against the ball and adjusted his stance. 'I prefer tungsten to these old fashioned things. More distance. But there, you're an old fashioned sort of fellow, with your old tweed jacket and those shiny brogues,' he grinned, teasing a friend that he had known for decades. 'You have to move with the times, James.'

Meigle swung, grunted slightly as the club made contact, and watched the ball soar up until it was lost against the blue of the sky. He shaded his eyes, nodding when the ball descended quickly and landed thirty yards from the green. 'Not too bad. You have to hit slightly to the left here.'

Drummond narrowed his eyes, waiting until Meigle's ball rolled to a stop. 'Let's see now. A slight breeze from the sea and damp grass underfoot.' He addressed the ball and swung, allowing his body to adapt to the follow-through. 'How's that for a man with old fashioned clubs?'

'Fair to middling.' Meigle watched Drummond's ball bounce on the fairway and roll to within a foot of his own. Sliding his hand over the handle of his buggy, he stepped forward, with the turn-ups of his trousers just breaking over his shoes. 'So how's the family, James?'

'Doing away, Sandy, doing away.' Drummond preferred to carry his bag as he strode, long legged, beside Meigle. 'Margaret's got herself the Architectural Chair at Glasgow University at last, which means that I don't see so much of her. She's hardly at home nowadays, what with conferences and researching and so on.'

'Good for her. I always thought that she was too clever for you.' Meigle stopped to admire the view over the bay, as he always did at this point. 'St Andrews looks its best at this time of year, don't you think?'

Drummond stood at his side. 'You say that every time you're here, Sandy,' he pointed out. 'Whatever the time of year is.'

'Maybe I do.' Meigle agreed. 'But it's true each time. And the children? How are they?'

'Fine. Andrew's just sent in his papers and he's entering Civvy Street. He found a job with a big American company.' Drummond scowled for a second. 'I'd prefer if he remained in the regiment, but there you are. Sarah is doing great things in Europe. She was in Frankfurt last I heard, but she said that she might be transferred to Strasbourg. Some financial matter with the EU.'

'Sarah working in Germany?' Meigle shook his head, 'It doesn't seem that long since you were complaining about her loud music keeping you awake all night!' He stopped and examined the lie of his ball. 'And Andrew resigned from the Guards? I thought he would follow in his father's footsteps.'

'So did I, but he's old enough to live his own life.' Drummond glanced backward. At seven in the morning the Old Course was fairly quiet, with only a handful of dedicated players braving the clock to worship at the shrine of golf. 'But I doubt that you've brought me here for an update on my family.'

Meigle addressed the ball, looking toward the green. 'You'll be introducing Andrew to the Society soon, then.'

'On his thirtieth birthday, as is the custom.' Drummond watched Meigle select a two iron. 'I'd chip it to the right and let the wind take it toward the hole.'

'It might be better to break the custom just this once,' Meigle chipped the ball long enough to avoid the Swilkin Burn, but hit it too far, so it rolled past the pin and nearly off the green.

'Bad luck,' Drummond sympathised. He drew out a club and, hardly pausing, knocked his ball directly onto the green. It landed, bounced once and rolled to within six inches of the hole. 'Is something happening?'

'Nice shot.' Removing the flag, Meigle selected a putter, lined up the ball and knocked it neatly into the hole. 'That's a birdie for me.' He stepped back. 'Yes, Jamie. There seems to be a threat to the Clach-bhuai'

Drummond looked up briefly, raised his eyebrows, and then returned his attention to the game. He putted gently and watched as the ball rolled directly into the hole. 'What sort of threat?'

Removing both balls, Meigle replaced the pin and walked slowly to the next tee. He eyed the distance to the green, allowing the North Sea breeze to fan his face. 'I'm not sure yet. The report was a bit garbled, but it seems definite enough.'

Drummond lined up for the hole, adjusting his tie so that it did not flap in the wind. 'Definite enough to justify a meeting of the Society?' He surveyed the fairway ahead. 'You know this course better than I, Sandy, so what do I do, drive left where there's plenty of room but the approach is awkward, or drive right, between these ugly bunkers and the gorse, and have an easier approach?'

'You're driving blind, Jamie, but hit left of Cheape's Bunker and go with the wind, Jamie. Always go with the wind at St Andrews.' Meigle watched as Drummond hit right, shaking his head as the wind carried the ball straight into a bunker. 'Bad luck.' He waited for a moment. 'Yes; the message did seem to justify an extraordinary meeting of the Society.'

Drummond waited until Meigle addressed the ball. 'That's unusual. When was the last extraordinary meeting held?'

'1941,' Meigle replied without lifting his eye from the ball. His driver struck sweetly and the ball soared toward the green, until a fluke of wind flicked it back, a full fifty yards short.

'Hitler's War,' Drummond hoisted his golf-bag onto his back and made for the bunker, with his nailed brogues leaving neat punctures on the grass. He studied the lie of his ball, selected a sand wedge and stepped quietly down. 'If I remember correctly, the Society had the Stone buried, together with all the associated paraphernalia.'

Meigle watched Drummond chip his ball expertly onto the fairway. A handful of sand drifted downwind.

'I haven't heard of any specific threats of war,' Drummond said as he climbed out of the bunker. 'And I would hear of that before you, so it must be something more direct.'

'I'll know more by the time we arrange the meeting,' Meigle sliced his next shot and the ball landed in the gorse.

'Damned bad luck. That's these tungsten shafts, fine for distance but poor for close work. You'd be better with the more traditional materials; centuries of experience and all that.'

'Damned bad play,' Meigle corrected. 'Never did like this game. I'll drop a shot and replace the ball.'

'How is your family?' Drummond asked. 'I heard that Anne has retired?'

'Two years ago,' Meigle agreed. 'We were married forty years then she decided to stop bringing in the money. Now she tries to help me all the time and manages a dozen different meetings for charities and the like.'

'Under your feet, eh? Hard luck,' Drummond sympathised. 'And the children?'

'Young Alex is doing well. He's in oil, you know; managing director of a multi-national. Just made a large strike in the Thar Desert or some other God-forsaken place. Rich as Croesus and a bigger sinner than Herod. Always got some stunner attached to his arm, or elsewhere.'

'You'll be proud of him, then.' Drummond lobbed his ball on to the green.

'Oh aye; chip off the old block.' Meigle smiled at some distant memory, and then examined the head of a number three iron. 'He lives his own life though; no time for an old duffer like me. You already know that Charles is in politics. He's an MP now, spending half his life working with the most appalling people.'

'They tell me that Westminster is like that. Terrible place.' Drummond watched as Meigle dropped a ball and knocked it a yard short of the green. 'And your girl? Young what's-her-name? Dammit, I should remember, I am her godfather for goodness sake.'

Meigle replaced his club. 'Young Rachel. They do say that the memory is the second muscle to fail, Jamie. She's not so young now, though. Caught herself a man and created a family. Quiet children; must take after the father. She's working on scientific research at Roslin. Something to do with environmental studies; God knows we need it with the world in such a state.' Meigle shook his head. 'You'll meet them later.'

'Of course.' Drummond looked behind him as two more golfers edged onto the fairway. One waved to him. 'Getting a bit public now, Sandy, don't you think?'

'Positively Princes Street,' Meigle agreed. 'Call it a draw shall we?'

'Fair result.' Lifting his ball, Drummond returned the wave and began to walk slowly back toward the clubhouse. 'You'll let me know in plenty of time about the meeting, I dare say?'

Meigle nodded. 'As soon as I get it arranged, Jamie. I'll have to allow time for the overseas members to come in.'

They walked past the golfers who had waved. One shouted over to them, enquiring if they had given up and Drummond stopped for a second. 'Too cold for an old man like me!' He waited for a response and grunted when none came. 'Poor quality. No sense of style at all.'

Meigle watched the golfer muff his drive. 'Poor golfer too, but that's no wonder when he's all padded up like that. He's got more layers of clothes on him than a polar bear. I was thinking of next month, Jamie. I don't want to wait any longer than that, in case anything happens in the meantime.'

Drummond nodded. 'That would be best then. You know my mobile number?'

'Of course.'

'Anytime, day or night, Sandy, if you need me.' They had reached the first tee, and people were gathering around the clubhouse to watch the golfers. 'I can come alone or with company.'

'Bring your son, Jamie; it's as good an opportunity as any to introduce him. And use your contacts; see if you can find out anything.' They shook hands, nodded and turned aside. Meigle rolled his clubs to the silver BMW and placed them carefully in the boot before sliding into the driving seat. It would take him nearly an hour to drive home to Edinburgh, and he had a meeting at ten. He looked up briefly as the helicopter lifted from the grounds of the Old Course Hotel, circled the town once and headed North West toward Perthshire. Trust Jamie to travel in style.

The news about the Clach-bhuai was disturbing, but it added interest to a life that was fast becoming dull. Perhaps people fantasised about retirement, but the path to enforced leisure was paved with boredom. He slammed the horn to warn a slow moving vehicle that he was coming, overtook smoothly and pressed down the accelerator. He hoped that the threat was genuine, so he could set his teeth into a challenge.

Chapter Seven : New York & Edinburgh: May

'The Honours have only left Edinburgh Castle twice in the last three hundred years,' Irene once again stood beside her laptop, lecturing her team. They listened intently, eyes focussed on the screen as she produced a series of images.

Patrick leaned across to Bryan and whispered something that made both smile.

'May I continue?' Irene's glare caused both to withdraw to their seats. 'In 1953 the Crown was taken for a national service of thanksgiving when Queen Elizabeth took the throne, and again in 1999 when the new Scottish Parliament was opened in its original building on the Mound.'

Irene flicked up a picture of the steep road that curved alongside Princes Street Gardens and pointed to the sombre structure that the Scottish Parliament used until their custom-built home was complete.

'And here are the Honours themselves.' Irene had located a further set of pictures of the Honours, and described each artefact in some detail. She noted that her team was much more focussed now that the hit was definite. 'One crown, one long sword and one sceptre.' She paused for a second before adding another click. 'There is also a mace, but that is reserved for Stefan. It is more modern than the others, so does not have the same historic value, although its intrinsic value is considerable. Added to your three-quarters of a million, Stefan, you should be able to retire on the proceeds.'

Stefan did not reply to her smile, but his eyes were sharp as they surveyed the picture.

'The Honours are being removed again, this year, when the Queen, Prince Phillip, Prince Charles and Camilla are all going to Edinburgh. The Scottish Government is hosting a European

Union conference, so various heads of state will be coming. The Honours are to be used to highlight the importance of the occasion.'

Irene did not know what type of persuasion Patrick had used to mollify Mary, but the driver looked nearly relaxed as she produced a cigarette lighter in the shape of a Formula One racing car and lit a cheroot. She looked to Patrick and raised her eyebrows.

'How are they to be transported?' Mary asked. 'Armoured car?'

'Nothing like,' Irene smiled. 'The British still have not learned about security. They are to be carried in a glass topped Rolls Royce so that the crowds can view them. The vehicle will drive slowly from the castle.' She clicked onto a map of the Royal Mile and traced the route with a pointer. 'Down here, passing these intersections,' Irene moved her pointer down the narrow street of Canongate to a roundabout at the palace. 'Then the procession goes around this roundabout and up to the Parliament building in Holyrood Road.'

'How wide are the streets?' Mary asked. She blew smoke toward the screen and smiled as Irene wafted her hand in front of her.

'Narrow; they are mediaeval, with hardly any room to move.' Irene clicked through her collection until she found a photograph of Canongate. The maroon-and-white double decker bus dominated the street, squeezing past a line of cars travelling in the opposite direction. 'Like this.'

Mary stood up and moved closer, bending forward to inspect the screen. Bryan immediately gave a wolf-whistle, to which she responded with a quick upward jerk of her middle finger. 'As you say, the street is narrow.' It was the first civil words that she had spoken to Irene, and the accompanying smile seemed genuine.

Irene nodded; her charisma was working at last. 'Ready?' On Mary's nod she returned to a map of the Royal Mile and reverted to flattery. 'Well Mary, you're the driver, so you know best. Where would you arrange the hit?'

'The broadest street, where we could have room to manoeuvre,' Mary said at once. She remained beside the screen, examining the map. 'I would wait in one of the intersecting streets, come out at speed and hit the convoy as it passed, then drive up here,' she jabbed her finger at the South Bridge, which cut a straight path north toward the centre of Edinburgh, and southward out of the city.

'That would be the sensible place to hit,' Irene agreed. 'So that is where the security will be tightest.' Relations between her and Mary might have thawed, but she would not allow the woman to dictate tactics.

'Security!' Patrick grinned, shaking his head. 'A glass topped vehicle!'

Desmond lifted his head. 'How much protection will there be?'

'Obviously I don't know the details,' Irene said, 'but the British like their Queen, and judging by previous royal occasions they will pack Edinburgh with police. They have lots of experience, and they did the 2005 G8 summit quite effectively, remember, and foiled that attempted attack on Glasgow Airport in '07.' Meeting Patrick's eyes, she winked. 'But let's start at the beginning. The Queen has a personal Scottish bodyguard, the Royal Company of Archers.'

'Jesus,' Bryan stared. 'Archers? You mean bows and arrows? Have the Brits forgotten about al-Qaeda already?'

Mary said nothing, but nodded to Irene to continue. The next picture showed a member of the Royal Company of Archers; everybody stared at the elderly man wearing a dark green tunic with black facings. 'These gentlemen have served as the sovereign's bodyguard in Scotland since 1822.'

'The same men, by the age of that one,' Bryan laughed.

'There are 530 of them, and they have to be Scots.'

'These men are for decoration. Show us who will really be guarding the Queen.' Mary raised her eyebrows in a manner strikingly similar to that of Ms Manning.

'There will be a ceremonial guard,' Irene said. 'Possibly of cavalry, such as these.' She showed a picture of the Household Cavalry, their breastplates and swords gleaming, plumes wafting in the wind and great horses clumping in front of London's Buckingham Palace. 'Or of infantry soldiers.' She showed an image of the Scots Guards, with red coats and bearskins, marching in procession.

'Toy soldiers,' Patrick gave his inevitable opinion.

Bryan looked over to Desmond and smiled. 'Targets,' he said, and pointed his index finger toward the screen.

'There will also be police.' Irene clicked onto a photograph of a Scottish police constable with his diced cap and truncheon. She allowed Patrick a minute to jeer, and then showed an image of an officer with a gun. 'Some will be armed.'

As she had expected, the sight of a police officer armed with an automatic rifle sobered the scoffers. They began to ask technical questions, which Irene allowed Patrick to answer. He had spent two days researching the type of weapons that British police were allowed to carry, and gave detailed information which the others wrote down.

'Maybe they carry guns,' Stefan said, his accent so thick that Irene had to struggle to understand him, 'but can they use them? Have they the will to shoot?'

Desmond grunted. 'Ask Jean Charles de Menezes.' His eyes were bright as he stared at the Ukrainian. 'That's the Brazilian that the London police murdered after the London bombing. They mistook him for a terrorist, so they said.'

'And ask anyone in the north of Ireland. The RUC were brutes,' Bryan added to Desmond's allegations. 'The British police are as capable of slaughtering civilians as any other enforcement agency.'

Irene waited until the emotional response had died down. 'So we have the Royal Company of Archers. We have soldiers, unarmed police and armed police.' She allowed her words to sink in. 'There will probably be plain clothed Special Branch officers amongst the crowd, and more than likely Special Forces ready somewhere nearby.'

'Jesus. They're animals.' Bryan shook his head. 'The SAS are trained killers. Savages. Uniformed murderers. Remember the three martyrs in Gibraltar?'

'I remember.' Irene had no recollection of any martyrdom in Gibraltar, but knew instinctively that it was best not to reveal ignorance to men such as Bryan Kelly.

There was a few minutes' silence as the team digested this new information. 'Are you certain that we should try for the Crown Jewels when they are in transit?' Patrick acted as spokesman for the rest.

'Yes.' Irene said. 'Now listen. View this objectively. As Mary pointed out, the soldiers are just for decoration. They are more concerned with pleasing their sergeant than in watching the crowd. They want to look their best, and they won't be carrying loaded rifles anyway. Discount them. And discount the Royal Archers. They are decorative old men. That leaves the unarmed police, a few police with weapons they'll hesitate to use in crowded streets, and maybe some SAS.'

'*Maybe* some SAS? Maybe is more than enough,' Bryan's voice rose an octave. 'Special Branch and SAS together? Count me out.' He frowned when Stefan laughed. 'Don't display your ignorance, Stefan. These people are killers.'

'And you are a frightened little Irishman,' Stefan taunted, 'full of big words but running from shadows.'

Irene allowed the testosterone to simmer for a few seconds. 'Nobody is running,' she soothed away the tension. 'Now tell me, gentlemen, what will be the priority of Special Branch and the SAS? The Queen and heads of state,' she answered her own question. 'To them, the Honours are just old baubles of little importance. Indeed,' she produced a smile that had even Desmond responding, 'the English would be pleased if the Honours were to disappear. That way there would be one less symbol of nationhood for the Scots. The English are scared that the Union might break up.'

'Are they?' Desmond showed more interest. He lit a cigarette.

'Of course.' Irene had been successful in her career because she thoroughly researched every project on which she was engaged. Now she could capitalise on the mind-bending hours she had spent studying modern Scottish history and the politics of devolution. 'That's why they allowed the Scottish Parliament, to quieten the threat of complete independence. That's why they lied to the Scots about the quantity of North Sea oil. That's why they crack down far harder on any militant Scottish nationalism than they do to Irish nationalism. The English need Scotland far more than Scotland needs the Union.' On an impulse she clicked back the PowerPoint to show the scarlet-coated Scots Guards. 'Without the Scots, who would fight England's wars? Without Scotland's oil, how could the English finance their cradle-to-grave welfare state?'

Desmond exchanged a glance with Bryan. 'Break the Scottish union and what has England left? Only the north of Ireland and Wales.' He leaned back in his chair, allowing smoke to trickle through his nostrils. 'Well now. Well, now indeed. Carry on, Irene, you are beginning to interest me.'

'So the English will have minimum security around the Honours, and maximum around *Her Majesty*.' Irene sneered the title to display her adherence to the Irish cause. 'What we have to do is divert even more of their attention to the Queen; thin out the security so the Honours are virtually unguarded when we hit.' Irene looked from one predatory face to the next to assess their enthusiasm.

Patrick was her current partner. He would do as she wished until she dumped him. Stefan had no concern about United Kingdom politics. He was a mercenary criminal, pure and simple; his reward was in dollar bills. Hatred of past English misdeeds motivated Desmond and Bryan; they lived on stories of the Great Hunger of the 1840s and reinforced historical tragedy with manufactured myth. Both men were bred on bitterness and indoctrinated with racial detestation. Mary was more enigmatic; Irene was not sure of her motive. Certainly she was of Irish stock, but she seemed to lack the fervour of the others. Perhaps gender issues drove her; a desire to prove herself equal to any man.

'Mary,' Irene decided to ask the direct question. 'You look uncertain. Are you still with us?'

'Still here,' Mary confirmed. When she looked up her eyes altered from lazy unconcern to intense concentration. She even managed a wan smile. 'But you seem to be keeping my part in this a secret. Where do you want me to drive?'

'I called this meeting to keep you all updated and to hear your input. When I have formulated a plan I will let you know.' Irene stopped as Mary frowned. She believed it was best to let her people have their say.

'You are taking too much on yourself,' Mary told her. She gesticulated to the computer screen. 'This all means nothing. If I'm putting my life on the line, I want to see the ground, not some map.'

Irene saw the sense in Mary's words. 'We'll all go over to Scotland,' she decided, 'and walk the route. Before the time comes for the hit, we'll know more about Edinburgh than the locals do.'

Since Stefan had demanded more than she had expected for his share, Irene had been carefully balancing her budget. She had only quarter of a million dollars to pay for everything, from hotel reservations to transport and weapons, so there would be no five star luxury on this trip, unless she dug deep into her own funds.

Mary surprised her with a smile. 'We didn't start off too good,' she spoke quietly, woman to woman in a testosterone charged room, 'but I've been watching you. I think we can work together.'

Irene ejected Patrick from his seat to move closer to Mary. Discarding the male-trapping charm, she allowed her voice to drop an octave. 'We'll have to learn to trust each other.'

'I trust your professionalism,' Mary's response was immediate. She repeated that taut smile. 'At first I thought you were just a spoiled little rich girl kicking out because *The Neophyte* failure had hurt you, but now I think there's more there.' She tilted her head, dark hair flopping and eyes assessing. 'I think that we both had to climb up a long ladder, with men pissing on us from above.'

Irene nodded. She had been right; Mary fought for feminism. She had not learned the advantages of being a woman in a world where most participants thought with their groins. As the object of life was success, empowering more women only increased the competition, so clearly Mary had misjudged the nature of Pandora when she campaigned to open the box. 'You reached the top of your ladder, Mary, and now *you* can pee on the *men* beneath. I'm still climbing.'

'Not many people could change course so quickly,' Mary's eyes were shrewd. 'Last fall you were all set for corporate success, now you are embarking on a criminal career.' She straightened in her seat. 'I wonder if the two are linked.' When Irene began to protest, Mary lit another cheroot. 'It's quite all right, Irene. I don't give a shit. I had to bend quite a few rules, but it seems that you are intent on completely burning the rulebook. Well, good for you, sister.'

Unused to being so expertly analysed, Irene withdrew into a smile; 'thank you for your approval,' she said.

'There's a lot to approve.' Leaning forward, Mary patted her thigh. 'We have more in common than you realise, Irene. Now, what was that about visiting Edinburgh?'

As a city geared for tourists, Edinburgh had more than its share of places to stay. Irene searched the Internet for somewhere within reasonable walking distance of the Royal Mile, but not within the orbit of the Parliament building. Central Edinburgh was infested with CCTVs and she had no desire to have her face, or the faces of her team, recorded.

Desmond had obtained a selection of blank passports and skilfully inserted false identities. He had altered Irene's nationality to Canadian, but even with her hair dyed black and a pair of frameless spectacles sliding down her nose, she was afraid that somebody might recognise her as the loser from *The Neophyte*.

'God, but I'm ugly,' Irene examined her new appearance in the bathroom mirror.

'Yes, but it suits you,' Patrick said solemnly, and ducked her emphatic slap.

Patrick also carried a Canadian passport, while the others retained their American identities. Mary's fame encouraged Desmond into some original thinking, so she wore tinted contact lenses to alter her eye colouring, padded the inside of her cheeks and cropped her hair. Subtle touches with a fine make-up brush deepened the lines of her face and added ten years to her age.

Eventually Irene found a hotel in a curved Georgian terrace five minutes from the city centre. Each room had an en-suite bathroom and as many facilities as a two star hotel should enjoy.

'Are you all together?' The booking clerk, a young brisk-eyed woman asked. Ordering a uniformed boy to carry their luggage upstairs, she offered each of them a complementary map of Edinburgh. 'You are on the first floor,' she said, 'four single rooms and one double.

'Thank you.' Irene handed a key to each of her team. 'Once we are settled in, we'll take a stroll around the city.'

'I'm sure that you will enjoy it,' the clerk said. 'I always believe that Edinburgh looks its best in May, before the main season begins and all the crowds come.'

Irene selected some brochures from the rack on the reception counter. 'Remember to take the camera, Patrick. We'll take some photographs.'

Only a hundred yards from the hotel, they came to the Dean Bridge, spanning an impressively deep chasm through which flowed a small river, the Water of Leith. Leaning as far over the wall as the sharp spikes allowed, Patrick pretended to fall. 'There's a waterfall down there; that's cool.' Bringing up the camera from its strap around his neck, he took a couple of photographs and hauled himself further up the parapet.

'Stop acting the fool, Patrick,' Irene snapped. 'We don't want to draw attention to ourselves.'

Patrick shrugged. 'I'm just acting like a typical American tourist,' he explained, jumping down. Mary smiled sympathetically.

'It's all that Marine training,' Irene explained. 'He responds best to orders.'

Flagging down one of Edinburgh's black taxi-cabs, Irene took them to the castle to look at the Honours, waited for their exclamations of awe and squandered a great deal of money in the castle book shop. Any scrap of information might be helpful. 'We'll pay in cash, ass-hole,' she said, pushing away Patrick's hand as he volunteered his credit card, reminding him 'your real name's on that.'

'Ease up on him,' Mary advised. 'After all, he's only a man.' When they exchanged an understanding glance, Irene realised that she might just begin to like Mary.

The uniformed stewards proved as helpful as before, relating something of the crown's history and answering every question that Irene asked.

'You mean the crown has hardly ever been out of the castle for hundreds of years?' Patrick could act the naïve tourist with skill, distracting the stewards as the others worked busily with their cameras.

'Hardly ever,' the steward confirmed. He was small and neat, with steady eyes and a face that revealed hard times.

'That's awesome,' Patrick said, as Mary pressed against him, smiling. 'We've nothing like that in Canada.'

'Maybe not, sir,' the steward agreed. 'But Canada has plenty other attractions. Your Calgary Stampede, for example. My sister speaks highly of it, and she lives in Edmonton. Which part of Canada do you come from?'

As Patrick hesitated, Irene answered, 'we're from Toronto.' She gave him a small nudge in the back. 'Come on, we've got the rest of Edinburgh to see. I want to visit the palace too.'

Comfortable with her position as tour guide, Irene walked them down the Royal Mile, pointing out the intersections where the route was most vulnerable, and the CCTV cameras that festooned the tall buildings.

'Lots of cameras,' Desmond said quietly. 'They'll be able to see everything that we do.'

'We can mask them,' Bryan told him. 'Or cut the cables.' He looked down the length of the street, with the slope gradually increasing and a number of small alleys leading away on the right. 'Plenty space here,' he said.

Stefan shook his head. 'It's too open. The police will be here to control the crowds.'

'And the army,' Patrick said. 'I would have marksmen up there,' he gestured to the upper flats with his chin. 'That building provides the best field of fire up or down the street.'

Irene touched his arm, attempting to make amends for her recent verbal humiliation of him. After all, she was not with him for his intellect, and her public criticism must hurt his ego. 'Thanks, Patrick. I knew that I brought you along for some reason.' He responded with a surprised smile.

'The police will have a block up there, too.' Stefan added. 'For crowd control.'

Irene did not offer him any reward. She was working out a plan in her head, but wanted to hear the input of these professionals first. 'How fast can you drive, Mary?'

'How fast is the car?' Mary responded with a shrug.

'Fast enough, then.' Irene led them down the Canongate, where dark tenements crammed claustrophobically over the narrowing street. 'This is my first choice of hit,' she stopped outside the centuries old Tolbooth. Two youths glowered at them from a pub doorway, one wearing a Burberry baseball cap, the other with a deep hood concealing his face.

Desmond shook his head. 'It will never do,' he said. 'Too cramped, and there's no space to escape.'

Mary pointed to the arched alley that pierced the massive stones of the Tolbooth and slid steeply downhill. 'If you mean for me to burst out of there and ram the Rolls-Royce, then that's fine, but there's nowhere to go but down there,' she pointed toward Holyrood Palace, then jerked her thumb in the opposite direction, 'or up there, back toward the castle and the soldiers.'

Irene ignored their protests. Waiting for one of Edinburgh's ubiquitous double decker buses to trundle past, she paced the width of the road. 'About five yards,' she said, 'and when the Queen comes there will be no other traffic and certainly nothing parked on the roadside.' She adopted her most serious look, as though their reactions disappointed her. 'So none of you think that it would be possible to hit here?'

'Not a chance in hell,' Bryan said definitely, as Mary shook her head. Patrick and Stefan said nothing.

'Good,' Irene allowed her man-killing smile to reappear. 'Then neither will the police. They are professionals, just like you, so they'll think the same way.'

'I have three questions,' Desmond said, looking decidedly unimpressed. 'One: how do we do the hit in this confined space? Two: how do we get away, and three: how do we stay free?'

'Take photographs,' Irene realised that the two youths had slouched closer. 'Try to look like tourists!' She waited until Bryan had pointed his camera at the Tolbooth with its projecting clock and exterior stairs. Patrick was more direct, focussing on the youths, who quickly withdrew, swearing. 'That's better. Well done, Patrick,' Irene favoured him again, before turning her attention to Desmond.

'Now, I'll take your questions one at a time, Desmond. One: we find out the order of this procession. I presume that it will be structured so that different sections of the crowd have something to keep them occupied. That means that there will be a gap between the Queen and the Honours, which is so much the better for us.'

'Why?'

Irene ignored Patrick's interruption. 'We wait at the entrance to Panmure Close,' she pointed to a gated narrow lane that ran at right angles to the Canongate, on the left side. 'The cameras can't see us there. When the Honours are approaching this spot,' she stamped her foot on the ground, 'then we create diversions to focus attention on the Queen and away from the Canongate. When the media and the crowd are looking somewhere else, then we come out of the close, blow open the glass and escape down there,' she pointed to an even narrower lane across the road. There was a name emblazoned on the stone above, but centuries of Edinburgh weather had worn it away.

'On foot?' Desmond shook his head. 'They'll catch us in minutes.'

'No they won't: all their attention will be on the Queen.' Irene shook her head. 'There will be hardly any security left here. There will only be crowds of tourists who will hamper the police, and lots of smoke to obscure the cameras.' She gave her most triumphant smile. 'We'll make sure that there is plenty smoke, so even if the CCTV cables are not cut, the cameras cannot pick us up. Now come with me.' She led them through the sloping anonymous close, and into Holyrood Road that ran parallel to the Canongate.

'There will be security here, to guard the Parliament Building, so we must divert them away. A nice bomb threat will do; either al-Qaeda or Irish terrorists; somebody that exists so it is treated as credible.'

Irene patted Mary's shoulder. 'Now Mary, this is where you come in. You will take over for the next stage.' She smiled. 'You'll need all your driving skills here. Come on!' she began to jog, with Patrick keeping pace at her side. Holyrood Road was more commercial, with a new hotel at one side and the new offices of the Scotsman newspaper and local authority housing opposite. Nobody looked up when they passed, and only when Desmond protested his age and years of nicotine use did Irene slow to a walk. 'You will drive up this street, back toward the castle, and then take a left into the Pleasance.'

'The what?' Desmond asked.

The Pleasance was a narrow, steep road, with a combination of ancient and modern buildings on either side. Groups of university students milled in casual unconcern as walked past. 'Straight on,' she encouraged, as Desmond began to falter.

'Even allowing for traffic, it will take about only twelve minutes until we reach the junction of Holyrood Park Road, then we take a sharp left. ' She pointed out her intended route.

'That goes back into town,' Bryan complained.

'Not quite,' Irene smiled. When Desmond had recovered his breath she increased her speed, walking briskly until she reached a roundabout. 'Left again here and we are within the Queen's Park.'

Matching her pace for pace, Patrick alone looked as if he were enjoying a casual stroll. He grinned down to her. 'That's another full day in Scotland and I haven't seen a man in a skirt yet.'

'Pity,' Irene warmed to his simplicity, 'as if we did, I could at least admire his hairy legs.' She winked as he laughed.

Behind a sloping green field, the red rocks of Salisbury Crags rose sheer in front of them, a semi circle of cliffs in the middle of the city. 'So we hide out here?' Desmond began to swear. His breath was coming in short gasps.

Irene allowed him two minutes. 'No. This is where Patrick meets us with the transport. I told you that he was in the Marines. I did not say that he was a helicopter pilot.' She waited until the expected exclamations subsided. 'Once we're in the air, we're home and dry. There will be so much confusion in Edinburgh that nobody will have time to bother about us.'

'I didn't know that you were a pilot,' Mary's eyes were contemplatively narrow. 'What did you fly?'

'Super Cobras and Hueys,' Patrick spoke quietly, as if he were ashamed of this undisclosed skill. He looked at Irene. 'Where shall I fly *to*?'

'You'll fly us to the Hebrides; that's the islands to the west of Scotland. I will have a chartered yacht ready to take us over the Atlantic.' Irene stepped back. 'So that's the plan, people. Mary has the hardest part in driving through Edinburgh.' She gave an encouraging nod. 'So it's good to know that we're in safe hands.'

Mary looked back over the road they had just walked. 'Not quite the wide open spaces of the Mid West, but certainly doable.'

'OK, then.' Irene rattled out orders. 'Stefan. I want you to get back to the Canongate and learn the ground thoroughly. You are our expert for the actual hit, so I want a detailed proposal.'

Stefan nodded and walked off without a word.

'Desmond. You and Bryan work out how to create diversions. I want smoke bombs at the actual site and alarms elsewhere. I want false telephone calls, warnings to the media, but the timing is crucial. I only want things to begin *after* the convoy has started; I don't want it cancelled. And I want enough diversity of warnings to thin out the security at the Honours and bunch them around the Queen.'

Desmond looked doubtful for a minute, but Bryan produced a smile. 'That will be a pleasure. We'll make the Brits hop.'

'Good. Mary, go and hire a car big enough to carry all of us plus the Honours. Drive over the route until you know it perfectly.'

Mary shrugged. 'It's a long journey for a short drive.'

'Learn it until you can drive the route in your sleep,' Irene ordered, and, with a brief nod, Mary left.

Irene smiled to Patrick. 'I feel better now that everybody knows their part. I presume that you can hire a helicopter somewhere in Scotland?'

'I would like an American craft, preferably the Bell 412.' On his home ground, Patrick spoke with authority. 'But if I can't get one, I'll try for the Aerospatiale Gazelle. It's French but built in Britain, so might be easier to obtain.'

'Why that one?'

'It holds five people including the pilot, which is not common for civilian helis. It also has a 220-pound payload, which will be handy as I'm not sure what other equipment we might need. Try and find out what the Honours weigh, so I can do the math.'

Irene enjoyed listening. Patrick had the capacity to irritate her, or raise her to heights of passion, but sometimes she just liked his company. Occasionally she even thought that it would be hard to let him go.

Patrick grinned to her. 'You'll like the Gazelle, Irene; it's pretty nippy too. Once we get airborne, we can cruise at 120 miles per hour, so we can cross Scotland in no time.'

Irene stepped back. 'I'm impressed,' she said. 'Did you work all that out just now?'

Patrick shook his head, still smiling. 'Not quite. You're too much the businesswoman to bring me along just for my incredible looks, so I must have had some function in your plans. Apart from sex, piloting is the only skill that I have.' He shrugged. 'I looked up the specs for helicopters as soon as you told me your ideas for the hit.'

Irene whistled, 'you've sure got me sussed, haven't you? July the 12th,' she told him. 'Go now and book.' Suddenly she was desperate to be alone. Taking responsibility for a corporate business was easy compared to giving personal orders to a small group of egoists and idealists. 'I must go for a walk.' She felt his puppy-dog eyes on her as she retreated, and reminded herself that he was expendable.

Chapter Eight Edinburgh: May

There seemed something essentially British about lying in bed listening to the song of a blackbird while early morning sun filtered through the curtains. Irene struggled to sit up, adjusting the pillows to create a comfortable nest for her head. Reaching to her right, she opened the top drawer of the bedside table, pulled out a joint and lit it. She drew sweet-tasting smoke into her lungs.

It was very rarely that Irene used even the mildest of drugs, but the pressure of this project demanded something more powerful than alcohol. She exhaled slowly, smiling as Patrick stirred into wakefulness. He lay on his side, muttering in his half sleep.

'Morning has broken,' Irene said.

Patrick pulled the covers further over his head.

Irene smiled, inhaling again, and gently eased the covers back to his knees. She ran her thumbnail down the entire length of his naked spine 'It's time for coffee.'

'Coffee and marijuana? The perfect combination to start the morning.' He eased onto his back, sat up beside her and reached out his hand.

Irene allowed him a few minutes to wake up. 'Off you go then. The machine is in the corner.'

He inhaled deeply, passed back the joint, gave that appealingly boyish grin and slid out of bed. Irene leaned back, enjoying the view as he walked to the coffee maker, replaced the filter and measured in the coffee. Her eyes followed the ripple of muscle down his back to the pert swell of his buttocks, and centred on the deep scratches on the offensive tattoo.

She grinned, admiring her handiwork as much as she appreciated Patrick's backside. She hoped that it really smarted. If she kept him for much longer, she must surely tear away Linda's name. Of course, she could take him to a professional and have the tattoo permanently erased; an Nd-YAG laser would be the most efficient, and probably fun to watch, but Irene knew that she would never do that. She liked having something on which to focus her aggression, and Patrick's tattoo could not be in a better position.

'Thanks, honey,' she sipped her coffee, patting the bed to invite him back to her side. He slid beside her, smiling, but she restrained his eager hand. 'Not just now.' She tempered her refusal with a smile. 'You'll wear me out.'

Irene let him press close. It would be hard to part with Patrick; he was an energetic lover, and easily controlled. Indeed, it would be difficult to find another man so suitable for her needs. Perhaps she could place him in a small apartment somewhere that Ms Manning could not discover, and visit him when she felt the inclination. She looked at him with growing affection; maybe later, when she was in full charge of the Manning Corporation, or the Armstrong Corporation, as it would then be, she could ease Patrick back into the centre of her life. Irene smiled as the marijuana relaxed her.

'You were really good last night,' she whispered into his ear. 'You really turned me on.' She waited for his small wriggle of pleasure. 'But I made a real mess of your butt. Let's have a look. Come on.' She gestured for him to stretch across her. 'I'd better put something on that,' she smiled and reached for the iodine cleansing wipes that she always carried in her handbag. 'Brace yourself; this might sting.'

Walking in Edinburgh was a new pleasure. Irene found that she appreciated the atmosphere of history that the city provided, as well as the crisp air of the Queen's Park. She wondered if James V had walked here, and smiled that she would be stealing his crown. 'Johnnie Armstrong's revenge,' she said to herself, and hoped that her father would be pleased.

The Palace of Holyroodhouse was not as large as she had expected, indeed smaller than the mansion of many American actors, but the history and the situation, hard by the Scottish Parliament building, enhanced its appeal. For a moment Irene imagined if the Queen would retire here to mourn the loss of her Scottish Honours, then dismissed the thought. She was here to research, not to daydream.

There was a guided tour of the palace, and stories of the murder of Rizzio, the secretary of Mary, Queen of Scots, and that queen's unfortunate marriages. 'Poor Mary,' Irene murmured as she learned about plots and counter plots, imprisonments and battles. In common with many thousands of others, Irene found herself captivated by the tragedy of Mary Stuart, and left the palace with a sense of sadness. If even a queen could suffer so many misfortunes, what chance was there for her?

A brisk walk up the Canongate helped clear her mind; she was far more astute than a Renaissance queen, and far better equipped to control her men. The memory of Patrick reassured her and she examined her nails with satisfaction. If the story of Mary Stuart taught anything, it was to maintain control of her own life.

After eating at a surprisingly good, but dangerously expensive restaurant in the High Street, Irene spent the rest of the afternoon exploring the closes of the Old Town, wandering from one narrow lane to another, glancing into dark doorways where murders and abductions had once occurred and stepped into a public house half way along Fleshmarket Close. The place was busy with tourists and locals, but nobody gave her a second look as she squeezed into a corner seat and sipped at her Glen Moray malt whisky and ice. Whisky was not her usual drink, but when in Rome...

Leaning back in her seat, Irene allowed the hum of conversation to wash over her as she contemplated her future. She had always sought power and wealth, but now all she had to do was perform one task successfully and she would have both in abundance, and would have helped right an ancient wrong. One task, and that required only careful planning and a few hours of direct, forceful action.

The whisky seemed stronger in Scotland, but she bought another and thought about Patrick. She would definitely find him an apartment, and once she was installed as head of the Manning Corporation she could openly bring him back into her life. That was a nice thought, although he might have to share her with others. Irene smiled at the prospect of having a host of men at her command, then remembered Ms Manning's swimming pool with its bevy of sculptures. Perhaps the head of such a vast empire would not have time for men. In which case, Irene decided, easing back her whisky, she had better make the most of it now.

She checked the time. Patrick had told her that there was American football on Sky Sports at three, so that would confine him to the hotel room; well, she had other plans for him this afternoon. Reaching in her bag for her cell phone, Irene was about to dial his number when she stopped. Better to surprise him. She grinned, bought a bottle of champagne from behind the bar and stepped outside, suddenly desperate for Patrick's company. Smiling, she examined her nails, clawing the air in anticipation.

With her footsteps quiet on the thick carpet, Irene hurried along the hotel corridor, threw open the door of her room and walked in, champagne held high. She stopped, momentarily unable to comprehend what she saw. Patrick lay face up on the bed, eyes closed and mouth open. Mary was on top of him, completely naked and making little noises of pleasure as she moved rhythmically back and forward. She looked over her shoulder as Irene walked in, and grinned.

'Fine man you have here,' she said, unashamed. 'I told you that we had more in common than you realised.'

Irene placed the bottle of champagne beside the bed. 'When you're done,' she said, 'you can celebrate with this.' She walked out, closing the door quietly behind her.

Chapter Nine : Pitlochry, Scotland: May

'Can you hear that?' Alexander Meigle stopped and lifted his head. Hacked from the living granite, the steps rose before him until they merged with the white mist that drifted across the summit of Ben Vrackie.

'I heard it.' Drummond paused in mid stride and allowed his boot to gently touch ground. He leaned on his cromach and met Meigle's eyes. 'I've been listening to it for the past ten minutes, ever since we left Loch Choice.'

Meigle blew softly, unwilling to admit that this ascent was tiring him. He wished that he could regain the athleticism of his youth, smiled and reassessed his years; man alive, he would even be grateful for the desperate energy of his middle age. 'Bagpipes, do you think?'

'No,' Drummond shook his head. 'Not powerful enough. Some sort of wind instrument, though. It's hard to tell in this mist.' He took another step upward. 'We'll find out soon enough.'

'No doubt.' Meigle looked upward. The steps seemed to go on forever. He was sure that this hill grew higher every time he climbed it. He followed Drummond, aware of the sucking drop on his right.

'Wait!' Drummond's hiss was urgent and Meigle instinctively froze. He saw the shape emerge in front, tendrils of mist clinging to the proud head as it pranced across the steps and stopped to test the scent. It was a young red deer, with immature antlers and huge eyes. For a second, deer and humans stared at each other, then the animal eased off the steps and disappeared. The mist closed behind it.

'That was worth seeing,' Meigle said.

'There are usually deer on Ben Vrackie,' Drummond's grin belied his age. 'But I still get a thrill of pleasure when I meet one.'

'I miss the hills,' Meigle regretted the self-pity in his own voice. 'I don't get up nearly often enough.'

'Well, Sandy, you're up today.' Drummond was walking faster now, pulled on by the thought of the summit.

Meigle followed, wishing that there was more opportunity for exercise in his life. He hated Jamie to show him up so easily. 'Nearly, James, nearly.'

Ben Vrackie was one of his favourite hills, partly because it was so accessible from Pitlochry, partly for the spectacular views from the top, but also because it was relatively easy to climb. With Pitlochry one of Scotland's premier mountain resorts, kindly hands had fashioned these stone steps from Loch Choice right up the cone to the summit plateau. If he had the power, he would confer sainthood on the owners of these hands that enabled an elderly man to ascend the staircase to his own particular heaven. He could still hear that damned noise, though, distorted by the mist so only faint snatches reached him, enough to tantalise, but not enough for him to recognise the source or direction.

Twice Meigle thought that the mist was thinning, but both times it returned with renewed density, so they clambered the final hundred steps in a cover of damp greyness that blocked out anything but the stone underfoot and the heather immediately to the side. Meigle walked slowly, testing each foothold, more concerned with retaining his dignity than the damage that a slip may cause.

'It's a shame we can't see the view,' he gasped at last, halting as if to admire the mist.

'As the old saying goes,' Drummond spoke as easily as if he were standing in his own garden, which, in a way, he was. 'If you don't like the weather, wait a minute and it will change.'

When the steps ended there was a muddied track that led on to the summit cairn, and only then did a slant of wind shred the mist to open the view around them.

'I must have seen this a hundred times,' Drummond said, 'but I still can't believe it.'

With the breath burning in his lungs, Meigle thrust himself up the volcanic rock on which the cairn was built and sank onto a suitably level surface. He sat there, dragging in oxygen as he hugged his heavy walking stick to his chest. 'That's some view,' he agreed. 'It's like half of Scotland is before you.'

For a full five minutes neither man spoke as they allowed the calmness of the scene to enter them. Drummond removed his deerstalker, as if in homage to the hills, then he addressed each summit, caressing the Gaelic names in a personal mantra of devotion. 'There's Meall an Daimh, Meall Garbh, Creag Breac, Crungie Clach, and Crungie Dubh,' he used his cromach as a pointer. 'Each with her own character and shape.' He replaced the deerstalker on his head and pulled the rim down low. Touching Meigle's arm, he shifted position so he overlooked the town of Pitlochry that nestled in its sheltering valley, and pointed to the west. 'And over there is Schiehallion, queen of them all. The fairy hill of the Caledonians.'

Meigle followed his finger, admiring, as he had so often done, the sheer beauty of Perthshire and the dominating lines of Schiehallion. He had travelled the world for business and pleasure and had seen mountain ranges that could dwarf anything that Scotland produced, but he had experienced nothing that could compare with the atmosphere generated by these Highland hills.

'Our hills,' he said quietly, and allowed the old feelings to seep through.

'Worth defending.' Drummond leaned on his cromach with the jut of his chin balancing the peak of his deerstalker hat.

They relapsed into silence, contemplating the panorama of the granite heart of Scotland as a kindly sun highlighted the peaks. Somewhere beneath them a buzzard keened.

It was then that the sound began again; a low whistling that seemed to emanate from Ben Vrackie herself. Drummond glanced at Meigle and grinned. 'I know it now,' he said. 'You wait here and I'll circle around.'

'Are you not a bit old for that sort of thing?' Meigle asked, but Drummond laid down his cromach, jammed his deerstalker firmer onto his head and winked.

Sliding around the base of the rocky mound, Drummond flitted above the dizzy drop to the southwest and vanished into a fold of ground. Watching from his seat, Meigle nearly smiled, knowing that the Colonel was enjoying using his old military skills once more, even although it was only to satisfy his own curiosity. Drummond could never be in any danger on one of his native Perthshire hills. The whistling continued for a while. When it stopped, Meigle raised his head, but a low murmur of voices and Drummond's distinctively genial laugh reassured him that all was well.

'Look who I've found,' Drummond paced across the springy heather with a slender, unsmiling man at his side.

'Morning, Kenny,' Meigle waved his stick. 'I should have known that it would be you making all the noise.'

Kenny Mossman lifted a finger in acknowledgement. Sallow faced, he carried a rucksack that seemed too large for his sparse frame, while his thick woollen hat was pulled low over his brow. 'I came up here for some peace,' he said. 'I didn't think it would be full of Society men.'

'No peace without Clan Donald,' Drummond misquoted cheerfully. 'And no peace with you tootling away on your penny whistle.'

'Penny whistle!' Kenny gave a baleful look. 'You're a bit out of touch, James. They cost a fortune now.' He showed the long, bronze-coloured tin whistle that he held in is hand. 'The wife complains when I play in the house, so I grab every opportunity I can.' Placing the whistle in his mouth, he blew gently, so the notes of *MacGregor's Gathering* sounded across the summit of the ben.

'That'll waken a few ghosts,' Drummond said soberly, 'having the MacGregors coming snooping around this area. The locals will be checking their cattle and locking up their daughters.'

'Not nowadays,' Meigle commented sourly. 'The daughters will be tearing off their knickers and hunting for the MacGregors,'

'Aye, the youth of today,' Drummond shook his head. 'Lucky buggers.'

Kenny grunted and changed to the more modern *Highland Cathedral*, so Meigle allowed the tune to fade into the landscape and drifted away into the reverie that the hills often evoked. That was one of the pleasures of the wild places; extreme exertion followed by a near-melancholic peace that rejuvenated a body and soul drained by city life. He allowed the hills to reenergize him, for he sensed that he might need all his strength for the forthcoming conference.

'Up there,' and when Drummond pointed skyward, Meigle followed his finger. At first he saw nothing, and then made out a distant speck that gradually grew in size as it descended.

'Another buzzard,' Meigle said.

'No; that's a golden eagle.' Drummond spoke softly. 'You don't see many of those around here.'

They watched the eagle for a long five minutes, admiring the immense wingspan and the ease with which it dominated the sky. There were no other birds visible now, even the buzzard having given way to the eagle.

'It's patrolling its territory,' Drummond said, 'searching for food.'

'There's a nice wee chippy in Pitlochry,' Kenny said, then closed his mouth as his attempt at humour fell flat. 'It's coming down.'

The eagle swooped so close overhead that its shadow flickered over them, and Kenny involuntarily ducked, but then it regained a little height and hovered on an up-draught of air just fifty yards off the hill.

'It's watching that deer,' Kenny said softly. He gestured with his whistle. 'Over there.'

Meigle watched as the eagle rose slightly higher, its wingtips quivering, before diving down upon the young stag that they had passed on the ascent. The stag ran a few steps and then tossed its head as if attempting to fend off the attack with its immature antlers.

'Christ,' Kenny blasphemed. 'They're going to fight. I've never seen that before.'

'Like I said,' Drummond spoke quietly. 'The eagle is after food. It's testing the deer, seeing how vulnerable it is. If it's weak, the eagle will try and drive it over the edge so it can feed its chicks with the dead body.'

'And I thought the Scottish countryside was a quiet place,' Kenny said. 'That's evil.'

'That's nature. The eagle has a responsibility; it must care for its young.' Drummond rested his chin on the crook of his cromach. 'As we must care for the Clach-bhuai. It's a protector as well as a predator.'

They watched the drama unfold as the eagle withdrew and dived again, beak open and talons outspread as it used its great wings to try and panic the deer over the edge. Just when it seemed as if it would strike, the eagle swooped upward, calling harshly. Without making contact, it drove the stag ever nearer to the lip of the summit, pushing it toward the sheer drop. The stag retaliated with its antlers, ducking its head as it retreated.

'Only another few assaults and the deer's gone,' Meigle said. He felt an unaccountable insignificance, for however powerful he was in the business world of Edinburgh, here was a life and death struggle between two dominant animals, neither of which cared anything for his existence. He watched as the eagle made a final sortie, screamed a last challenge and the deer broke, but instead of tumbling down the cliff, it jinked forward, its antlers nearly grazing the outstretched talons of the eagle, and trotted into a gully. Brown heather shrubs shielded the animal from their view.

'Trust the red deer to know its own territory,' Drummond sounded quite relieved. 'It's safe now; the eagle can't reach it there.'

Meigle nodded. He watched as the eagle attacked again, its beak wide with frustration, and then it spiralled upward, screaming its harsh challenge to any other bird that dared intrude on its air space. Two creatures, each supreme in their own environment, each destined to dominance, meeting on the border between land and air. It had been an elemental encounter, with neither loser nor victor, and he had been a mute observer. But now he must be prepared to take charge again, to take responsibility for his own affairs.

'So the eagle's chicks might go hungry,' he said quietly. 'We had better learn that lesson, and ensure the safety of the Clach-bhuai. Whatever method we have to adopt.' He looked over to Kenny. 'We might have to call on your family expertise, if that's all right?'

Kenny shrugged. 'That's what we're here for. Just say the word.'

The sound of voices broke his reverie as a party of walkers clambered up the steps.

'Time to return,' Meigle decided. Up here with a slight wind skiffing the mist and the rock gleaming wet beneath him, all the business worries of Edinburgh seemed insubstantial. Balance sheets and interest rates, international deadlines and self-important clients all thinned into nothingness beside the eternal presence of the mountains. When companies and banks vanished, these hills would still be standing, unemotional, solid, seemingly serene yet home to more drama than existed in any company take over or financial crash. The hills were the heritage of every person of Scottish descent; it was Scotland's duty to preserve them, as it was his duty to guard the Clach-bhuai.

A group of walkers clattered onto the summit, exclaiming at the view as their garish coats contrasted with the subtle shades of Perthshire. One man plumped down beside the summit cairn and unfolded a map, while a woman produced a plastic packet of sandwiches. Their loud voices chased the peace from the hills.

'The Society will soon be arriving,' Meigle said. 'We'd better be there for them.' He nodded to Drummond. 'I'm looking forward to meeting your Andrew again.'

Drummond nodded. 'I have not told him much,' he said, jogging down the path. He waited for Meigle to catch up. 'Just that it's a family tradition that he has to attend.'

'Nicely put.' His time at the summit of Ben Vrackie had strengthened Meigle for the descent so he negotiated the steps with more ease. Although his knees complained at every jolt, he kept pace for pace with Drummond all the way back to Loch Choice. For all his apparent lack of muscle, Kenny had no difficulty in holding his position. After stopping to slide his whistle between the straps across the front of his pack, he caught up within a few dozen paces.

'What's this all about, Sandy? I've never been to a full Society meeting before.'

'I've never held one before,' Meigle said. 'But you'll know soon enough.' He halted to rub at his left knee. 'I'm getting too damned old for all this.'

'Just a short stroll now,' Drummond encouraged. He had walked slowly, but Meigle knew that he was impatient to increase his stride. Although climbing Ben Vrackie was a major expedition for Meigle, Jamie would consider it a casual jaunt, a warm-up for greater things. He scanned the loch for ducks, nodded as a coot bustled away from the bank and allowed Drummond to move in front.

Meigle sighed. There was always something sad about leaving a hill. This meeting of the Society bothered him, for the full responsibility descended on his shoulders, and at his age he was not sure if he could cope. His whole world might alter before he returned to Vrackie. So might the world of everybody in the Society. He checked the path, to see

115

Drummond watching him with his deceptively mild eyes and Kenny rolling along with his hands deep in his pockets, humming. Maybe he was not so alone. That was the essence of the Society; a supportive group of varied talents dedicated to one objective.

Rebuilt at the height of Victorian Scottish Baronialism, Tummel House was only a couple of miles from Pitlochry. Set in nearly a hundred acres of informal and formal gardens, its profusion of bartizans, towers and turrets overlooked the town and enjoyed splendid views across the River Tummel to the Perthshire hills. The house and its predecessors had belonged to James's family since the early 1530s, when King James V had rewarded an earlier Drummond for military support on a Border expedition.

At first Meigle had thought to book a hotel for the Society conference, but on reflection he had decided that Drummond's house was more private and certainly large enough. With the Society paying for the catering and equipment, the only problem would be some disruption to James's family, but James solved that by sending them to Paris for the weekend.

Meigle had worded the invitations in person, and had insisted that everybody foregather beneath the portraits and hunting trophies in the great hall. He knew only some of them, and this was the first full gathering for nearly seventy years, so there would be many introductions to make.

'All right, Sandy?' Drummond was at his side, looking every inch the country gentleman with his tweed suit and tie beneath the walnut brown face.

'All right, Jamie.' Despite his years of experience in chairing board meetings, this event was going to be difficult. Things were always more serious when the subject matter was close to one's heart.

He stood outside the varnished doors, glanced at Drummond, took a deep breath and entered. The Society stood in small knots, engaged in the awkward, desultory conversation of strangers. There were men dressed with the casual ease of the truly wealthy, and men uncomfortable in off-the-peg suits that were probably only released from the wardrobe for weddings and funerals. There were women in faded denims and cheap jackets and women whose power clothes would impress the least impressionable of City merchants. All they had in common was the topic of their conversation as they discussed every possibility that they could conceive for their presence in Tummel House.

Meigle moved easily from group to group, reacquainting himself with people that he had met only once or twice before but knew well from their membership papers, renewing friendships with men or women that he had known since childhood and gripping the hand of new members.

'I am Sandy Meigle,' he said, looking hard into the eyes of a middle-sized man with a Hunting MacPherson tartan kilt and the most determined chin that he had ever seen.

'Lachlan MacPherson,' the man crushed Meigle's hand enthusiastically, 'from Halifax.'

Meigle disengaged his hand. 'Good to have a Nova Scotian here,' he said. 'How is the timber business nowadays?'

MacPherson grinned widely. 'Fine, Mr Meigle, just fine.'

'You are very welcome, but the name's Sandy. We're all friends here.' Meigle moved on, paying particular attention to the younger faces. He had met most members individually, but never collectively, and recognised the newcomers from family portraits and the photographs that were an essential prerequisite of membership. He crossed the floor to greet the tall young man at Drummond's side.

'Andrew, man you've grown.'

Andrew Drummond was as tall as his father, but perhaps three inches broader in the shoulder. 'Mr Meigle. You're looking well.'

Meigle shook his hand and pointed to the collection of decanters, bottles and glasses that stood on a side table. 'The drink is free, Andrew. Covered by Society funds.'

'The Society must have plenty money to spare then,' Andrew said frankly, 'for there are a lot of thirsty people here.' He widened his eyes that seemed an even more youthful copy of his father's. 'I don't really know much about this Society that I seem to have inherited,' he said. 'Dad hasn't told me much.' He deepened his voice in a bad copy of his father's brisk bark. 'You're too young yet. Plenty of time for that.'

Drummond's frown could not hide the pleasure in his eyes.

'Your father is quite right,' Meigle said solemnly. 'But you'll learn more today. In the meantime, mingle freely. We're all friends as well as members.'

Andrew grinned. 'I wouldn't mind making friends with that member there,' he nodded toward a confident looking woman in a flowing blue dress.

'Another new face.' Meigle watched the woman for a minute, mentally searching through his photographs. 'If you would excuse me?'

'I am Sandy Meigle,' he thrust out his hand to the woman. 'The chairman of this Society.'

'Doctor Eileen Wallace.' Her grip was firm and cooler than her intense grey eyes. Experience had taught Meigle that he could find out a lot by examining the eyes and mouth of a person. The eyes were said to be a window into the soul, but people fashioned their own mouth. Eileen's lips were held tight, suggesting a resolute personality.

'You are very welcome, Eileen.'

'I prefer Doctor Wallace, on first acquaintance.' Eileen's gaze did not waver. 'And I would like to know what this meeting is all about.'

Meigle smiled. 'I quite understand that, Dr Wallace, but everything will be revealed in the fullness of time.' He could place her now. Dr Eileen Wallace, the daughter of Mr and Mrs Wallace of Stonehaven. She was born into the Society from her mother's side, the late Emily Wallace, nee Rutherford.

'I hope so, Mr Meigle.' Eileen did not drop her eyes as Meigle moved on, winking to Andrew.

'Good luck with that one,' Meigle whispered, and Andrew grinned.

'I like a challenge.'

'Sandy!' Drummond slid up, his brogues silent on the marble floor. 'Everything is set up in the ballroom.' He ushered Meigle to a huge room where rows of seats faced a platform intended for a dance band. 'I'll get them moving.'

Drummond had directed the members of the Society to their seats before Meigle mounted the three steps to the platform. He expected the stir of interest as he entered, and lifted a hand in acknowledgement to the nods of respect and recognition. Checking that everybody was present, Meigle took his place in front of the white screen that stretched across two of the room's tall windows.

He waited until the murmur of conversation died, pushed the button that closed the curtains behind him, and raised the level of lighting. The twin chandeliers emitted a soft glow, light that permeated into every corner of the room and highlighted the original oil paintings that graced the muted colouring of the walls. Drummond walked to the double doors, ensured that they were shut and stood with his back to them, facing Meigle across the room.

'Ladies and gentlemen,' Meigle started in the traditional manner, 'members of the Society. If only because we have never all met in the same place before, you know how unusual this gathering is. For that same reason, you will realise that it must be important.'

He surveyed the faces. 'You are all welcome, especially Lachlan, Andrew and Dr Eileen Wallace.' Extending his hand in their direction, he invited them to stand. 'As the next generation, you do not yet know the responsibilities that will be heaped on your shoulders. You are about to learn.'

There was a ripple of laughter from the older members, and one or two began to clap, or stand and hold out their hands to Lachlan, Andrew and Doctor Wallace. Meigle allowed the noise level to rise as the new members were received into the Society. He hid his satisfaction as Andrew and Doctor Wallace leaned across to formally introduce themselves to each other, and nodded as Drummond lifted a single finger. Of the three, Lachlan seemed most pleased to acknowledge his membership, grinning broadly to everybody that shook his hand. That was how things should be. Only when the members sank back into their seats did Meigle continue.

'As a reminder, this Society has existed for many centuries, in many different forms. We adapt to suit the era in which we live, but our function remains the same. We are here to help each other through life, but our primary reason for existence is to ensure the security of the Clach-bhuai.'

As he had expected, Andrew and Lachlan looked mystified. It was unlikely that either had ever heard the name before. Andrew looked to his father, who gave a solemn nod, while

Doctor Wallace straightened her back and looked attentive. She held up a hand.

'May I ask a question?'

'Of course,' Meigle believed in encouraging the young. 'But I will explain everything.'

'Is that not rather an outmoded concept?'

Meigle knew the background and occupation of every member of the Society. He was aware that Eileen Wallace was a lecturer in Celtic Studies at an Aberdeen university. 'To which concept do you refer?'

'The name Clach-bhuai is Gaelic,' Doctor Wallace spoke with all the authority of her education, 'and it could mean Stone of Power or Powerstone. I presume that you are referring to the Stone of Destiny, which, despite the colourful legends, most experts believe to be a chunk of Scottish sandstone with no mystical powers whatsoever.'

Meigle allowed the murmur to die down. He could see that Andrew Drummond was looking intently at Doctor Wallace. No doubt he was calculating his chances of impressing such a knowledgeable woman. 'Your translation is correct, Dr Wallace. The name is Gaelic, although of an archaic form, and it can mean either Powerstone or Stone of Power. However the object in question has no connection with the Stone of Destiny.'

Doctor Wallace lowered her eyes, obviously unsettled.

'Nevertheless, I thank you for your point. It is always good to meet somebody with independent knowledge.' Meigle glanced at Drummond, who took his cue nicely and smiled over to Eileen.

'That's the ticket, Dr Wallace; keep the old man on his toes!'

The resulting laugh removed most of Doctor Wallace's embarrassment. When Meigle saw Andrew lean across to speak with her, he thought that the incident had passed without rancour.

'Our stone is rather smaller than the Stone of Destiny,' Meigle continued. 'For you members who know this story already, please forgive me for blethering on. For those members who know something of it, please bear with me, and for those newcomers to the Society, please listen with great attention.'

Further dimming the lights, Meigle flicked the switch of a projector and an image of the Honours of Scotland appeared on the large screen at his back. 'These are the Scottish Crown Jewels,' he said. 'They comprise the Crown, the Sword of State and the Sceptre. There are also a number of rings and the Mace.'

As most of the members leaned back, Andrew and Doctor Wallace fidgeted slightly in their seats. Meigle continued. 'Beautiful, are they not? Mediaeval workmanship of the highest quality. Nobody is exactly sure of the age of the crown but we know that an Edinburgh jeweller named Mosman reworked it for King James V in 1540. The Sword of State and the Sceptre were both Papal gifts, dating from 1507 and 1494 respectively. In themselves, each is intrinsically priceless and historically invaluable. All have survived war and raid. When Cromwell invaded in 1650, the Honours were smuggled to safety from Dunottar Castle, by the wife of the minister of Kineff.'

Meigle fixed his eyes on Doctor Wallace. 'She was a member of the Society.'

Doctor Wallace looked up. Her eyes were remorseless.

'When the Union of the Parliaments occurred in 1707, one clause of the document stipulated that the Honours were never to leave Scotland. To ensure that the Westminster parliament kept its word, the Society persuaded the powers of the time to lock them up in the Castle. They remained there, safe, for over a century. Only when the Society deemed that Westminster might be trustworthy after all, did Walter Scott, another member, reveal their existence.'

One of the English members gave an ironical cheer.

Andrew Drummond opened his mouth to speak, but when his father shook his head he relapsed into silence. Doctor Wallace covered her yawn with a slim hand.

'Only last century, when Hitler's War broke out, the Honours were again in danger. Hitler wanted Edinburgh Castle as his summer residence, so he did not bomb it in the early years. In 1941, however, he knew that he could not invade the country, so the Castle, and the Honours, were endangered.'

Doctor Wallace looked up. 'By what?'

'Aerial bombardment.' Meigle said. 'What Hitler could not get he tended to destroy, and the Castle was a target. The Society met and the Honours were buried for safety.'

Doctor Wallace shook her head. 'Are you saying that the Society was more concerned with pieces of jewellery rather than the well being of women and children? It was all right for Hitler to bomb the houses but not the Castle?'

'Not quite,' Meigle was slightly surprised at the venom of the attack. 'The Society's function is to protect and preserve the Clach-bhuai. That is what we do. Individual members were, of course, serving in the forces.'

'In that case, Mr Meigle, your terminology is incorrect,' Doctor Wallace said. 'Even if you persist in using Gaelic, the crown jewels are not the Clach-bhuai.'

'Indeed not.' Meigle agreed. 'The term relates to one stone.' He flashed an image of the sceptre onto the screen. 'This is the sceptre, and this,' he pressed again for a close up of the polished crystal that sat on top, 'is what we are dedicated to protect. This is the Clach-bhuai. The Stone of Power, the Powerstone.'

As he had expected, every member leaned forward intently. Even Doctor Wallace paused to inspect the shining globe that he presented.

The Clach-bhuai would have fitted comfortably inside the fist of anybody that was present. Except for the setting, it did not look different from the ball of any fairground fortuneteller.

'That's only crystal,' Doctor Wallace pointed out.

'Yes.' Meigle agreed, 'but crystal with a history of much greater significance than you would suspect.'

'God!' Doctor Wallace stood up. 'You mean you've called me here to look at pictures of a crystal ball? Don't you realise that some of us have a life?' Pushing back her chair, she stepped toward the door. Drummond stepped aside. 'I should have known that I was wasting my time when I saw all you old men in tweed jackets!' Pulling open the door, she spoke over her shoulder. 'This is straight from the pages of Harry Potter and I have real work to do. Just wait until the media hear about this!' She slammed the door shut so the draught rocked the chandeliers.

Meigle held up his hand for silence. 'Does anybody else feel like that? If you do, I apologise for wasting your time and invite you to leave now. Naturally your transport costs and all expenses will be reimbursed.' He waited for a few minutes. 'Good. Then I think we should have a break. We will reconvene tomorrow morning. In the meantime, please feel free to enjoy the facilities of Drummond House. There is a putting

124

course and a swimming pool, as well as a tennis court, and, of course, the beautiful garden to walk around.'

There was a murmur of appreciation and a slow movement toward the door. Meigle nodded to Drummond, who had taken position beside the window. 'James, I think that we have work to do.'

Drummond nodded. 'Unfortunately,' he sighed. 'This is not how I had hoped the day would turn out.'

'We are here to ensure the security of the Clach-bhuai.' Meigle reminded. 'It is our responsibility.' He smiled as Andrew walked up, his face concerned. 'Andrew, my boy!' They shook hands, until Meigle winced under the pressure of the younger man.

'What was all that about, Sandy?'

'A small local difficulty, shall we say,' Meigle nodded to Drummond, who slipped quietly into a corner of the room and dialled a number on his mobile phone. 'You take a stroll around the grounds, Andrew, or perhaps try the putting.' Glancing around the room, he indicated a smallish, plump-faced man in a dark suit. 'That's Iain Stewart from Peebles. He's a scratch player.' Iain raised a single finger in acknowledgement.

Andrew nodded to Iain, 'sounds about right. And when he's hammering me all over the course, what will you be doing?'

'Your father and I have things we must do.'

Andrew opened his mouth to speak, but Meigle had a lifetime of experience in dealing with people. He gestured to the door and Andrew left without a word.

Chapter Ten : Perthshire: May

'Well James?'

Drummond nodded. 'She got into a bronze Nissan 350Z,' he quoted the registration number, 'and she was in a right tizzy. She stormed right down the drive like a maniac.'

'Nissan 350Z? That's a powerful vehicle. Expensive too.' They left the ballroom together, running to the car park.

'Dr Wallace must be in love with herself to drive such a fancy vehicle on her salary.' Drummond slid into the driving seat of his Landrover and waited for Meigle to join him. 'Young woman, good job, big ego. That one's got too high an opinion of herself. Perhaps we should vet our members more thoroughly. People are not as dependable as they once were.' He started the engine and pulled smoothly down the drive.

'We'll never catch her in this.' Meigle said. The Landrover Defender was as reliable and robust as its driver, but lacked the Nissan's speed. 'We should have taken my car.'

'This one is better for what I have in mind,' Drummond told him. 'Where do you think she is going?'

'In that mood? Back to Aberdeen to continue with her *very* important job. And then to the press. We cannot allow that.'

Drummond nodded. He worked on the sat-nav system that was on his dashboard and studied the results. 'She has four options then. One, she can take the A9 to Perth, change to the A90 to Dundee and head northward to Stonehaven and Aberdeen. Two, she can take the A9 to Dunkeld, then cut across Perthshire on the A923 to Blairgowrie, then the A926, joining the A90 near Forfar. Three, she can… wait!'

Leaving the sat-nav, Drummond answered his hands-free mobile phone. 'Drummond.'

'MacFarlane, sir. There's a bronze Nissan 350Z heading northwest along the A924. Just passing Kinnaird and motoring. Man, is it motoring.'

'North?' Drummond eased the Landrover into Pitlochry. 'Damned woman's going toward Strathardle. She's taking the hill road.'

Meigle nodded. 'Good man, James. Helicopter?'

'Of course. I phoned MacFarlane. He was on stand-by in case of emergency.' Drummond slammed the Defender into fifth gear and overtook a tour bus as he turned from Atholl Road. He ignored the sudden fear in the faces of the occupants and acknowledged the justified anger of the driver with a raised hand.

'Do you have a contingency plan?' Despite the seriousness of the situation, Meigle felt the adrenalin begin to work through him. He had experienced the same feelings when about to announce a take-over bid, or launch a new financial package with his company.

'That's a narrow road that she's chosen.' Drummond said. 'There are plenty of positions for a successful ambush.' Glancing ahead, he negotiated the climb out of Pitlochry, squeezed past a lumbering tractor and powered ahead. To their left, rolling mist had completely obscured Ben Vrackie.

'I did not expect this,' Meigle did not conceal his concern.

'Not quite like your usual decisions, Sandy?' Drummond took a hairpin bend so wide that he forced an approaching car to brake. He said nothing as the driver swore loudly through his open window.

The Defender pulled up a steep hill, with the surroundings becoming wilder by the mile as they entered the range of mountains that acted as a protective barrier for Pitlochry. Sheep scattered as Drummond sounded his horn.

'Somebody should teach these damned creatures the highway code.' He raised his voice, speaking toward the hands-free. 'MacFarlane! Where is she?'

'Just approaching Straloch, and she's still travelling. You'll no' catch her in the Drover.' The sound of rotors made MacFarlane's voice even more disembodied.

'Pick me up,' Drummond ordered. 'There's a level piece of ground a mile ahead.' He looked at Meigle. 'I want you to keep driving and do exactly as I say.' When his eyes met Meigle's they were as devoid of expression as Perthshire granite. 'All right?'

'All right.'

Drummond nodded and looked ahead. The helicopter was already coming in to land. 'Have you driven a Drover before?'

Meigle shook his head.

'She's wide at the corners. Keep the hands-free alive and follow my instructions.' Meigle slowed and halted, leaving the vehicle on his last word. He walked quickly to the helicopter that sat, rotors turning, ten yards from the road. The noise of the blades reminded Meigle of old films about the Vietnam War.

Meigle slid into the Defender's driving seat, checking the controls and involuntarily ducking as the helicopter lifted. Sheep scattered, bleating to their lambs when the machine chopped overhead. Meigle gunned the motor and drove on, struggling with the steering wheel that seemed very stiff after the luxury of his BMW. Trust Jamie to buy a state-of-the-art helicopter for his estate, but drive in a ten-year-old basic Landrover without even power steering.

'She's taking the B950, after Kirkmichael,' the voice seemed to echo in the cab of the Defender. 'Don't follow her.

Keep to the road that you are on, but put your foot down. You're driving like an old woman!'

Meigle had driven this road before, and remembered the turn-off that cut across some rough country to Glenshee. By taking that route, Eileen was committing herself to the hill road by the Cairnwell and Braemar to Aberdeen. She had a long, lonely drive in front of her. He pressed his foot onto the accelerator, feeling the surge of power from the engine as the Defender responded. He took the next corner too wide, adjusted his steering and nearly clipped a dry stane dyke, straightened up and pushed down harder.

'Sandy!' Drummond's voice was calm as ever. 'When you reach Bridge of Cally, turn left on the A93, and then take the first left after Milton. That way you will be heading toward her, on the same road.'

Meigle grunted. 'Her route is far shorter than mine and she has the faster vehicle. By the time I reach the road end she'll be long gone.'

'She won't.' There was something so final about those two words that Meigle sat back and said nothing. He pushed the accelerator as far as he could and concentrated entirely on the driving, hurtling through a small village without reducing speed, so that an elderly woman hardly had time to stare as he passed.

'There's a tractor in front of her,' Drummond spoke over the sound of rotor blades. 'That's slowing her down nicely,' he chuckled. 'She should have stuck to the main roads.'

There was a Range Rover pulling away from the small shop at Bridge of Cally, but Meigle ignored the driver's protests as he hit the junction at fifty, veered across the road, straightened up and pressed on, heading north toward the end of the road that Doctor Wallace was travelling. He had left the hands-free on and could hear Drummond's voice, distorted by static, giving sharp orders to MacFarlane.

'Those sheep there. Drive them, shift them onto the road. She'll have to slow down again.' There was the sound of Drummond's short barking laugh.

Meigle visualised the scene. Drummond was using the noise of the helicopter to drive sheep from the surrounding land onto the road. 'How are we doing?'

'Fine. There are about a hundred sheep milling about in front of her, running every which way.' Drummond sounded satisfied. 'She's pulled in to the side until they clear.'

'How far over the road is she?'

'About half way. At the quarries of Bleaton; it's the only unfenced part of the road.' Drummond's laughter was more sinister than reassuring. 'She's left the car now and she's trying to chase the sheep away.'

Meigle passed the monotonous conifers of a forestry plantation and turned sharp left onto the B950. He was only a couple of miles from Doctor Wallace, and driving toward her. High up, he could see the helicopter hovering ahead, and was not surprised when the machine came closer. 'Stop just there,' Drummond ordered. 'And move into the passenger seat. I'm coming back.'

There was a level piece of ground to the right, but the helicopter did not land. Instead it hovered a few feet above the ground and Drummond jumped out, rolled once and leaped up as if he were a twenty-year-old youth rather than a man approaching his pension. As the helicopter lifted, he ran toward the Defender and slid into the driver's seat.

'All right, Sandy?' Drummond drove for a few minutes, pulled into the shelter of a copse of trees and cut the engine. After the clatter of the helicopter and the hum of the diesel, the sudden silence was welcome. Taking a can of oil from the back of the Defender, Drummond walked a few paces and poured about half a litre onto the road. The dark golden liquid spread easily, slicking over the irregularities in the tarmac to lie in venomous innocence, a trap for any oncoming vehicle.

'Now we wait,' Drummond said, returning the can to the back of the Defender. He pressed the switch to ease down the side window.

Meigle looked ahead, not quite sure what Drummond had in mind. Directly in front of them the road dipped, and then rose into a sharp bend. Sunlight glinted from oil that dripped into a drainage ditch on either side.

'We'll hear her coming before we see her.' Drummond sounded very calm. 'I've sent MacFarlane away. Better if there is only the two of us.'

Meigle nodded. He felt as if something tight was being fastened around his chest. He had been introduced to the Society on his thirtieth birthday, and had accepted the responsibility willingly, rising with pride to be Chairman and head decision maker. Now, for the first time in three decades, he was experiencing some doubt.

'Listen.' Drummond lifted a finger. There was the sound of rising and falling gears as an oncoming motor vehicle negotiated the intricate curves and hills of the road. Drummond checked his seat belt. 'Ready? This will be over quick.'

'I'm not sure,' Meigle looked toward him, but it was already too late.

The Nissan appeared with startling speed. One second the road was empty, the next the bronze vehicle was hammering down the slope and approaching the corner. Drummond pulled out, directly in Doctor Wallace's path, with his lights on full and his hand pressed hard on the horn.

Doctor Wallace must have reacted instinctively, switching her right foot from the accelerator to the brake and slamming her left foot onto the clutch. There was the painful scream of brakes and the Nissan slowed, until the front wheels made contact with the oil. Bereft of traction, they slewed sideways and the Nissan skidded from the road, carved great grooves in the rough grass verge and thumped nose first into the ditch. The engine whined its protest.

'My God.' Meigle watched the devastation in horror. 'She might be dead.' He reached for the door handle to get out but Drummond forestalled him.

'Stay inside.' His eyes were as calm as ever, but there was no mistaking the steel in his voice. 'As Kirkpatrick said at Greyfriars, I'll mak siccar.' He reversed the Defender to its previous position and killed the engine before walking slowly to the Nissan. Meigle saw him slide into the ditch and try to open the driver's door. There was a pause, and then the noise stopped as Drummond switched off the Nissan's engine. He returned a few minutes later, his sleeve smeared with blood.

'She's dead.' He said laconically and picked up his telephone.

'What are you going to do?' Drummond fought down his nausea. He knew that it had been necessary to protect the Clach-bhuai, but the incident had still shocked him. He was a businessman, used to the cut and thrust of negotiations and the ruthless demands of money, but he had never before witnessed a violent death. He shook his head: he knew the rules. Generation after generation of the same family served the Society, but if the first demand was to protect the Clach-bhuai, the second was loyalty. Any hint of dissent meant a threat to the existence of the Society; there could be no wavering.

'I'm going to call the police and an ambulance,' Drummond replied. 'We were witnesses to a tragic accident. We have to report it; after all, I am a Justice of the Peace.'

'Of course,' Meigle agreed. He heard the distant bleating of sheep. At one time it had been a spider that saved the Kingdom of Scots, now it was a different animal. 'Then what?'

'Return home.' There was a trace of surprise in Drummond's voice. 'You have to inform the Society of the threats to the Clach-bhuai.'

Chapter Eleven : Edinburgh: May

At first Irene had felt sick, then humiliated and dirty, and finally angry. After leaving the bottle of champagne she had shut the door and retreated from the hotel room as quickly as she could. The receptionist looked up enquiringly when she rushed past, but Irene ignored her hesitant offer of assistance, thrust through the front door and back into the street.

She had known Patrick for nearly eighteen months and thought that she understood him. 'Bastard,' she mouthed, 'dirty, two-timing, double crossing, cheating bastard.' The avalanche of abuse did not help, so she increased her speed, walking without direction as she struggled with this new concept. Patrick was the first man to ever cheat on her; she had always called the shots in a relationship, deciding on its direction and when it should end. The fact that it was Patrick, compliant, obedient Patrick, only made it worse.

Patrick had always been there to listen to her problems and to bolster her plans. She had turned to him unthinkingly for support in her bid to become Ms Manning's neophyte and had automatically enlisted him in her campaign to steal the Honours. God, it had been Patrick who recruited everybody from his circle of Irish dissidents and other malcontents. Now he had betrayed her, and with a woman who was neither particularly young nor particularly attractive.

Walking on to the Dean Bridge, Irene stared over the parapet. What had Mary got to entice a man? She was short and slender, wiry even, with stringy muscles and hair that lacked even a pretence of style. What could Patrick see in her? Mary could offer nothing, except free sex. Obviously that had been enough to tempt him. She closed her eyes, reliving the images from her bedroom until she could unfreeze her natural prejudice and try to see Mary through Patrick's eyes. She shook her head; there was nothing to see, no shape, minimal curves, no personality even.

Irene swore, shouting a string of the foulest words she knew into the deep gorge that gaped beneath. Balling her fists, she hammered at the unforgiving stone parapet. If Patrick had betrayed her with such an unprepossessing creature as Mary Kelly, then how many others had there been? Was their relationship that frail, that meaningless? Pushing herself away, Irene allowed her anger to drive her in an aimless march that continued until her legs burned and the orange glow of streetlights softened the severe stone tenements.

The images repeated themselves in her mind; Patrick laughing as Mary gyrated across his hips, Mary turning slowly to the door with her face triumphant, Patrick's expression of serenity gradually changing to shock.

Irene stopped and looked around. She was in a broad street with a mixture of tall stone tenements and more modern buildings. A sign above a row of street level shops announced the single word Grassmarket. Above her, eerily lit by floodlights, the castle seemed to hang from the sky as if separate from the city that it dominated.

The sight of the castle quietened Irene. If she had a landmark, then she knew where she was. She took a deep breath, putting things in perspective. After all, she was a professional, a corporate executive, and Patrick was only an ex-marine. She remembered Ms Manning's stipulation that she must journey alone, so that Patrick was no longer a fixed star in her firmament. Taking a deep breath, Irene began to view the situation with more objectivity. Her hurt, like Patrick, was only transitory. It was a pity that she had grown to like him, but there were many more men that she could use for sex, when necessary.

Irene looked upward at the curving stonework of the castle's Half Moon Battery, whose cannon had threatened the city for half a millennium. That, like her ambition, was permanent. She was in Edinburgh to steal the Honours. The theft would further her career. If successful she would become one of the richest women in the world. Patrick had been her boyfriend. He had cheated on her. But she had intended to dump him anyway.

Ordering her thoughts always calmed Irene down. Now she had to find some advantage for herself. She assessed the situation logically; working out what angle she could best use. She had to play the part of the wronged woman, while retaining both Patrick and Mary in her team until such time as she could discard them both.

Patrick would expect her anger, so she could take immediate revenge on him, but Mary was more difficult. She was proud of her motoring accomplishments, so that was where Irene would hurt her. Once she had control of the Manning Corporation, she could buy over Mary's sponsorship and then cut it off entirely. Or perhaps she would sponsor a rival female driver? The prospect of removing Mary from her top spot put Irene in a better humour, so she looked forward to meeting Patrick again. God but she would make him squirm.

A group of youths burst singing from the nearest pub and the momentary flicker of light from the interior illuminated the shop next door. A heavy grill protected the window, but Irene realised that it was a jeweller. She stepped closer, trying to peer inside, but the noise from the pub distracted her and she walked on, slower now, as ideas worked through her head. Obviously

Patrick had to go, but she could make the most of their final few weeks.

Back at the hotel, she found him in their room.

'God, Irene, I'm sorry, so sorry,' Patrick stood before her with his head down and his hands spread wide. 'It just happened, you know? I did not plan it or anything.'

Sitting in front of him, Irene allowed him to grovel. She could nearly enjoy her feeling of power, although she still hurt and wanted to retaliate. Patrick continued to profess his sorrow, offering a dozen forms of penance to assuage his guilt and her anger.

'What can I say? What can I do to prove it was an accident?'

'Nothing.' Irene kept her tone flat; unsure whether it would be more effective to slap him or storm out the door. 'You can do nothing, Patrick. You've done enough.'

'I know.' His head was down again. 'I'm sorry.'

'And would you be so sorry if I had not caught you?' She allowed the fire to light behind her eyes, moved her hand to the side and saw him flinch as if he expected a blow. Really, men were soft beneath the muscles. She felt like a puppet mistress.

Patrick said nothing. He stood directly under the central light of the room with the crisp hairs of his chest showing in the vee of his shirt.

'I don't know what to do,' Irene said softly, allowing him some hope as she injected doubt in to her voice. She was punishing him, playing with his emotions as he had toyed with Mary's body.

Patrick stepped one pace forward. He was a full seven inches taller than her, with a forty-four inch chest and powerful arms, but at that moment he looked like a small boy caught out in some infantile transgression. He reached out to her.

'Don't touch me!' There was no need to act as Irene recoiled in genuine disgust. 'Not after you've been rolling around with that woman!' Her slap was instinctive and so fast that Patrick had no time to duck. It caught him full across the face with a sound that rebounded from the walls of the room. 'Get back.' Irene held her ground, forcing him to retreat by the power of her will. 'Get back from me, I said.'

'Sorry, I'm truly sorry,' Patrick stumbled backward, one hand to his face. He looked shocked at the intensity of her anger.

'Oh, get out,' Irene pointed to the door. 'Go on.' As logic battled with anger, Irene knew that she was making the wrong decision. She would be better to forgive him, to allow him back into her favour, but she could not. 'Get back to that woman.' She could not bear to say Mary's name.

Patrick opened the door.

'Oh for God's sake, go!' Irene pointed outside, turning her face away to hide the tears that were burning at her eyes. She heard the soft click of the door closing before she collapsed onto the chair.

It was early in the morning before she could control her sobs, and she could not return to the bed that Patrick had defiled. She knew that she should never have allowed emotion to rule her, but at that moment she would have swapped every jewel in Scotland, and every artefact in Mannadu, for one man on whom she could rely.

Dawn in Edinburgh was subtle rather than spectacular, with a silvery sheen slowly seeping from the east, adorning the stylish stonework of the Georgian architecture and the greenery of the gorge below. Irene leaned against the parapet of the Dean Bridge, listening to the increasing rumble of traffic that combated the soft singing of blackbirds. She had slept fitfully but awoke with new purpose; she had to control her emotions today, and show forgiveness to Patrick. Somehow she also had to face Mary. Retaliation would wait until the Honours were secure.

Taking a deep breath, Irene returned to the hotel and ordered a huge breakfast. She was still eating when she saw Patrick stagger into the room, unshaven and obviously having spent the night outside. Irene felt some satisfaction that he had not seen fit to return to Mary, but did not smile when he hovered beside her chair. His first words were predictable.

'I'm sorry, I really am. I won't do it again.'

Irene looked up slowly, aware that a waitress was watching from a corner of the room. She allowed the tension to build up. 'Well now; we'll have to see, won't we? Oh for God's sake, Patrick! I'm having my breakfast. Go and get washed and shaved, you look like something the cat refused to drag in.'

'Can you forgive me?' Patrick raised his head slightly.

Irene reached out but dropped her hand before she made contact. 'I'm not sure yet. But if I let you back,' she narrowed her eyes and half rose from her seat, 'by God you'd better not let me down again!'

'I won't,' Patrick promised, 'I swear that I won't.' He waited a moment as Irene returned to her breakfast, and then walked away, his shoulders hunched.

Irene looked directly at the waitress and smiled brightly. 'Men, eh? You have to keep them under control all the time, or there's no knowing what they'll be up to. They're just children with oversized libidos.'

The waitress smiled and shook her head. 'That's true. You wouldn't believe the things they get up to in here, but some of the women are just as bad.'

139

Irene had no desire to swap gossip with a hireling. 'I'll bet they are,' she said, and looked up as Mary came in, arm in arm with a smug looking Desmond. 'And talking of bad women,' she raised her voice so it carried around the room, 'here's one now.'

Mary sat opposite her and smiled directly into her face. 'Don't look so upset, Irene. He was only a man. There are plenty more, you know.' She patted Desmond's arm, as if to prove her point.

Irene examined her, wondering anew about the attraction. With her cropped hair and gaunt face, Mary was anything but pretty, while breasts and hips that appeared not to have developed since puberty could hardly interest a man.

'What did Patrick see in me?' Mary read her thoughts with an ease that made Irene suspect that it was not the first time she had faced a cheated woman over the breakfast table. 'He saw success, Irene. Men like to have a successful woman, and you only got second prize.' She dropped her voice. 'Remember that we all watched *The Neophyte*, Irene, and saw you squirm.'

'Yet I'm calling the shots now,' Irene kept her voice calm. Instinctively she realised that shouting would avail her nothing with this woman.

'Do you think so?' Mary kept her voice low. 'You need me, but I can return to the States any time, and you can do no more about that than you can stop me taking Patrick. You can't even fire me, Irene, because I know too much.' Holding out her hand, palm up, she said, 'I have you here.' She slowly closed her fist.

Irene controlled her anger. Everything Mary said strengthened her resolve for vengeance, but she could wait. She forced a smile. 'Well then, I'd better keep our relationship on a professional basis then, hadn't I?'

'That's the way,' Mary's smile was just as wide, and looked more genuine. She leaned forward and whispered, 'especially as I can guess who you are working for. It's no secret that Rhondda Manning is an art collector. Trying to get back into favour, are we?'

For a moment Irene was shocked. She had no idea that her life was so transparent. The old maxim came to her, when in doubt, attack. 'Whoever I am working for, Mary, I do not have to boost my ego by seducing a man half my age. I let you borrow Patrick's body once, but he's back in the fold now, and he won't be straying again.' She dropped her smile, hoping that Mary could not hear the rapid hammering of her heart. 'Now that the shepherd is aware of the wolf, she'll be much more ready to defend her sheep.'

'What are you saying?' Desmond leaned forward to listen, 'I can't hear you when you whisper like that. Are you talking about me?'

'Always, sweetheart,' Mary withdrew and placed her fingers on his arm. 'I was just telling Irene how talented you were in bed. Far better than the panting youths I have had before.' She smirked into Irene's face.

Bryan and Stefan came in together, with Bryan's eyes scanning the entire room before he sat down, while Stefan stared stolidly ahead. Only when Patrick joined them did Irene give her orders for the day. She told Mary to continue to learn the portion of Edinburgh that she was to drive, checking every back street and alternative route in case of roadworks or hold ups. 'Desmond, you and Bryan have to work on diversions. I want you to devise methods of taking everybody's attention away from the Honours. Smoke, bomb alerts; anything like that. OK?'

Desmond nodded while Bryan glanced from Mary to Patrick and back. His eyes narrowed thoughtfully. Patrick did not look up from the table.

'Stefan. You have to work on the actual hit. That's your speciality.'

Stefan shrugged. 'Sure.' Although his accent was still more Ukrainian than American, Irene knew that he was the only member of the team she entirely trusted. Stefan was a professional working for money; Irene could understand his motives far better than she could the idealism-driven Irish.

'And me?' Patrick looked up briefly.

'You and I are working together today,' Irene said, 'lucky me.' She was very aware of Mary's mocking eyes.

The Grassmarket looked different in daylight, with the pubs closed and the shops open. There were more tourists probing into the historical corners and more students doing anything apart from study. Two women gossiped at the foot of a flight of steps that led into a common stair. Irene looked up, seeing the castle impressive on its rock, a reminder why she was here.

'You let me down,' she said to Patrick, breaking a long silence.

He nodded. He was walking one pace behind her, as if too ashamed even to be at her side.

Irene swallowed. She needed his help to steal the Honours, but could not let him off too easily. She had to play this cleverly. 'You hurt me badly.'

Patrick nodded again and Irene quelled her rising irritation. Why did he not argue? Shout back? Try to put some of the blame on her so that they could have a blazing argument that would allow each to vent their anger and get things out in the open? She shook her head; she always picked men who were so much less than her, men who looked strong, but who proved to be moral weaklings, unable to match her in temperament or wit. What was wrong with them?

'Well, say something then!' She stopped and faced him, not hiding the anger that forced his eyes to slide from her face.

His answer was predictably humble. 'I'm sorry. I didn't know what I was doing.'

'She forced you, did she?' Irene raised her voice, aware that the two women had stopped talking to listen. Men hated public humiliation so she hoped that Patrick was squirming with embarrassment. 'That woman forced you into her bed and raped you? That woman of nearly twice your age and half your size?' Irene deliberately raised her voice with each word, watching Patrick's face redden.

The women were very quiet, one shaking her head in disapproval.

Irene waited for a response, relishing his discomfiture. When he eventually raised his eyes to hers, there was no fight in them.

'All right,' she said, quietly, knowing that she had won, but perversely disappointed by his lack of spirit. 'I agree that she is a man-eater, a predator. You were her victim.'

Patrick nodded, willing to accept his own weakness.

'You're a fool, Patrick. She was just using you.' Irene eased some compassion into her voice. What did she ever see in this spineless creature who was unable even to defend himself? He could only offer boyish looks and muscles. She stepped back, reminding herself that his ability to fly a helicopter made him indispensable. A sudden image of wealth and power of the Manning Corporation thrust into Irene's mind. Patrick was crucial to her campaign; she had to relent.

Stepping back, Irene turned and quickly crossed the road, hoping that she did not trip on these old-fashioned granite setts.

The last thing she wanted to do was land in an undignified sprawl on an Edinburgh street. She heard the echo of her steps and then, when she was half way across, the clatter of Patrick racing in pursuit.

'Irene!' When he came beside her, snatching for her hand, she knew that she owned him, body and soul. 'I am sorry. I was not thinking and I don't even like the woman.' His voice was urgent, pleading, as he walked at her side. She shook her hand free and stopped just outside the jewellers that she had seen the previous night.

'If you don't like her, then why did you sleep with her?'

'It just happened. She was there, I wanted you, but she came into the room and things just happened.'

He was as immature as a small boy, Irene thought, reaching for forbidden sweeties just because he could. She knew that there had been no malice in his actions, only a lack of thought, a triumph of desire over judgement. God, men were so childish! She turned away and stared into the window. The shop was tiny, with a dark interior and a collection of cheap trinkets on display. She focussed on the one tray that seemed even moderately interesting.

Patrick followed her eyes. 'They're nice,' he seized the opportunity that she offered. 'Would you like one?'

The temptation to continue her cruelty nearly overcame her, but instead Irene nodded. 'Quite nice,' she said.

'Come on inside.' There was desperation in his eyes. 'Please, Irene. I want to buy you something.'

Irene allowed him to take her inside.

Inadequate light from brass oil-lamps reflected from a score of locked glass cases, while the sanded floor sounded hollow under their feet. Two men stood in muted conversation across a counter of polished wood. The overall effect was so quaintly

Victorian that Irene was not sure whether to walk out or laugh, until she realised that the display in the window did not express the quality of the jewellery inside. Most of it was unique, handcrafted pieces that reflected the character of the designer more than the mass media tastes of modern society.

Ignoring Patrick, she studied the stock with growing interest, spending time over each case. There was nothing on display that would sell in New York or Paris, but the originality intrigued her.

'You've some nice stuff here,' she said at last.

'Aye. No' bad.' The man was slight, with a thin face and sandy hair. He leaned across the counter. 'Was there anything in particular that you were after?'

'I'm not sure.' Irene examined a tray of amethyst rings. 'I don't think I've ever seen anything quite like these before. Where are they from?'

'Scotland,' the jeweller said baldly. 'Everything in here is Scottish made. I make a lot of it myself.' He lifted out the tray for Irene to examine. 'We used to mine gold in Scotland, but not now. Some of the stones are Scottish though. Amethyst, cairngorm, pearls from the Tay.' He shrugged. 'You don't get many Tay pearls nowadays. Apart from me, there is only one other shop licensed to sell them, and that's in Perth.' He looked up sharply. 'The diamonds aren't Scottish though. Nor the rubies and such like.' His gesture seemed to dismiss the non-Scottish stones into secondary importance.

'I did not know that Scotland made jewellery,' Irene slipped a ring over her finger and held it up to the light. The amethyst sparkled as Patrick hovered, demanding to know if she would like it.

'Give the woman a chance,' the jeweller reproved.

Irene thought that if he improved his customer care skills the shop owner might be able to afford more impressive premises. 'We've just had an argument,' she explained. 'He's desperate to buy me something so we make up.'

The jeweller grunted. 'Is that right? Well, my family have been making good in this profession for centuries, so we've got a wee bit experience.' He looked Patrick up and down. 'How much money is the gentleman willing to spend to get back in your favour?'

Irene could not help smiling. 'A lot,' she said at once, 'but I won't let him spend above his budget.' She had been slowly growing aware of the third man in the shop and looked up. He was leaning against the counter, watching. 'Do you always listen to private conversations?'

'Every chance I get,' the man replied. 'They're the most interesting kind.'

Expecting him to apologise and withdraw, Irene was not sure how to respond when he merely smiled.

'I can suggest these,' the jeweller continued as if nothing had been said. He produced a tray of silver brooches, each one a variation of the same pattern. Two love hearts intertwined, some topped with a crown, others bare. 'We call them the Luckenbooth brooch. My great-great-great-something grandfather made one for Mary Queen of Scots, and we've been making them ever since.'

'Mary Queen of Scots?' Irene looked closer. 'That was James V's daughter.'

'Aye. Contrary Mary that got her head chopped off,' the jeweller looked up. 'The intertwined hearts are meant to signify a romantic attachment, so it would be a perfect gift to bring you both back together.' He glanced at Patrick. 'If you're sure that's what you want.'

146

The third man stepped forward, lifted a brooch and placed it in Irene's hand. The silver watch on his wrist looked old but expensive. 'The original brooches were given to the shopkeepers of Edinburgh to prove they had the right to have a locken, or locked booth. That was what they called the shops in Edinburgh in the old days. They only became romantic when Kenny's ancestor made one for Mary, which she gave to Henry Darnley, her man. That's why some have a crown.'

'Can you keep quiet?' Kenny the jeweller sounded irritated. 'I'm telling the story. I don't get much chance to talk to good looking women so let me enjoy it.' He looked up and winked at Irene, who wondered if his customer care was perhaps better than she had thought. 'Aye, Drew's right, though. The Luckenbooth brooches became popular in Edinburgh, with couples exchanging them when they became engaged. They also kept bad spirits from babies, so I'm told.'

Irene examined the brooch that Drew had selected. It was one of the simplest in the tray, Sterling Silver topped by a crown, but lacking the amethyst or cairngorm that adorned the centre of others. 'I like this one,' she said, 'you have good taste.'

'I like this one better,' Patrick picked out the most ornate brooch in the display and handed it to Irene. She could have resisted the contrition in his eyes, but was determined to patch up their relationship.

'So do I,' she said, immediately aware of his pleasure at her agreement. She granted him a smile and some mellowing in her eyes. 'We'll have it,' she told the jeweller.

Drew frowned. 'If you're sure,' he said, 'but the other is less ornate. It would complement your appearance, rather than distract from it.'

'Let the lady make her own mind up,' Kenny pushed an elbow into Drew's ribs. 'You ignore him, hen, and choose whichever you like best. What do men know about jewellery anyway?'

'I'll wear it now,' Irene said, and allowed Patrick to pin it in place. His hand brushing her breast had a new, strangely forbidden thrill.

Kenny stepped back, his head to one side as he looked over his customer. 'Aye, no' bad,' he said. 'It suits you.' He nodded. 'You'll be wanting my card for your next visit?' Reaching under the counter, he produced a simple business card with *Kenneth Mossman, Jeweller to the Scottish Royalty* written on it.

Drew examined the card. 'He likes to boast of his family's royal connections' he said, 'even though they ended centuries ago.' He exchanged a glance with Irene, scribbled something, and handed her the card. Their eyes locked for a second, and then she looked away. When she glanced back, he was still watching her.

'Centuries don't seem to mean much over here,' Irene said quietly.

'We can be patient when we need to,' Drew said, 'but very impatient for what we want.' He was not as tall as Patrick, but every bit as broad, with challenging eyes and a face whose colouring betrayed a life spent mostly out of doors.

'And what do you want?' Irene asked. She saw Drew lift his choice of Luckenbooth brooch and produce his wallet, but Patrick had stepped closer. He paid Kenny and guided her out of the shop, into the comparative brightness of the Grassmarket. This time when he reached for her hand, Irene could not shrink away; she still needed him.

Chapter Twelve : Fortingall, Perthshire: June

'Pretty, isn't it?' Meigle indicated the village that straggled along one side of the narrow road. Apart from the church and the hotel, there were a score of houses facing onto open farmland, with a wooded ridge growling down in the rear. Meigle reached into the boot of his BMW and withdrew a walking stick and a leather case. 'The name stretches beyond antiquity,' he said, 'Fortingall, the fort of the strangers.'

Where MacPherson looked suitably impressed, Andrew shrugged. He had grown up in and around Perthshire so one more village, however picturesque, did not interest him. 'Why are you showing us this?'

'You'll see,' Meigle told him. 'It is part of your introduction to the Society.' He led them the few steps from the car park to the kirk yard and stopped beside a walled enclosure that held a massively battered yew tree. 'This is the famous Fortingall yew.' He looked to MacPherson, 'you're a tree man, Lachlan. What do you think of this one?'

MacPherson surveyed what remained of the tree. 'It's old,' he said. 'Very old, I would say, but not much use for timber. If it was on my patch I'd get rid of it for something more useful.'

Meigle shook his head, 'Oh, the pragmatism of the New World. This is reputedly the oldest tree in Europe, maybe five thousand years old. That means that it was ancient when Christ was a boy. You might cut it down, Lachlan, but holy men have taken saplings from this tree and planted them at Glastonbury and Roslin Chapel and Scone.' He glanced at MacPherson. 'These are all religious sites,' he explained.

Andrew looked surreptitiously at his watch.

'Why? I mean, what's the religious significance?' MacPherson asked. Sliding over the wall, he touched the bark of the yew, and then grinned. 'I thought there might be some sort of feeling, but it's just a tree.'

'They say that Christ's cross was fashioned from a yew,' Meigle said, 'and the Druids were said to have worshipped them.'

'What worshipped them?' MacPherson looked confused.

'Celtic holy men,' Andrew explained. 'To them, certain trees and rivers were sacred. The Druids are supposed to have harvested great quantities of knowledge. A bit like the First Nation shamans of Canada, but in long white robes.'

'So they say,' Meigle nodded, 'but I think most accounts are second, or even third hand. If you look over there,' he indicated the ridge that dominated the village, 'you are looking towards the site of Dun Geall. When this tree was only middle aged, around 3000 years old, Dun Geall was the home of a chief, perhaps even a king, known as Metallanus. So they say. Come with me.'

It was years since Meigle had been in Fortingall but his feet found the path without difficulty, panting up the hill a few steps ahead of the two younger men. Refusing offers to relieve him of the weight of the case, he stopped twice for breath while MacPherson tactfully admired the view.

'This is Dun Geall,' Meigle said at last. 'You don't think that it's very impressive, do you? Yet a dun was a fort, and at one time this Pictish settlement was so important that the Romans sent an emissary here.'

Andrew looked around him. The hillside was bare of any trace of fortification, with neither stone wall nor battlement. 'Why?'

'It was Roman policy to send an ambassador to tribes that bordered the Empire. They made alliances, secured trading treaties, assessed the tribal strength and extracted tribute. Most

Empires do something of the sort.' Meigle eased himself onto a suitably rounded boulder and waited for MacPherson to join him. He placed his case on the ground, with the walking stick on top.

'The Picts were an unusual people in that their women had equality in just about every respect. They certainly had great sexual freedom and one woman became very friendly with the Roman envoy. So they say.'

'Talk about the boot being on the other foot,' MacPherson grinned. 'In Canada, the Scottish backwoodsmen slept with every native woman they could find.'

Andrew laughed as Meigle continued.

'Anyway the couple had a child, and when the envoy returned to Rome, he took his son with him. The mother, naturally, decided that she should also travel with him. According to the story, Metallanus, the Pictish king, also gave the envoy rich jewels as a gift to the Emperor and the Roman Gods.'

'And I'll bet the woman made sure that she had her share,' Andrew said.

MacPherson laughed. 'Of course she would. She had her son to take care of.'

'Perhaps so,' Meigle agreed. 'In time the Roman, his woman and their son settled in central Italy, a province known as Samnium, and the boy became accepted into the family. When he reached maturity he wore the Pilateus, which was a felt cap worn by freedmen, and he used his father's name of Pontii. Or so they say.'

MacPherson frowned and looked up. 'Pontii?'

Meigle nodded. 'I think you know where I am headed. Put the names together and you get Pontii Pilateus: Pontius Pilate.'

'Christ!' MacPherson blasphemed.

'They knew each other,' Meigle agreed. 'But the story is getting even more interesting. From this point on we are on firm historical ground. Pontius Pilate made a very good marriage to Caudia Procula, who was the grand daughter of the Emperor Tiberius. She was illegitimate, but the connection was strong enough to ensure Pilate's advancement.'

'Royal patronage, eh?' Despite himself, Andrew was listening. He moved closer.

'Imperial, indeed. With his wife to guide him, Pontius Pilate became an Equus, a knight, and so one of the privileged. Lucius Sejanus, the Prefect of the Imperial Guard became his mentor and in AD 26 Pontius Pilate became governor of Judaea.'

'That's the infamous Pilate eh?' Andrew shook his head. 'Trust Scotland to get involved in things that don't concern us.'

'I've not finished yet.' Meigle said. 'As we know, Pilate was a hard man. He ruled Judaea for around ten years, and there were many complaints about his severity. Around AD 33 he agreed to have Christ crucified, after a personal interview. That incident was eventually to make him one of the baddest of the world's bad men, but at the time it hardly raised a ripple in Rome. It certainly was not the cause of his removal from office. However, three years later he suspected a group of pilgrims of being terrorists and had them all killed. That's when Rome got rid of him.'

'So what happened to him, then?' Perhaps it was the atmosphere of Fortingall, but Andrew found himself listening. A rook rustled past, croaking loudly.

'What usually happened to inefficient Roman officials. He was found guilty and exiled to Vienne, in Gaul, and there he disappears from official records.' Meigle shivered as the wind picked up. He stared toward the hills of Glen Lyon, pushed himself upright and walked slowly downhill. 'Come with me.'

'Is this story relevant to us?' Andrew asked.

'If it was not, I would not be speaking,' Meigle told him. 'So far there is nothing secret in what I have told you. You can find the legend of Pilate's birth in a hundred books, and his later career is well known. What I am now about to tell you is not known outside the Society.'

Andrew looked politely impressed. MacPherson just looked impressed.

'Pilate's mother was not just anybody. As you would expect, the best quality women sought out the Roman envoy, and it was a Druidess who eventually claimed him as her man. When Metallanus gave the envoy precious jewels, the Druidess carried her own stone all the way to Italy.'

Meigle climbed slowly over a stile, with MacPherson carrying his walking stick. He did not relinquish hold of his case.

'When Pilate was sent to Judaea, his mother came to say goodbye for the last time, and she gave him her stone.'

'For luck?' Andrew asked.

'Something like that, but a bit more. It was a Druidical stone, a sacred stone.' Meigle reclaimed his stick back and crossed the final field to the village. 'It was a stone of power.'

Andrew grunted. 'It did not do him much good, did it?'

'Perhaps there was more than just Pilate at stake,' Meigle said quietly. He entered the churchyard and again stopped in the shelter of the yew. A blackbird sang somewhere nearby.

'He took the stone with him, and we have proof of that.' Opening the case, Meigle extracted two slim files and handed one each to Andrew and MacPherson. 'Open these.'

There were photographs inside. The first was of a worn Roman coin, depicting a crooked staff. 'The coin was struck in Judea during the reign of Pontius Pilate,' Meigle said, 'and the staff is a lituus.'

'Of course it is,' Andrew said, shrugging. 'And what is a lituus?'

'The wooden staff carried by augurs, holy men,' Meigle explained quietly. 'They used it to proclaim their authority, a bit like a bishop's crosier. Pilate was the only known Roman Governor of Judea, or anywhere else come to that, who used the lituus as the *only* object on the face of his coins. It meant something to him personally, as well as being an insult to the Jews, who were very much opposed to augurs or any other fortune tellers.'

Lifting the photograph, Meigle pointed to the centre of the lituus, where the staff curled around on itself. 'Now look closely and tell me what you see?'

'There's something in the centre of the loop,' MacPherson said. 'Another object?'

He studied the picture. 'It's something round.'

Meigle produced two magnifying glasses from his case. 'Try these.' He was smiling, but his eyes were watching.

'It's like a stone. Is it the Powerstone?' MacPherson looked up. 'Is that the druidic stone that Pilate's mother gave him.'

'So we believe,' Meigle said. He sat down on a recumbent tombstone and invited them to join him.

'That is the Stone of Power. When Pilate called Christ into his presence to be questioned, he had the lituus and the stone with him. The Society believes that Christ would have touched both.' Meigle waited for the information to settle in. 'And when Pilate was recalled to Rome, he took the lituus with him.'

154

'So where is it now?' MacPherson looked at the case, as if expecting Meigle to pull the lituus out like a conjurer producing a white rabbit.

'I presume that the lituus disintegrated with time, but the Stone returned to Scotland. You see, Metallanus had a son, a man named Mansuteus. He was a bit of a wanderer and when he visited Rome he naturally enquired about his stepbrother. He heard that Pilate was in Gaul and sought him out. Most legends claim that Pilate committed suicide, but we think that Mansuteus brought him back here, to Fortingall, and the Stone of Power came with him.'

'I think I can guess what's coming next,' Andrew said.

Reaching across, Meigle flicked over the second photograph, an image of the Sceptre of Scotland. The third photograph was a close up of the polished globe of crystal that topped the sceptre. 'The Powerstone,' Meigle said quietly. 'This is the stone given by his Druid mother to Pilate, and the stone which was in his lituus. This is the stone that returned to Scotland to be used by the Arch-Druid of the kingdom, and which the kings and queens of Scots took as their own.' Meigle allowed his voice to drop further, so that Andrew and MacPherson had to strain to hear him.

'With this stone, the Scottish monarchs had power over the druids. Without it the throne could fall. We know it as the Clach-bhuai.'

Only the wind brushing through the branches of the yew disturbed the silence, until MacPherson spoke.

'That's the stone that you were speaking about at the Society meeting.'

'That's the stone that the Society was created to defend.' Meigle said. 'So from this day onward your lives will have a different focus.' Rising from his seat, he nodded toward his

155

car. 'Now come with me and I'll tell you about the current threat.'

Driving fast down the A9, Meigle was back in Edinburgh in an hour and a half, pulling into the double garage of his detached Victorian house.

'Is that you Alexander?' Anne Meigle thrust her head around a corner as Meigle guided his charges toward his office. Paint dotted her blue overalls and she wiped at the speck on her glasses, succeeding in smudging it further.

'I've got company,' Meigle told her. 'This is Lachlan MacPherson from Nova Scotia, and Andrew Drummond, James's son.'

Tall and dignified behind the paint, Anne Meigle held out her hand to each. 'Pleased to meet you both,' she said. 'Is it business, Alexander?'

'Business,' Meigle confirmed. 'We'll be an hour or so.'

'I'll leave you to it, then,' Anne produced a professional smile and disappeared.

'That was my wife,' Meigle said, unnecessarily. 'She never enquires about the Society. It is best that you keep the same secrecy.'

Meigle's office was situated on the third floor, with splendid views over the adjacent Botanic Garden toward the Castle and Arthur's Seat. 'I often use this for Society business,' he said, 'please take a seat.'

There were four to choose from, deep green leather armchairs that crouched around a highly polished table. An old-fashioned roll top desk stood against one wall, with a state of the art computer on the other and a television with integrated DVD at its side. Three filing cabinets and shelves of books filled the remainder of the room.

'Now listen.' When both Andrew and MacPherson refused his offer of a cigar, he sat on one of the unoccupied seats. 'The Society has survived for centuries, but most of the time we don't have to do very much. We know where the Clach-bhuai is, and that it is safe, and that is enough. However, sometimes we have to act.'

'When?' MacPherson leaned forward.

'The Vikings were a bit of a threat when they burned Dunkeld in 903. At that time we held the Clach-bhuai in the church there, so it was a quick dash over the hills to safety.' Meigle grinned, as if he had been personally responsible for the move. 'Then we had to act again when Edward Longshanks of England came on his plundering expeditions. Historians will tell you that he was after the Stone of Destiny, but he actually sought the *Stones*, plural. That's why he came back to Scone again and again; he was hopping mad that we whisked it away from him.'

MacPherson laughed. 'I've heard all about Longshanks. My mom used to scare us with horror stories of Edward of England.'

'Yes?' Meigle nodded. 'Your mom was a sensible woman. He would have given Hitler a run for his money.'

'But why?' Andrew asked. 'Why was the Clach-bhuai so important to Edward?'

Meigle lifted his head, smiling, as the buzz of a vacuum cleaner sounded from below. 'That's Anne busy, then. Never stops, that woman. You remember that a later English king, Edward III, I believe, fastened the garter of the Countess of Salisbury around his knee and formed the Order of the Garter? Well, legend states that the Countess was also the reputed high witch of England, and by wearing the garter Edward was safe from witchcraft. Edward Longshanks wanted the Clach-bhuai for the same reason. He knew that he could not conquer Scotland until he possessed the spiritual symbols of the nation as well as the castles.'

Meigle shrugged. 'In the event, of course, he failed in both.' He smiled to Andrew. 'It's difficult to defeat Scotland when there are men of the calibre of your father. The next real threat was Cromwell.'

MacPherson nodded, listening eagerly.

'He defeated us at Dunbar Drove and sent his uglies north, so the Society had to bury the Stone at Kineff in Aberdeenshire. Then there was the Union, and threats to carry the Honours to London.' Meigle shook his head. 'That took some bargaining, but we got there. The English were so desperate for a Scottish union that they threatened war and economic blackmail, they used bribes and threw dukedoms at the Scottish commissioners like confetti, but in the end they got what they wanted. Security for England, Scottish soldiers for their wars and political control over Scotland.'

'And what did we gain? I mean Scotland.' MacPherson was leaning forward in his seat.

'Scotland got access to an extensive trade network that probably prevented mass starvation,' Meigle said frankly. 'We had lost some of our main trading partners because of the 1603 Union of the Crowns, and we had just come through a shocking famine. Scotland needed trade to live, and the 1707 Union supplied it. Within fifty years we were beating the English at their own game. We exploited the Union with England, gentlemen, just as they exploited us. Don't ever get the idea that we were victims. We're not that weak.'

'It was a marriage then, and not a takeover bid?' Andrew asked.

Meigle smiled. 'Call it a shotgun marriage, where the English groom expected a compliant bride, but instead found that he had married a thistle. The wife had her own ideas.' He shrugged. 'However, I have not brought you hear to discuss politics, gentlemen, but to inform you of the current threat to the Clach-bhuai.' He waited until he had their attention. 'We know that somebody wants to steal the Honours of Scotland, but we do not know who. We also know that somebody has organised a criminal group who intend to snatch the Honours when they are carried between the castle and the Parliament building on the 12th July.'

'Criminals? Surely the police can handle that, then,' Andrew said.

'Certainly. We can send the police some information, but we prefer not to. After all, they might ask awkward questions, like who we are and how we know. We are a small and very secret group, remember, and we exist to protect the Clach-bhuai, not to guard the Crown Jewels, however pretty they may be. As far as I am concerned, the thieves can have all the rest of the Honours and good luck to them, but the Clach-bhuai is our concern.'

'*How* do we know?' MacPherson wondered.

'We have a man within their group. Quite by chance, I may add. We do not possess an all-seeing eye or anything, but the Scots are a far travelled people, so we do have members in many parts of the world.' Meigle smiled to MacPherson, 'even in Nova Scotia. Now; it's four o clock by our time, so he should be up and around.' Meigle spoke to himself, and then woke up his computer. 'I have a video link with various people,' he explained, 'so I can see to whom I am speaking.'

After a few minutes a face appeared on the screen. 'Is that you Mr Meigle?' The voice was distorted by distance, but it was plainly Eastern European.

'It is. I have two new members here. Andrew Drummond, and Lachlan MacPherson.' Meigle leaned back. 'Say hello.'

The face on the screen nodded. 'Hello.' He stared at them, expressionless.

'He doesn't say much.' Meigle excused him. 'But he's as dedicated to the Clach-bhuai as we are.'

'They are pushing ahead with the arrangements,' the man said, his voice distorted by distance. 'What do you want me to do?'

'Just go along with them,' Meigle said. 'I don't want you to upset anything. Indeed, I want the operation to be a success.'

'Why? I could stop them anytime.'

'Not yet,' Meigle said. 'I want to find out who is behind this threat. If it is something official, then there might be big trouble, but if it's only some thief, there's no real problem. We'll let the Clach-bhuai reach its final destination and then get it back.'

'So I help these people?'

'That's your job,' Meigle agreed. He stepped back as the screen faded.

'He did not sound Scottish,' there was a question in MacPherson's voice.

'We are a world wide Society,' Meigle explained. 'One of our past members was a mercenary soldier in Russia, and like many other Scots, he settled there. Stefan Gregovich is his descendant.'

Chapter Thirteen : New York City: June

Irene had examined her plan thoroughly. She had inspected the ground from every angle, on foot and by car. She had spoken with every member of her team until they could recite their part perfectly, and she had held brainstorming meetings where everybody was invited to seek out flaws. As she had expected, Mary was the most critical, but some of her ideas had proved useful and Irene had accepted the minor modifications. Neither of them mentioned Patrick.

After two weeks in Edinburgh, they had flown back to New York with all the arrangements made and nothing to do but wait. Irene was glad to wash the dye from her hair and dispense with the spectacles, to eat American food again and bask in the atmosphere of the city at the hub of the world.

'This is the hard part,' Irene said as she walked across Bow Bridge. She liked to pause on the apex of the arch and look backward toward the wooded Ramble with its crazy paths. There were always birds here, candying the air with their calls.

Patrick nodded. He looked much more at home in Central Park than he had done in Scotland, a New Yorker in New York, with his black baseball cap tilted back on his head and his tee-shirt boasting the New York Jets logo. He also fitted his American role far better than his Irish, with all the historical baggage that country appeared to pile onto its exiles. 'You've got it all covered,' Patrick said, and gave that enormous grin that had first captivated her.

They walked on, skirting the Lake as they headed toward Cherry Hill. Joggers panted past them and a young mother stopped to talk to the baby in her pram. Everything seemed so normal that Irene could not believe the enormity of the task that she was contemplating. She was planning to steal the Crown Jewels of the Queen of Great Britain.

The thought was suddenly so frightening that she wanted to cancel everything and run away. She had lived so much of her life on a second best basis, never quite reaching the targets that she had set, but always fighting, clawing her way to get somewhere. She had entered *The Neophyte* determined to win, despite protestations to her work colleagues that she was merely broadening her experience. The more progress she had made, the more positive she had felt, until she had thrown up her job and staked everything on victory.

Defeat had sickened her. Reaching for the stars, the moon had not satisfied her. If Ms Manning had not offered a second chance, Irene was not sure what she would have done. But now her life had altered. She looked sideways at Patrick, trying to recapture her feelings for this man, but knowing that she could never trust him again.

Patrick looked back, his arm draped around her shoulders and he squeezed reassuringly. 'It will be astounding,' he said. 'In one month you will have pulled off one of the most outrageous undertakings that the world has ever seen. We will have shaken the throne of England and you'll be one of the richest women in the world.'

The words sounded good. Irene could not care less about the throne of England, or the throne of Scotland for that matter; it was the richest woman title that she wanted. She knew that she was playing for very high stakes, for if she failed, God only knew what the British would do to her. They could not cut off her head or anything, not in the 21st century, but they would probably throw her in jail forever.

For a second Irene contemplated herself chained to the wall in one of the dark dungeons of Edinburgh Castle, with a hooded jailer throwing scraps of bread to her. The Honours were centuries old and nobody had ever managed to steal them; what made her think she could succeed? She shivered in sudden fear, but the sights of Central Park helped her shake away the gloom. She was from a country where anything was possible. The United States had won her freedom from the jaws of the British lion; prising trinkets from its paws was surely easier.

'Come on, Patrick,' she challenged, wriggling free and dancing ahead. 'I'll race you up Cherry Hill.'

It was good to run in Central Park, to hear Patrick's whoop as he followed and to know that he allowed her to win. When they reached the top of the hill they threw themselves onto a bench to admire the view of the Lake. An elderly man smiled to them and made a comment about enjoying their youth while they could, while a middle aged woman stopped to peer at Irene.

'Were you not on a television show?'

Irene shook her head. 'Not me, I'm afraid,' she denied the accusation and deliberately embarrassed the woman by reaching across to kiss Patrick. He responded with so much enthusiasm that they grappled for a few minutes before she broke free. The woman was no longer there.

'This is better,' Patrick said.

'Just like it used to be,' Irene agreed, adding quickly, 'before I entered that foolish competition.' She had enjoyed that kiss, strangely, and briefly wondered if things could return to normal.

They were quiet for a few minutes, until Patrick said, 'do you know, Irene, I don't think that you did lose. I think that Ms Manning wanted to put somebody on a final trial and that

Kendrick guy wouldn't have the balls to do anything illegal. He's only holding the fort for you.'

Irene toyed with the idea for a few minutes. It felt good. She pushed herself closer again, sitting hip to hip and arm linked in arm, until her innate restlessness forced her to stand up. 'Come on Patrick; let's walk.'

They passed the statue of the Falconer, dodged the traffic by 72nd Street and ascended the hill at Strawberry Fields with its memory of John Lennon before heading to Eaglevale Arch and the Naturalists Walk. Irene slid her hand around Patrick's hips and cupped his buttock. That felt good, too, she decided, and she ran her thumb over her nails. Maybe she should make him get a matching tattoo on the other side. The prospect of scratching out Mary was delicious.

'Edinburgh was ace,' Irene said, 'but you can't beat New York.'

'Let's grab a burger,' Patrick suggested, so they reversed their direction until they found a stand near the Tavern in the Green and lay on the grass in the Sheep Meadow, enjoying the Manhattan skyline.

'Is there beer in the fridge?' Patrick asked. 'Real beer, not that British stuff.'

'Real beer,' Irene confirmed. 'Golden honey in colour and cold as an Arctic winter.' She looked over to him, tipped forward his baseball cap and smiled, discovering anew why she had fallen for him. Mary had been a bad episode, but it was past.

'Real beer,' Irene repeated, 'and a real firm bed.' Taking him by the hand, she headed for the East 66th Street exit and Fifth Avenue.

It felt right, walking through the streets of New York, with the purposeful bustle and the sense of achievement, good to be part of a city that looked to the future rather than dwelling on its history. Irene moved faster here, held her head high and swung her arms. Patrick hailed a cab and they clambered in. Exchanging pleasantries with the driver as she gave him directions, Irene revelled in his New Jersey accent.

'I'll be glad when this is all finished,' Patrick said, 'and we can get back to normal.'

'Normal?' Irene watched the tall buildings that soared up to a nearly hidden sky. 'Change is normal.'

'That's what I mean,' Patrick told her. 'This is how it should be.' As the cab stopped at a red light, he gestured toward a construction site, where yellow cranes swayed and a swarm of workers were busily erecting another spectacular building. A green-and-yellow billboard proclaimed 'In one year, this will be the Manning Manhattan Art Centre.' In smaller letters beneath was the message, 'For further information, try our web site or contact Kendrick Dontell, Project Manager.'

The name drove the breath from Irene even as the cab moved forward. The pleasure of the day left her, being replaced by a sickening sense of failure. She had lost *The Neophyte* competition, despite all her best efforts. She was a failure, a loser, a plaything of Ms Manning, who offered her promises while Kendrick enjoyed the luxury of success and power.

'We can't fail, Patrick,' she heard the grit in her own voice. 'We must pull this Scottish thing off.'

'We will,' the pain was reassuring when Patrick squeezed her hand. His eyes were intense. 'You can do it, Irene, and I'm with you all the way.'

'Let's go home,' Irene was suddenly desperate for the physical security of this man's body. She needed him to hold her, to tell her that everything was all right.

They nearly ran from the cab, paying the driver with a large denomination bill and leaving without waiting for the change. Nodding to Mark the commissionaire, Irene jumped into the escalator, admired herself briefly in the brass mirror that covered one entire wall and pulled Patrick in beside her. She pushed the number eight button, allowed Patrick a brief fondle and tumbled out at the door of her apartment.

It seemed to take an age to locate her key and then they fell inside, laughing together as if they were teenagers. They undressed as they crossed from the front door to the bedroom, leaving a trail of clothes in their wake. Both were naked when they reached the giant bed, but it was Irene who took the initiative with a passion for Patrick that she had not felt since she first entered *The Neophyte*.

He seemed surprised at first, but she knew how to manipulate his body, so he was soon responding, his hands exploring and caressing in all the familiar ways. Her hand sought out that tantalisingly offensive tattoo, curled into a claw and dug in deep. Patrick reacted as she knew he would and Irene forgot all about Ms Manning and *The Neophyte* and the Scottish Honours for a space and entered a different world.

'That was intense.' Patrick lay on his back, staring at the ceiling. Turning his head, he grinned over to her.

'Just a bit,' she agreed. She smiled back, allowing her eyes to drift across his body. She liked to watch the bulge of his biceps and the smooth chest of which he was so proud.

'That's the best it's been for a long time,' Patrick sounded serious. 'Sometimes I thought we would never get back to that again.'

'We experienced a glitch,' Irene shrugged away bad memories. 'We were too busy.'

Patrick nodded. He struggled to sit up, and pulled her head onto his stomach. She lay there, luxuriating in the feel of firm muscle beneath her ear.

'It will be better when all this is over,' Irene said. 'We will have everything that we've always wanted.' She lay still for a few minutes, allowing the daydreams to dominate. She could see the penthouse suites, the chauffeur driven limousines and the clothes from Chanel and Christian Dior, Geoffrey Beene and Morgan Le Fay. Irene smiled; yes, Morgan Le Fay; that would suit her height. For a moment she imagined herself entering a board meeting in a chic French dress, with all the men's eyes admiring her as she gave cutting insights into the future of the Armstrong Corporation, then she realised that Patrick was stirring beneath her.

'Ready, honey?'

But Patrick could never be ready for the storm that Irene could create. She left him sleeping on the bed, contemplated his recumbent body with a slightly regretful smile and stepped into the kitchen. She always needed coffee after sex.

Irene opened the cupboard and checked her supply. She kept a variety, from the Wal-mart brand that she used every day to the more specialised blends that were retained for special occasions. Today she selected her favourite Columbian and measured out two mugs. Even the smell was invigorating, so she was humming as she waited for the machine to complete its work.

Without realising it, she had been listening to the slow chimes of Patrick's cell phone. Now she padded through to the hall and raked through his discarded clothes until she located the phone in a pocket of his jacket.

She switched it on.

'Pat?' The voice was urgent. 'Are you free tonight?'

Irene replaced the phone in Patrick's jacket and walked back to the kitchen to pour herself a mug of coffee. She slipped slowly, glancing back to the bedroom where Patrick still lay across the bed. She shook her head slowly, for the voice on the telephone had been that of Mary O'Neill.

The coffee tasted bitter as she returned to the bedroom. Patrick looked up and smiled.

She smiled back. 'Coffee? Do you want some?'

He shook his head. 'I'll have something stronger, I think.' He got up slowly, rubbing at his latest collection of scratches. 'And I'll have a shower, I think.'

'You do that,' Irene watched as he padded naked to their lounge and poured himself a stiff shot of bourbon. 'Your cell phone was ringing, so you'd better see who it is. I'm going for a walk.'

Patrick tossed back the bourbon and poured himself another. He nodded. 'Coffee and a walk. That means that you are thinking about something.'

'How well you know me,' Irene flattered. Suddenly anxious to be out of the house, she pulled on a pair of faded blue jeans and a white tee shirt, slipped into her oldest and most comfortable sneakers and threw a very out-of-season leather jacket on top. Lifting her bag from its repository at the back of her favourite chair, she pulled the door quietly shut behind her before she started to swear.

Irene did not notice Mark opening the door for her, and she checked her purse as she walked the familiar streets. The small card oblong seemed to cling to her fingers, with its bragging claim to a royal connection and the telephone number scrawled across the back.

Irene held the card in her hand as she walked across the city. There were many places in New York from where she could make a transatlantic call.

Chapter Fourteen : Edinburgh: June

'Well now; this is an unexpected pleasure.' Drew held out his hand.

Irene took it. For years she had calculated every move, ensured that all the angles were covered before she committed herself to anything, but now she had acted on the spur of a very insubstantial moment. She looked up at this smiling Scotsman and wondered if she was being completely stupid, decided that she probably was and then decided that she did not really care. 'It's good to see you again.'

They strolled a few paces with the sound of birds in the air and the castle a friendly giant in the background. Princes Street Gardens may have been much smaller than Central Park, but the scenery was just as interesting.

'It's good to see you, too,' Drew stepped back, 'but don't tell me that you've come to Scotland just for my sake.'

'Of course not.' Irene dismissed the notion with a slight shake of her head. 'No. I was coming here on business and I thought that I'd look you up.'

'I see.' There was an awkward silence for a few moments, and then Drew shrugged. 'Well, here we are. Do you want the tourist bit? Or a meal in some fancy restaurant? Or what?' He shrugged, suddenly serious. 'I've never been out with an American before, so I'm not sure what to expect. I'm not even sure if this is a formal date, or just a casual hello.'

Irene laughed. 'I don't think I'm any different to any of the thousand Scottish girls that you've dated in your life.'

'God, I hope so,' Drew met the laugh. 'They all dumped me, and the last one slapped my face.'

'Oh, I can do that too. You probably deserved it anyway.' They found a handy bench and sat side by side, with the world strolling past them and the hum of traffic pleasant in their ears. A squirrel scurried close, hoping for nuts.

Drew nodded. 'Probably, but that's hardly the point.' He said nothing for a few minutes, but Irene saw his eyes roaming over her face. 'So what brings you back to Edinburgh? Apart from an overpowering desire for my company, of course.'

'Is that not enough?' she answered at once. If she was brutally frank, she did not know why she had arranged to meet him. Her telephone call had been made in anger, a spur-of-the-moment decision. This liaison was madness, considering how close she was to committing a crime that would dominate every media outlet in the world.

He was quiet again as Irene examined him. His clothes were different to those of Patrick, not quite tweedy, but certainly conservative. She could not imagine Drew wearing a baseball cap and tight denims, and there was an aura of quiet confidence about him that she found nearly disturbing. He seemed so sure of himself that she felt somehow superfluous, yet simultaneously completely secure.

'Who are you, Drew? I don't even know your last name.'

'Me?' His shrug was characteristically self-deprecating. 'I'm just myself. It's who you are that is more interesting. You don't know my last name; I don't know any of yours.'

'I'm an American tourist in your city.' Recognising his attempt to turn the conversation, Irene refused to be drawn. 'And my name is Ire…Amanda,' she used the name that was emblazoned on her false passport, and then stood up. 'Take me to the castle.' It was an insane idea, returning to the target so soon before the hit.

'Come on then, Ire…Amanda.' Drew was on his feet on the last word, automatically reaching for her hand in a gesture that Irene found quite appealing. 'As I still don't know your real name, and I object to using a nom-de-plume, I'll settle for no name at all.' When he did not press for an answer, she stepped in front, until she realised that she was unsure of the route.

'That way,' Drew helped her out. 'Over the railway bridge and up to the left.'

He took her up a steep path that skirted the base of the Castle Rock and ended at a small gate into the Esplanade. The place was busy with workmen erecting scaffolding, their Edinburgh accents raucous with abuse.

'What's happening? Is this for the Queen?' Irene felt a slight thrill of apprehension, in case there was something new to add to her calculations.

Drew shook his head. 'The tattoo. It's like a military pageant they hold every year. Lots of tartan and pipe bands. '

He led her past the scaffolding and into the castle. The soldiers at the gate stared directly ahead, wooden-faced.

The castle was much busier than during her previous visit, with more visitors crowding the open spaces and the military more active than ever. Drew pulled her back as an army Landrover roared past, and a small group of soldiers wandered past, chattering cheerfully to some children. She watched them for a second, trying to reconcile her images of the military in Iraq and Afghanistan with these noisy, laughing young men who lacked any of the machismo she had expected.

'Awright?' The word seemed a common greeting among British soldiers, until Irene realised that the soldier was addressing her. He was smiling, his freckled face alive with recognition. 'Are you still here?'

'Hello there!' Irene tried to bring the memory back. 'We met in the pub didn't we? I thought you were off to Afghanistan or somewhere.'

'So we were,' the red haired private said, 'but they brought some of us back. We're going in the Tattoo.' He sounded proud, but there were new lines on his face and a shadow behind his eyes. 'Wee Tammie's here too,' he indicated the private with the scarred lip, who acknowledged Irene with an inclination of his hand. 'So who's this then?' The red head nodded to Drew. 'Did you dump the marine? Quite right, he looked a complete wanker.'

Irene nodded, surprised at his frankness. 'He was.' She saw no reason to explain herself to a couple of Scottish private soldiers. The memory of a slogan came back to her. 'Up the Royals!'

'Up the Royals!' Both privates returned the words, one looking sideways at Drew, as if expecting him to complain.

Drew grinned. 'Wrong regiment,' he sounded quite comfortable in their company. 'I was a guardsman.'

The red haired Royal surveyed him for a second before shaking his head. 'Nah. You've got the height, right enough, but too many brains.' His companion laughed. 'So where are youse off to then?' The question was directed to Irene.

'Nowhere, anywhere. It doesn't matter.'

'Aye, there once was a fairy,' the private with the scarred lip shrugged. 'We'll have to be getting along. You two enjoy yourselves.' He moved away, with the red haired man giving a final grin.

'There once was a fairy?' Irene looked at Drew for an explanation.

'There once was a fairy,' Drew grinned, 'and she was called Nough. Fair enough?'

Irene laughed and, linking her arm with his, walked up toward the battlements. She knew that she should be missing Patrick, that she should feel guilty, that she should feel hurt, but she felt none of those things. Instead she allowed the Edinburgh wind to blow her hair free across her face, and jumped at the sharp crack of the One-o-clock gun, the artillery piece that fired every day at one in the afternoon.

'I forgot about that,' she giggled like a child. Drew had taken the opportunity to grab her arms and was now holding her tight.

'It's a thing we do in Edinburgh,' Drew told her solemnly. 'It helps us to distinguish the locals from the tourists.'

'What do you call this, the Edinburgh bear hug?' He released her immediately and she stepped back. 'I was not complaining, you know.'

The view from the battlements was as breathtaking as she remembered, with Drew producing a camera for the highlights that she pointed out. A friendly Japanese couple took their photograph as Irene straddled one of the eighteenth-century cannon, with Drew's arm light but supportive around the waist.

'Down you come,' he lifted her as if she were a child, and she laughed, impressed by his strength.

They spent a contemplative quarter hour in the War Memorial, with Drew leafing through the Book of Remembrance for the Scots Guards, and then brightened their mood with a pair of giant ice-cream cones complete with chocolate that dripped crumbs down Irene's shockingly expensive blouse.

'I'll brush it off for you.'

'You won't bother.' Laughing, Irene pushed away his hovering hand and guided him inside the Royal Apartments. 'My accustomed lifestyle,' she explained. It seemed only natural that they should graduate toward the Crown Room, and both gaped at the Honours as they glittered in splendour in their glass case.

'That's something,' Irene muttered, as though she had never seen them before.

'Aye. Not bad. Not what I'm used to at home, of course,' Drew's sudden grin took her by surprise and Irene could not contain her laughter.

She was quiet again as she stared at the glory under the lights. Here was history and sacrifice and splendour. She knew their story so well now, from the simple coronet that Robert Bruce had slipped on at Scone to the gunfire and powder smoke of the siege of Dunnottar and the long century when the Honours had been believed lost. 'What are they worth, do you think? In the open market, I mean?' Irene did not know why she asked the question; perhaps she just wanted to hear Drew's opinion.

He shook his head. 'Incalculable. Intrinsically they are probably worth millions, but the historical associations would multiply that a hundredfold, or more.' When he looked up, there was a quizzical smile on his face. 'If I said a king's ransom, I would not be far wrong, but they're worth more than any monarch. And yet,' he pointed to the rough oblong of sandstone that sat nearby, 'to the Scottish people, that is probably worth more.'

'It's just a lump of stone,' Irene complained. 'It's ugly.'

'I've heard it called the soul of a nation,' Drew said, 'and that's probably ugly too, given its history.'

Irene smiled and shook her head. She allowed her fingertips to brush against Drew's arm as she moved past him. 'Enough history now. Surely there's more in this city than old things.'

'Surely there is.'

Drew knew of an intimate French restaurant tucked into a basement in a New Town side street, but his impressive knowledge of the cuisine was spoiled by a poor command of the language. Laughing, Irene helped him out.

'My father insisted that I learn a foreign language,' she explained, as the waiter bowed toward her. 'He said it would help my career.'

'Good for him,' Drew approved, not in the least embarrassed by his display of ineptitude. In a similar situation, Patrick would have withdrawn into a tongue-tied sulk, with his male ego wounded.' You'll know about French food too, then. Recommend what's best.'

They lingered over the meal, with Irene insisting on lighted candles for the wine and Drew barely flinching at the bill. By the time they left, the traffic had calmed down and long evening shadows picked out the dressed stonework of the architecture.

'Take me somewhere nice,' Irene demanded. 'Somewhere quiet where we can walk and talk.'

Drew nodded, catching her mood, and guided her down a short hill to a walkway beside a river. 'This is the Water of Leith,' he explained, and she did not object when he took her hand. There were the ubiquitous blackbirds singing nearby, and a brood of mallards paddling in the water.

'This is nice.' Strangely disinclined to stride in her usual fashion, Irene stood for a moment, listening to the ripple of the river.

'Not bad,' Drew agreed, and led her slowly down a flight of steps. They were in a gorge with wooded sides that were alive with birds, while insects hung on the shafts of sunlight. They walked for a few minutes, passing under the massive arches of the Dean Bridge over which she had once peered, pausing to stare at the thunder of a small waterfall before reaching an area of red-stoned houses unlike anything Irene had seen before.

'This is the Dean Village,' Drew told her.

Irene smiled and looked around. 'When I first came here I expected small cottages with thatched roofs, or ugly stone buildings with no plumbing. This is more like fairyland. Who lives in a place like this?'

'I do,' Drew said. He stopped at a low bridge overlooking the water, with a converted mill opposite. Trees from the riverbank reached gently over the parapet. 'Top floor flat with one of the best views in Edinburgh.'

Irene looked at him. She knew that she was on the rebound, reacting to Patrick's infidelity and it would be far more sensible to keep a low profile. She also knew that she had to ask her next question. 'With your girlfriend?'

'I think we both know that I do not have one.' Drew's smile was gentle. 'If I had, I would not be here with you, and that would be a great loss.'

'Oh.' Irene looked away. She focussed on a man walking a nondescript dog beside a terrace of houses. The dog was pulling at its lead, determined to squeeze every last ounce of pleasure from its outing while the man looked harassed. Which was she, the dog or the man? More like the lead, she thought, a connection between two worlds, and unsure to which she belonged.

When Drew slipped a hand into his inside pocket, Irene thought that he was going to produce a pipe. She could imagine him as a pipe-smoker, calm and serene among agitated people, but instead he pulled out a small brown box.

'I kept this,' he said quietly. 'In case we ever met again.'

Irene snapped open the box. Sitting on a bed of green silk, the Luckenbooth brooch shone in silver simplicity. She looked at it for a long moment, aware that its symbolism was far greater than any intrinsic value that it may possess. In itself the brooch was nothing, a piece of inexpensive silverware, but if she accepted it, she felt that she would be making a commitment that she would be reluctant to break.

Drew shared that knowledge. He perched himself on the low stone wall with the water beneath him and the blackbird's call soft above. He said nothing.

Irene slipped her fingers beneath the brooch. It felt reassuringly cool, but the silk was the same shade of green as used by the Manning Corporation. 'No,' she withdrew. 'No, Drew. I do appreciate the gesture, but I cannot take it. I have work to do, a career to build.'

'It's a brooch,' Drew said softly, 'nothing else.'

Irene drew a deep breath. 'I cannot accept your gift,' she said.

'As you wish.' Drew retrieved the brooch, looked at it and snapped shut the box.

There was silence for a long minute as Irene looked away. The man and his dog passed unheeding and the blackbird sang with subdued notes.

'Perhaps I had better be getting along,' Irene said.

Drew shook his head. 'There's no urgency. You decided not to wear my brooch, that's all.' He smiled, 'after all, you haven't slapped me yet.'

'I could do that,' Irene told him. The thought was there, simultaneous with the desire to kiss him, accept the brooch and allow him to pin it on her breast. She closed her eyes, fighting personal images that could only betray her career aspirations. 'I could so easily do that.'

'I'll walk you back to your hotel instead,' Drew suggested.

'Just point me in the right direction.' Reaching out, Irene touched his arm. 'I should not have contacted you. I am sorry, but business…' she shrugged, unsure what to say, and unsure how she felt.

Drew nodded. 'I'm not sorry,' he said. He nodded up the steep street from where the dog walker had come. 'Princes Street is up that way and straight ahead. You know your way from there.'

Cursing herself for allowing emotion to control her logic, Irene stalked up the hill. Why had she contacted Drew, when all she needed was to keep quiet for a few more weeks? Now there was a further complication in her life. When she reached the top of the hill, she realised that she was at the edge of the Dean Bridge, and turned around. Drew was leaning against the wall, watching her. She did not respond when he raised a hand in good-bye.

Chapter Fifteen: Edinburgh: July 12

'Are we all set?' Irene felt the tension gnawing inside her. The events of the next few hours would change her life, one way or another. Either she could present Ms Manning with an addition to her collection, or she would be staring at the blank walls of a Scottish jail. Either she would be the heir to immense wealth, or endless years of confinement would turn her into a broken woman with neither a past nor a future.

'All set.' Desmond tapped the transmitter at his side. He looked more nervous than Irene had expected. She had thought that men with a history of armed struggle against the British state would be completely composed, but instead his hands were trembling, and sweat filmed his forehead. Hollywood was never like this.

This time they had booked into two separate hotels, with an arrangement to meet outside the Canongate Tolbooth. Irene had insisted that they arrive at different times, and drift into their pre-arranged rendezvous at Panmure Close as though they were strangers.

'Plenty people here,' Bryan said, looking around at the crowds that were gathering all along the Royal Mile. Most were tourists, enjoying this additional spectacle to add to their holiday memories. A few hundred were elderly citizens of Edinburgh, come to watch their queen. One small group carried placards protesting about the royal presence and demanding a Scottish Republic. The republicans pushed through the crowd, and for a moment they surrounded Desmond. A blonde woman thrust a red leaflet in his hand and kissed him briefly, before they moved slightly uphill.

'Freedom for Scotland,' they chanted. 'End the rule of privilege!'

A man opened a can of Irn-Bru and took a long swallow, while a family argued about where they should best stand. There was none of the intense patriotism that Irene had witnessed when the President drove in his motorcade, no forest of national flags or outpouring of sentiment that the press loved to capture.

'What a place for a bomb,' Desmond muttered, licking his lips.

Irene glanced at him. 'What do you mean?'

'Just what I said. Look: dense crowds, dozens of shop fronts to provide glass splinters, a public event to ensure media coverage. This is the sort of event that I would hit.'

'Nice thought,' Irene looked away. She could not afford any distractions from the task in hand. 'Concentrate on your timing.'

More people came, jostling forward to the simple metal barriers that the yellow-coated police patrolled. There seemed a forest of cameras, a constant barrage of noise as fingers pointed up the length of the Royal Mile in the direction from which the cavalcade would come. Irene put her hand to her face, adjusting the sunglasses that covered her eyes and nose. Together with the blonde wig over her black-dyed hair, they helped disguise her face. The theory was simple: anybody spotting the wig would not expect the hair beneath also to be dyed. The long white coat with its thick padding was intended to conceal her body shape, but it drew curious stares on such a warm day.

'There are the TV cameras.' Desmond lowered his head and turned away, as if sheltering to light a cigarette. 'Jesus, I forgot about them!'

'I didn't,' Irene reminded. 'That's why we're disguised. They will be concentrating on the Queen, anyway.'

'Listen,' Desmond held up a hand. 'Can you hear it?'

Irene had been mildly disappointed not to hear bagpipes played every day in Scotland, but there was something so distinctive about the sound that she could not help raising her head. Drifting between the tenements, the sound seemed not to belong; it was as if an entity from a wilder world had intruded on the safety of civilisation. Now more heads were turning, more voices exclaiming.

'It's the pipes,' an elderly Edinburgh man stretched across the grey metal barrier for a better view. A young policewoman ushered him back, smiling.

'The Queen must be coming,' a Yorkshire voice said. 'She's got her own pipe band, you know. They play for her every morning.'

'Do they? Poor woman. That's a horrible noise.'

Irene watched as the Scottish Republican group moved closer to the barrier, watched closely by the young policewoman.

The music was increasing, accompanied by the rattle of drums and a rhythmic thunder that Irene decided could only be the marching of hundreds of men. Suddenly she felt sick. Why was she here? Was it too late to call the entire thing off? She was a businesswoman, not a master criminal.

'Jesus,' Desmond breathed harder. He looked upward at the overhanging clock of the Tolbooth and crossed himself. 'They're four minutes early!'

'It's OK,' Irene reached for his arm, her management skills forcing her into calmness. 'We've allowed for some time deviation. Relax and focus.' She looked into his eyes, seeing only the unashamed fear that mirrored her own.

'Here they come!' The crowd pushed to the barriers, staring up the long corridor of the Canongate as the high lilt of the pipes increased in volume. There was a rattle of drums, and then a body of tartan-clad men appeared, marching solidly down the street. The pipes fell silent.

'Pretty, aren't they?' Desmond fingered his transmitter. A bead of sweat trickled down the side of his face.

'Lovely. Watch what you're doing.'

The band was level now, a mixture of young men and more mature NCOs, all made tall by their feather bonnets. Tartan kilts swung around bare knees, light reflected on bright buttons and buckles. Irene watched, wondering if Mary, Queen of Scots had stood in this very spot watching a similar spectacle hundreds of years ago. It all seemed very archaic in this world of computers and advanced electronics, but there was still something fascinating about these sights and sounds. She touched the glittering Luckenbooth brooch that Patrick had pinned on her coat.

'For luck,' he had said.

'If you wish,' she had replied, but her smile had been hollow and she had to turn away to hide her hurt anger. As soon as the Honours were secure, she would tell him exactly where to go. The thought gave her a thrill of pleasure amidst her anxiety.

'Now?' Desmond poised his finger.

'Not yet!' Irene snatched at his hand. 'I'll say when.'

The band marched past, drums tapping, and the crowd buzzed. Cameras clicked busily. The policewoman guided an elderly man across the street, his feet shuffling slowly. Irene smiled as the urgent sound of police sirens sounded in the distance. That was the first part of her plan in operation. Bryan had withdrawn to the depths of the close, from where he was making a number of telephone calls to divert the police to different sites around the city. A child began to cry.

'Here's the next lot!'

There was the sound of horses, hooves ringing on granite setts that had been re-laid to enhance the appeal of the street. With their breastplates gleaming and horsehair plumes jigging, a score of cavalry walked slowly between the tenements. The crowd were cheering, but Irene noticed that at least one rider had difficulty controlling his mount, and a sergeant eased beside him with less-than-gentle words of advice.

Irene's cell phone rang. She jumped, berating herself for not turning the damned thing off. She tried to ignore the sound, concentrating on the time, but the ringing was insistent and an elderly woman in front turned round.

'I think that's your mobile, dear,' she said helpfully.

'Thank you,' Irene bit back her temper. She put the phone to her ear.

'Amanda?' Drew sounded concerned. 'I've just heard that there might be trouble at the procession today. Best avoid it.'

'What?' Irene nearly bit her tongue with agitation. She was very aware of Desmond beside her, his hands twitching. She pushed the phone closer to her mouth and bowed away from the crowd. 'What sort of trouble? What have you heard?' She looked around, expecting to see armed police descending upon her, or black-hooded SAS men abseiling down from the rooftops. Sweet Lord, was there some way out of this?

'I can't say. Just be careful. All right?'

'Yes, yes,' Irene could feel the increased beating of her heart. 'I'm waiting for the parade now. What sort of trouble? What should I watch for?'

'Now! It must be time.' Desmond was glaring at her.

'Not yet!' Irene reached over just too late to prevent him from pressing the red button on his transmitter.

'Not yet? What do you mean?'

But Irene had no time to answer Drew's question as the loud bang of an explosion echoed down the Royal Mile.

'You're too early! It's not here yet!' She reached for the transmitter, but Desmond stepped back as the crowd surged toward the barrier, eager to see what this new spectacle could be. Desmond jabbed his thumb on the button a second time and another explosion sounded. The noise seemed to cascade upon them, deeper than the sudden roar of the crowd, so loud that it vibrated from the ancient buildings and rattled the windows of the shop fronts.

Somebody screamed 'It's a bomb!' and began to push down the street, toward Holyrood Palace. A large woman led a surge to the crash barriers, where the police were attempting to keep the crowd calm while simultaneously staring toward the sound. Thick, choking smoke rose from higher up the street.

'There!' Desmond grinned at Irene.

'You're too early! Where's the parade? You're too fucking early!' Irene slipped forward, heading upward, toward the smoke and against the downward thrust of the crowd. Scores of people were screaming in panic, a baseball-hatted youth was helping an old woman who had fallen while a man in a smart business suit tried to push them aside in his hurry to flee.

'Here! Here it comes now.' Desmond pointed upward.

A unit of Scottish infantry, all tartan trews and jaunty glengarries, jogged toward them. Among their ranks was the glass-topped Rolls Royce that Irene knew held the Honours. The vehicle looked too large for the confines of the Canongate, too shiny for the tall grey gulley through which it passed. Even through the jostle of the crowd, she could see the gleam of gold, the glitter of precious stones. Her destiny was rolling down an Edinburgh street and she was determined that Desmond's stupidity would not rip it from her.

'Amanda! Are you all right?' Irene had forgotten all about Drew in the madness, but now she lifted her cell phone. 'I'm fine Drew, but I have to go. All hell's breaking out here.' She killed the phone, returning it to the pocket of her bulky coat. At least if anybody had heard, they would be looking for somebody called Amanda, and she had her real passport carefully hidden away.

Desmond laughed softly, 'and another one!' This explosion was quieter, possibly through distance. The soldiers did not even look round.

'Give me that!' Irene snatched the transmitter and shoved Desmond aside. He staggered backward, swearing as she held on to the device. It fitted snugly into her hand.

It had been Irene's idea to create major distractions with false bomb alerts that would take the attention of the security forces away from the Honours, but Desmond who decided just where to plant the ex-British Army thunder flashes, the smoke bombs and the canisters of CS gas that he had obtained from Irish Republicans in Scotland. Only Desmond had the technical expertise to wire the devices so they could be detonated by remote control.

Now Irene studied the transmitter. There were two buttons and a small dial. She knew that the red button detonated the thunder flashes and smoke bombs, and the green the CS gas, so the dial must control the order in which the devices exploded.

'This way, please, ma'am. There seems to be some sort of disturbance.' Close to, the policewoman looked even younger, with a fresh face that belied the calm assurance with which she gave orders. 'Keep back from the road now, until all the vehicles have passed.'

'Don't touch that!' Struggling through the crowd, Desmond reached for the transmitter. For a moment he wrestled with

Irene as the crowd surged around, then he pressed his finger on two buttons simultaneously and there was a series of explosions. Somebody began to scream incoherently.

'You ass hole!' Irene screamed at him as the mass of people scattered, knocking down the protective barriers and brushing aside the thin line of police. Her plan had been for a number of diversions followed by a controlled sequence of harmless explosions that would divert most of the security from the Honours to guard the Queen. Instead there was pandemonium, with people panicking while smoke and tear gas rolled down the Royal Mile. Irene began to cough as the fumes caught at her throat and stung her eyes. Streams of mucus ran horribly from her nostrils.

'Move! Now!'

Irene gasped as the words grated hoarsely in her ear. At first she could not recognise the tall figure with the obscene gas mask, but Bryan pulled her into the shelter of the Tolbooth Wynd, beneath the great square clock. He pointed to her over-the-shoulder bag. 'Your mask!'

Nodding, Irene opened the bag and hauled out the mask. Wiping her nose first, she slipped off her sunglasses and hauled the clammy rubber over her head. It fitted snugly, so she could both see and breathe with more clarity. Beside her, Desmond was doing the same.

'Look!' Bryan had taken command. Hefting an innocuous Tesco's carrier bag, he pointed to the Rolls Royce, which was isolated in the centre of a mob of terrified, gasping people. 'Everything's fucked up but we can still do it. Keep your heads and follow me. Stefan is keeping our escape route clear.'

Irene nodded. The officer in charge of the soldiers was using them to help the police, concentrating more on humanitarian aid than on his duty in guarding the Honours.

Coughing and swearing, the soldiers were scattered, with only two men posted beside the vehicle.

Keeping low, Bryan crossed rapidly to the Rolls Royce. The first soldier was bowed double, coughing and vomiting as the CS gas thrust into his lungs, but the second moved forward. 'Back! Stand clear of the vehicle!' His voice was hoarse from the gas, his eyes were swollen and mucus streamed from his nose, but still he pointed the squat SA 80 rifle directly at Bryan, who slouched on. Without hesitating, Bryan pulled a silenced pistol from inside his leather jacket and fired a single shot. The sound was muted, hardly heard amidst the clamour of the crowd.

'No killing! I ordered no killing!' The gas mask muffled Irene's scream as the soldier immediately dropped. The rifle clattered to the ground. Bryan fired a single shot into each offside tyre of the Rolls Royce and replaced his pistol.

Stepping over the soldier's body, Bryan poured fast acting superglue into the lock of the Rolls Royce door, trapping the driver and escort inside. Ignoring their frantic efforts to escape, he removed a small square of what looked like yellow putty from his bag and placed it at one corner of the glass box that held the Honours. Producing a small detonator, he stepped casually over the prone body of the shot soldier. He pushed Irene out of the way.

'Keep back. Don't get involved.'

Despite her shock at the murder, Irene watched in fascination as the men inside the Rolls Royce hammered at the sealed door. She knew that Desmond had obtained the C5 from his Irish connections, but had never seen it in operation before.

The sound was less loud than she had expected, but the force of the explosion was shocking. Rather than shattering, the reinforced glass roof lifted clean off the frame, before sliding down the body of the vehicle, trapping the driver inside his cab. The escort at last wrenched open the door and staggered out, holding a pistol in his right hand. Blood seeped from his ears.

With his gas mask making him appear like something from the First World War, Stefan pushed his way through the crowd from the opposite side of the road. Lifting a massive hand, he chopped straight-fingered at the escort's throat.

'Don't kill him!' Irene heard the panic in her voice, but knew the mask would muffle her voice. She could only watch as Desmond produced a brace of yellow-bodied smoke bombs and rolled them down the road. They rattled away, emitting choking white smoke that further confused the situation.

'Oh Jesus Lord help me,' Irene prayed. She had expected something clean, with the professionals executing a clinical robbery, but here she was in a scene reminiscent of Dante's Inferno. Viewed through her eyepieces, the Canongate was a shambles of retching, gasping people lumbering from patches of yellow smoke, or wiping helplessly at their eyes.

She saw a child lying on its face, spewing helplessly as its mother held it; she saw the policewoman guiding an elderly woman toward a close, both doubled up with the pain of constant coughing; she saw the baseball-capped youths supporting each other against the Tolbooth steps while a group of tartan-bedecked tourists huddled against the harsh stone wall of the Tolbooth.

'Oh, I'm sorry, I'm so sorry. I did not know, I truly did not know.' Irene shook her head, sobbing her shame into the mouth of the gasmask.

Even before Stefan had disposed of the escort, Bryan had dived onto the Honours. Producing a folded bag, he reached for the crown.

Irene choked back her tears. She had not expected horror like this; she hesitated, torn between her ambition to complete the procedure and her desire to help these stricken people. 'Oh suck an elf!' Having come so far, she could not stop now.

'Hurry up!' Bryan was gesticulating, his eyes angry behind the smeared eyepieces of his mask.

Stepping over a middle- aged man who was attempting to crawl under the smoke, Irene scrambled to Bryan's side. Reaching for the sceptre, she curled her hand around the stem and pulled, but it would not move.

'Shit, shit, shit! It's stuck!' Irene pulled again, swearing, but the sceptre did not move. 'It's bolted down!' She looked at Bryan. He glared back through magnified, alien eyes. She leaned closer, hissing urgently. 'Use your gun! Shoot them free.' She raised her voice above the continuing racket of the crowd. 'Use your gun!'

They had to be quick, before Edinburgh's notorious wind cleared away the smoke and gas. Irene had to consciously control her bladder as a hard hand tapped her shoulder.

Desmond pushed between them, scrabbling at the massive Sword of State, his thin body wriggling with effort. Pushing him roughly aside, Bryan produced his pistol, pressed the muzzle against the first of the two steel clamps that held the crown and fired. The clamp parted and he repeated the procedure. The crown jumped slightly as it was free.

'For God's sake, don't damage it!' Irene heard her voice rising. She could hear Bryan's breath rasping through the muzzle of his mask as he pressed his pistol against the clamps that held the Sword of State.

Irene winced at each shot. Each impact felt like somebody was striking her, but Desmond snatched the sword the instant the clamps split, yelling his triumph. 'Up you, you Brit bastards!'

Ignoring the gilded scabbard, he swore as he lifted the four and a half feet of steel and silver gilt. 'Damn but it's heavy! Erin gu Brath!' Lifting it high, he dodged into the crowd, jinking around a soldier who pawed feebly at him while guiding a wheezing woman away from the worst of the gas.

Stefan appeared at the opening to the un-named close. He lifted his gas mask, shouted 'this way' and replaced the mask, looking tall and immensely capable.

Irene watched Desmond cross to Stefan, even as Bryan shot the sceptre free.

The dense mass of people had combined with the summer heat to confine the tear gas within the Canongate, but now the wind gusted through the closes. The gas and smoke were thinning, just as the officer in charge of the escort realised that the Honours had gone.

'That man! Stop!' The officer thrust an arm out, finger pointing directly to Desmond.

'Move! Move! Jesus, move it!' Thrusting the sceptre into her hand, Bryan pushed Irene away from the Rolls Royce. 'Come on!' He had the crown in his left hand and waved the pistol in his right as he barged down a slender teenager and ran across to Stefan.

Irene followed, gasping to breathe inside the gas mask. The sceptre was heavier than she had imagined, and clumsy to carry. It felt more like a burden than a national treasure half a millennium old. She saw a mob of people crowd around a policeman, a soldier wiping mucus and tears from his face, a tourist in a tartan shirt leaning against a barrier, and then Stefan was holding her arm and pulling her into the close.

'Down here!'

The passage was short and dark, with uneven cobbles beneath her feet and faded graffiti on one wall. Bryan kicked an empty beer can and swore, glancing over his shoulder. He began to struggle with his gas mask, but Desmond put a hand on his arm and shook his head. Although Irene could hear heavy footsteps in the close, she dared not look back. In her hands she held a prize that would make her one of the most powerful women in the world, if only she could keep her nerve for the next few hours. There was no time for faltering, no time for regrets; she must keep going.

Sweet Lord, she had succeeded in stealing the Crown Jewels of Scotland. It was a theft that would make headlines throughout the world, an accomplishment that would be discussed for centuries to come.

Desmond was well in front, holding the sword as if it were a lance, with Bryan not far behind. Ignoring Desmond's previous instructions, he tore off the gas mask, revealing a face bright red with exertion.

'Where's the car? Where's Mary?'

Irene pulled off her own mask. Either the gas had not seeped so far down or the wind had dissipated it, for the air was as clear as in any other Old Town close. 'Down here. Not far.' She ran on, keeping her face down in case the CCTV cameras penetrated this far into the close. If not, she hoped that her wig was sufficient disguise.

Stefan was at her side when she reached Holyrood Road, but instead of Mary and the car, hundreds of people packed the street. He muttered as his foot caught an empty bottle, sending it spinning into the street. Irene tried to hide the sceptre inside her bulky coat, but everybody was too concerned with their own problems to pay them attention. She started at the wailing of sirens, but whether of police, fire brigade or ambulance she did not know.

'Shit,' Bryan said, 'and shit again. These are refugees from the High Street. Where the fuck's Mary with the car?'

'Not here yet,' Surprisingly, Desmond was the calmest of them all. He leaned on the Sword of State with a nonchalance that Irene could only admire. 'We are ahead of time, after all.'

Irene glared at him, but he shrugged. 'It only took three minutes from the first explosion,' he explained, 'and it takes Mary four minutes to drive here.'

'Three minutes?' Irene glanced at her watch, astonished to see that Desmond was correct. She thought that they taken much longer.

'That's all,' Desmond said. 'The whole thing went like clockwork. There!' He pointed as a red Cherokee thrust through the crowd, sounding its horn. It pulled up beside them and Mary blinked through heavy goggles at them.

Irene closed her eyes. Maybe this would work, after all. They had achieved the impossible, now all they had to do was escape. She fought the bout of relieved hysteria that nearly reduced her to giggling uselessness and stepped toward the vehicle.

'Hey! Youse!' The voice was pure Edinburgh as two tartan-trousered infantrymen erupted from the foot of the close. The man in front was hatless and his hair was distinctively red. He levelled his SA 80 so the silver blade of the bayonet glittered evilly. Bryan had been confident that the army would not carry loaded rifles through the city. He had not mentioned that Scottish infantrymen were quite adept with the bayonet. 'Gie's them back!'

Irene heard herself shriek as she saw her dreams dissolve in front of her.

'Get in!' Mary's scream sounded above the noise. She gunned the engine. Jerking open the passenger door, Bryan threw in the crown and launched himself inside before reaching for Irene.

'Come on, for God's sake.'

Stefan slipped into the passenger seat beside Mary.

'Desmond! Get in'

'You shot my brother, you British bastards!' Desmond glared at the two advancing soldiers. 'You killed him in Armagh!'

As the second soldier knelt and aimed his rifle, Irene saw the scar on his lip and remembered him laughing in the Ensign Ewart only a few months ago. He was not laughing now.

'Bryan! You told us that the army would have empty rifles!'

'So they have; he's bluffing!' Bryan raised his voice, 'Desmond! We're doing more for the cause this way! Erin gu Brath!'

'Erin gu Brath!' Desmond echoed, but rather than climbing into the Cherokee, he lifted the great sword around his head and ran at the kneeling Royal Scot.

Irene did not know if she was prompted by a desire to retain all the Honours, or if she had some loyalty to Desmond, but she dropped the sceptre and slid out of her seat. 'Desmond! Don't be a fool!'

Desmond ignored her. As he swung his sword, the red-haired Royal lunged forward. He ducked the great blade with a quick jerk of his head, grunted and plunged in the bayonet. Desmond squealed as it entered his chest, and screamed again as the Royal Scot twisted the blade before withdrawing. Desmond seemed to stiffen; he looked down at the torrent of blood that had already soaked through his jacket, swore softly and crumpled to the ground. The sword clattered at his side.

Before that day, Irene had never seen a man shot or stabbed. She opened her mouth in horror, as Stefan's huge hand closed around her arm. 'It's over. Get in. Hurry.'

'Up the Royals!' The red haired private lifted his bloodied blade and advanced toward them, with his companion at his side. 'Come on you bastards! Come oot and fight!'

'The sword!'

'Forget the sword, the soldier boys can have it!' Stefan bundled Irene back inside as Mary threw the Cherokee into a crazy three point turn that nearly knocked two pedestrians off their feet and had the Royal Scots swearing in anger. The red haired soldier lashed out as the Cherokee passed, his boot thumping from the bodywork.

'Come oot you cowardly bastards!' Stooping, he lifted the empty bottle that Stefan had kicked and threw it after the retreating car. It spun in the air, crashed against the rear windscreen and clattered away.

Mary thrust down the accelerator and the vehicle powered along Holyrood Road.

Irene looked back. The second soldier had lifted the Sword of State and gestured obscenely at them. Desmond lay where he had fallen with his blood a spreading puddle. Leaning forward, Irene vomited onto the floor of the car.

Chapter Sixteen: Edinburgh: July

'Go! Move!' Bryan leaned over the back seat. 'Just motor through.' The crowds in Holyrood Road were increasing as people pushed down the closes to escape the gas and smoke in the High Street. Police in yellow jackets struggled to establish order as a long line of ambulances helped the coughing casualties.

Irene leaned back, gasping for breath as she relived the horror of Desmond's bayoneting, and wondered where it had all gone wrong.

'Are you happy?' Mary shouted over her shoulder. 'You've got your trinkets now.'

Irene shook her head, wordless. Hollywood had not prepared her for this sordid reality. Was Ms Manning's lifestyle worth it?

'Move it!' Bryan had removed his gas mask but pulled a green baseball cap low over his face. 'Keep rolling, Mary.'

With her hand firm on the horn, Mary weaved from side to side to negotiate the crowds. Twice they passed people lying retching on the ground, and once a man tried to flag them down. He carried a child and looked desperately at them, mouthing the word 'hospital.'

'The diversions worked then,' Bryan had already recovered. 'We should be home free in a few moments.'

Irene shook her head. 'Oh, God, I didn't expect it to be like this.'

'No? What did you expect, Irene? Disneyland? A film set with lots of tough heroes and only the villains being hurt?' Mary's laugh cut deeply. 'Better hope that's not right, because in this film, we're the villains!'

'Watch your driving.' Stefan said quietly. 'Police.'

The Edinburgh police had acted swiftly to place a line of orange and white cones across Holyrood Road, and manned it with four uniformed officers. Two were busy giving first aid to the injured, but the policewoman who stepped forward had sergeant's stripes on her arm. She held up her hand.

Mary slowed until she was within five yards of the barrier, then rammed down the accelerator and swerved around the sergeant, who jumped aside, her mouth working rapidly. The Cherokee hit the cones at speed, flicking one high in the air. A second jammed beneath the front axle and scraped along the road for the next fifty yards until Mary stopped, threw the vehicle in reverse and curved around the cone.

'Lost it,' Mary said briefly. 'Who needs Hollywood when we can have Edinburgh, eh? Here's our junction.' She turned into the Pleasance, dropped down a gear and threw the Cherokee onward.

Irene looked behind her she heard the approaching wail of sirens. 'Police. No, it's a Landrover.'

'Redcaps,' Bryan told her. 'Military Police. Bastards with snouts.'

'We can outrun them,' Mary said calmly. 'Watch this.' Dropping her gear again, she moved to the right side of the road, forcing an oncoming car to swerve across the road, and then quickly returned to the left side. Faced with the suddenly approaching vehicle, the Military Police Landrover abruptly braked, skidded, and slammed sideways into a lamppost.

'Amateurs!' Mary raised her gears again and powered on. 'There might be more ahead though. It depends how many were diverted to the High Street.' She overtook a BMW, flicked on her lights to make the driver think she was braking and laughed when he dropped behind. 'That's another obstacle for the police.'

'Well done, Mary,' Bryan approved.

Stefan glanced at his watch. 'How are we for time?'

Irene glanced upward, hoping that Patrick was there with the helicopter. She thought of the man Bryan had shot, and of Desmond lying in his own blood, and of the casualties the CS gas had caused. She had not intended such hurt. She had not realised the pain and suffering that her idea would cause. Shaking her head, she looked down at the gaudy crown that squeezed in the space between the back and front seats, and the sceptre that she unconsciously gripped in her hand. These trinkets were her tickets to power but she no longer knew if the price justified the prize.

Ignoring red traffic signals, Mary eased around slower moving traffic, weaving around a toiling cyclist. 'Nearly there.' She laughed again as a solitary police car emerged from a side street just behind them. Irene shuddered at the wail of sirens and sunk lower in her seat.

Mary shook her head. 'Don't they realize that sitting behind me is useless? I won't go any slower and people in front just clear out of the road quicker.'

There was a build up of traffic ahead, but Mary jinked around the congestion like the superb driver that she was. Turning left at the Commonwealth Pool, she circled both roundabouts and slammed through the entrance to the Queen's Park.

'He's not here! Jesus and Mary, he's not here!' Bryan stared beyond the red crags of Salisbury, scanning the sky. 'The police will be with us in a minute.'

'Calm down.' Mary's voice was sharp. 'Paddy won't let us down.' Heading left, she veered off the road onto the wide stretch of grass. 'He'll be here.'

Putting a hand over her face, Irene glanced backward. The police car had negotiated the roundabout but had had been halted by a slow moving bus.

'There he is.' Stefan gestured upward just as Irene became aware of the slightly sinister beat of a helicopter rotor.

Mary pushed the Cherokee into a wide curve, waited until the helicopter hovered above them, and then braked. 'All out, and don't forget the crown jewels.'

'Never travel without them,' Bryan assured her.

Irene felt her legs trembling as she nearly fell from the seat and staggered outside. The helicopter hovered above them, the downdraught from its rotors flattening the short grass and causing their coats to flap madly around their legs.

'Oh look,' Mary sounded terribly calm. 'It's not very large.' She shrugged toward Irene, 'I hope that we can all fit in.'

'Of course we can,' Irene snapped back. 'Patrick worked out the passenger capacity months ago.'

The helicopter touched down smoothly, its blades rotating. The passenger door slid open and Patrick looked out. 'Hurry! The bastards have put an air exclusion zone in place, there's a police car coming into the park and army Landrovers driving from Holyrood!'

'Oh Fuck! Fuck, fuck, fuck!' Keeping low to avoid the rotor blades, Irene ran toward the helicopter. Mary was there first, laughing as Patrick pulled her on board. She eased into the seat at his side. Stefan waited by the door, shouting above the noise of the engine.

'Come on Irene. I'll hold that while you get on board.'

Nodding, Irene handed over the sceptre. She paused at the door. 'This is not the same chopper!'

'No!' Patrick shook his head. 'This is a much faster craft. Much smaller too. It only has space for two passengers.'

'What? Irene stared as Bryan tossed the crown to Mary and eased on board.

'Sorry, Irene, but there's no room at the inn.' Reaching into his pocket, Bryan pulled out a pistol and shot Stefan through the head. The Ukrainian fell without a sound.

'No!' Irene screamed the word.

'I'll get the sceptre,' Bryan volunteered, but Patrick shook his head.

'No time! The crown will do! It's the best of the bunch anyway.' When he looked round Patrick wore the familiar boyish grin that Irene knew so well. 'Bye, Irene. I'll think of you clawing ass in jail, you perverted bitch.'

'Patrick!' Irene reached forward, grabbing at the door of the helicopter, but Mary was quicker. She placed her foot against Irene's chest and pushed hard. Irene screamed as she fell back, her fingers scrabbling uselessly.

Mary leaned out of the open door, grinning. 'Paddy prefers a real woman to an arrogant child!' Extending her fingers, she blew on her nails, mocking. 'But don't you fret, girl, I'll treat him real good, better than you ever did!'

As the helicopter began to rise, Irene jumped up. Her fingers closed on the rounded steel lip of the doorframe. 'You can't leave me! Patrick! Please!'

'Bye, Irene. Thanks for the crown.' Mary placed her foot on Irene's hand and exerted a little pressure. She leaned closer, 'we'll talk lots about you.'

'No!' Irene looked up, but Patrick was concentrating on the controls. Mary lifted her foot and stamped down hard.

As the pain lanced through her fingers, Irene jerked back her hand and felt a sickening second of nothingness as she fell the fifteen feet that the helicopter had risen since she had taken told of the doorframe. She yelled again at the immediate agony down her left side as she thumped on to the ground.

The churning throb of the helicopter receded into the distance, carrying off the Scottish crown and her dreams of success.

She lay on the short grass for a long moment, hearing her breath gasping in her lungs and waiting for the first thrust of pain to diminish. The temptation to remain down was very strong, but she knew that she had to rise, for she could hear oncoming police sirens. Pushing herself to her feet, Irene gasped at the sickening pain in her right hand and down her left side. She began to hobble backward until she kicked something soft and solid.

Stefan lay face up with a tiny hole between his eyes. There was an ugly patch of blood and a puddle of brains behind his head, and the sceptre lay just outside his outstretched fingers. For a second, Irene could only stare at the glittering item with the clear bauble on top, and then she stooped, scooped it up and stuffed it inside her coat. If she was going to prison, at least she could hold the damned thing that sent her there.

The sound of sirens increased and a car slithered onto the grass. A policewoman emerged, gesticulating at the crowd of onlookers that was gathering.

'God,' Irene glanced behind her. There was a stretch of smooth grass, and then a scattering of trees; while to her right were the scree slopes that led to the red crags of Salisbury.

'You there! That woman!'

Irene heard the police moving toward her. She had no choice. She had to run. With the pain begging her to stop, she began to move through the crowd and toward the Crags.

'There it is!' A man pointed upward, where Patrick's helicopter was a rapidly diminishing speck. 'They shot that man and escaped! A woman tried to stop them but they pushed her out!'

'Bastard! Bastards, bastards!' Irene drew strength from her anger as she increased her speed. Intent on the helicopter, the crowd parted to allow her passage, and then closed again as a hundred faces concentrated on the free drama that she had provided. A small convoy of police cars rolled along the road that encircled the park, and a score of uniformed officers descended on Stefan's body.

'She was one of them!' A small girl jabbed a finger toward Irene, but nobody listened to the accusations of a child.

Irene moved on, heading right, away from the mob. She contemplated the Radical Road that led around the Crags, but the slope was too steep and she limped on, with the noise gradually diminishing behind her. Holding the sceptre tight beneath her coat, she reached the smooth black tarmac of the road that encircled the Queen's Park. Her dreams were shattered, Patrick had betrayed her and she was a stranded fugitive in a foreign country. When Irene closed her eyes she could only see the panicking crowd, children gasping for breath and an old woman with tears weeping from her swollen red eyes.

There were more sirens ahead, but a low iron railing to her right suggested sanctuary. She glanced over hopefully, but she could not have negotiated the steep cliff even when she was fully fit. She had no chance with her present injuries and the sirens were coming at speed. Sobbing with pain, Irene crossed the road, and angled back, up a short incline that led to the edge of the Crags. Keeping her head low, she forced herself to keep moving, fighting the weakness and the agony but grasping the sceptre as if it would repair all her ills.

This part of the park was unfamiliar and virtually empty of people. Sinking onto a shattered red rock, Irene looked for somewhere to hide. She sat in the rear of Salisbury Crags, where the ground declined in uneven undulations to a straight path and then rose again in the rougher slopes of Arthur's Seat, the eight-hundred-foot high hill that dominated the eastern section of Edinburgh. There were a dozen people walking here, but none gave her more than a passing glance. Incongruous in the midst of a city, a rabbit jinked from cover and scurried upward among tangled undergrowth.

Moving uphill toward the rearmost lip of the Crags, Irene found an area of broken ground, screened by yellow gorse. She slumped down, swearing, dashed away tears of frustration and scanned her surroundings. The crags provided cover from any searching police, but she knew that any asylum was temporary. As soon as they learned that she had been thrown from Patrick's helicopter, the police would scour the park. However, the confusion in the Royal Mile would keep them occupied for some time yet. Lying on her back, Irene closed her eyes.

She should be cruising over the Hebrides now, approaching the tiny pier at Bunnahabhain in Islay, where her chartered yacht was waiting. Within the hour she would have been out in the Atlantic, heading west. Instead she was cowering in a gouge in the ground, grasping only one third of the treasures that she planned to take to Ms Manning. Irene glanced at her watch. It had been just after two when Desmond triggered the first of the smoke bombs. Now it was nearly four. What had happened to the time? She lay back, fighting the nausea of tension, CS gas and fear. The memory of Desmond's death was so vivid that she had to think about something else, she had to use her analytical brain to get out of this mess.

There were three questions. How could she get away from Edinburgh, how could she reach safety and should she still hand the sceptre to Ms Manning?

The first question was more immediate. The city was already crammed with police and security. They could hardly fit any more in, but most would concentrate on the safety of the heads of state. What remained would pursue the trail of the thieves. Once the police heard what had happened, they would expect her to run out of the city as quickly as she could. The best answer then, was to remain in Edinburgh, perhaps even as herself. Dispose of Amanda and recreate Irene Armstrong.

That answer helped the second question. If she kept her nerve, she could use her own passport to return to the USA. With her original plans in disarray, she could not yet think how to carry the sceptre.

The third question was more awkward. With the worldwide publicity that this day would create, Ms Manning might be reluctant to accept the stolen sceptre, however valuable it was. At present she could do nothing to alter that, so she must concentrate on the first two points. She was an intelligent, logical woman; she could think her way clear of this situation.

Taking a deep breath, Irene viewed her situation rationally. Despite the smoke, CCTV cameras would have caught her image, but the wig and dark glasses should have provided a disguise. Now she had to lose them, together with her outer clothing, so she was not immediately recognisable. After that she could plan her next move.

Removing the wig, Irene stuffed it inside the pocket of her coat, which she took off, reversed and draped over her shoulder. The sceptre was a larger problem. It was longer than she had thought, and bulged awkwardly around the crystal ball. Lacking any choice, Irene stuffed the lowest part into the waistband of her jeans and thrust the upper half under her loose tee shirt. It felt extremely uncomfortable, but there was little else she could do. Standing up, she hobbled downward, toward the rough track.

With every step, the shaft of the sceptre scraped against her leg and ribs, but Edinburgh in summer was used to eccentrics. She was just another tourist among thousands. When the track merged with the road that encircled the park, Irene turned right, away from the Royal Mile. She could hear the continual scream of sirens, while the air still held the sting of CS gas.

Irene checked her watch again. Nearly five in the evening and it was still full daylight. This far north, darkness would not come until well after ten, so she had no natural shield under which to shelter. Her choice now was stark; either she walked out of the park in full view of the police, or waited for night. She glanced ahead, seeing a small loch to the right, beside which a group of mothers-and-children fed a horde of ducks, uncaring of the drama that had happened only a few hours ago. Beyond the loch was a road junction, with two police cars, lights flashing, and a group of dark uniformed officers.

Irene turned to the loch, lifted a piece of discarded bread and pretended to join the happy feeders. She could feel the frantic hammer of her heart and hoped that she did not look conspicuous.

'It's a lovely day,' she said to the nearest of the young mothers.

'Certainly is,' the woman replied. 'Big trouble in town though.' She looked about seventeen; far too young to be responsible for the child that stood at her knee, and the second that wriggled in the pram she rocked back and forth.

'Oh? I wondered why there were so many police. What happened?'

The woman shrugged. 'Don't know. Somebody attacked the Queen, I think. Something like that. They're closing off all the park exits anyway.'

Irene looked up. The police were speaking with a small group of men. 'So I see. Was anybody hurt?'

'Don't know.' The woman shrugged. 'Anyway, I'd better be off. I'm on night shift.' She gave Irene a small, frightened, smile. 'Are you all right? You're bleeding.'

Irene raised her left hand, for her right was throbbing painfully. For the first time she felt the dried blood and mud on her face where she had fallen from the helicopter. 'I had a bit of a fall,' she explained. If this busy young mother had noticed, then so would the police at the park entrance. Forcing a smile, Irene waited until the woman wheeled away her pram before she began to walk slowly back toward the park. She would have to wait until night before trying again.

Standing on a prominent knoll, the ruin of an ancient building overlooked the loch. It might have been important at one time, but now consisted of a stone shell with only three walls and no roof. Irene struggled up the slope, stopping to nurse her ribs or her leg every few steps, and collapsed thankfully into the angle of two of the walls. Now she had shelter and a viewpoint. The sceptre was hard and warm against her body so she slipped it free and placed it at her side.

Perhaps it was the strain of the previous few hours, but she suddenly felt very tired. As she closed her eyes, images from the day burst into her mind. She saw Desmond being bayoneted; yellow smoke slithering between the Canongate tenements; the retching casualties in Holyrood Road, Mary's sneer as she stamped on her hand, Patrick's taunting face as he left her behind.

Irene woke with a start, aware that she was shivering and in a very unfamiliar place. She looked around, seeing utter blackness in one direction and the glow of streetlights in another. Something splashed coldly in the loch beneath. She checked her watch. It was two in the morning, with stars pricking the sky and the breeze moaning through the gaps of her ruin.

Where could she go? Not back to the hotel, for if she had been identified the police would be waiting for her. Where then? For a second she thought about approaching the United States Consulate, but dismissed the idea immediately.

The memory of Drew's calm presence came to her. Drew. Although she hardly knew him, something instinctively told her that he would provide sanctuary. Drew would know what to do. Irene shivered and straightened her legs, gasping at the renewed pain in her side and the constant throbbing of her knuckles. Lifting her coat, she held it tight in her left hand as she replaced the sceptre under her clothes, flinching when the cold metal touched her skin. Her injuries had stiffened while she slept so the descent from the ruin to the loch was jolting agony.

Guessing that there would still be police at the main entrances to the park, Irene reluctantly turned away from the orange glow of Edinburgh and headed into the darkness. After ten stumbling minutes, she came to the tarmac road, crossed quickly and slipped down a slope of grass. She fell, stifling her moans as the sceptre scraped against her side, and slammed against a stone wall.

Lying still until the waves of pain subsided, Irene rolled away as headlights gleamed on the road. A police car grumbled past, its blue lights flashing a warning. Fear forced her to her feet and she pulled herself over the wall, feeling the rough stone rasp against her ribs, renewing yesterday's pain.

There was a short drop on the opposite side, and a piece of mercifully soft ground on which to land. Irene shuddered as she saw an array of windows, some dark, some lit. She was in what appeared to be a communal back yard, with a smooth lawn and a garden shed. Voices murmured above her, and somebody laughed. She lay still as a figure appeared at one of the illuminated windows and a man peered outside.

As soon as he ducked back again, Irene ran forward, tripped and stumbled down an unlit flight of steps. She landed with a clatter, bit her lip to kill her yell and remained still in case somebody came to investigate. Somewhere in the night, a cat yowled. After a few minutes she rose, whimpering.

A doorway gaped before her, and Irene stumbled forward until she emerged from the dimness of a passageway into the orange glow of street lamps. She staggered onward, passing dark tenements and dingy basements, rows of parked cars and small clusters of graffiti-garnished shops. There was a main road ahead, with traffic lights and what was obviously a sporting stadium.

Irene hesitated for a second and turned left, holding the sceptre close to her body and moving as quickly as she could. Her watch told her that it was four in the morning but already the light was strengthening, and people were on the move. A red Royal Mail van hummed past, then a double-decker bus.

'Where the hell am I?' Irene wondered.

It was another hour before Irene came to a part of the city that she recognised, weaving around the orderly streets of the New Town with their end-to-end parked cars and identical cliffs of buildings. Her feet were sore, her ribs ached constantly, but she had to keep moving. She had to reach Drew. He would help her.

The hill sloped abruptly downward, its opening nearly hidden in the half-light of morning. The street was narrow, nearly mediaeval in its crooked descent but Irene paused only briefly, frantic to reach shelter before full daylight revealed her to the remorseless stares of Edinburgh's godly. Limping, she held onto the iron rail that ran down one wall, and allowed her feet to follow the uneven pavement. Drew's apartment was down here, but so much had happened since last she saw him last; it was hard to believe that only a few days had passed.

She had to reach Drew. He would help her.

The fairy-tale towers of the Dean Village seemed to exude mystery. Irene stood outside, staring upward; she knew that Drew lived on the top floor of one of those buildings, for he had mentioned the views, but she did not know exactly where. She had to reach him. He would help her. But not if he found out that she was a thief. Irene felt the sceptre pressing against her side. She must hide it somewhere, so that Drew would never know.

She looked around frantically, searching for a suitable hiding place, swearing in a low monotone that alarmed a passing teenager. She gave a parody of her most charming smile and the girl hurried on, looking over her shoulder.

'She must think that I'm a junkie,' Irene told herself, and recognised her immediate laughter as hysteria. 'Oh shit, how did I get into this mess?'

The sound of leaves rustling in the wind inspired her to duck to the walkway beside the Water of Leith. Birdcall and whispering water soothed her nerves, but desperation drove her over the iron railing that separated the path from the riverbank. She sobbed as her feet sunk into the hole- pitted earth of the banking, until she realised that the inconvenience was a muddy blessing. It was the work of a moment to wrap the sceptre in her coat and thrust it deep into one of the holes, and another minute to conceal her handiwork with a tangle of bracken. Barely noticing the sting of nettles, Irene hauled herself back onto the path. She waited until the pain in her ribs subsided, and then returned to the street.

It was lighter now, full daylight by half past five, and she still had to find Drew. Each building in the courtyard had its own entrance, and with no names displayed on the ground floor, and no commissionaire to give friendly guidance, Irene had to labour up each stone stairway to the top flat. There were four towers, each five stories high, and two doors on each flat. The first two doors had no names at all, so she noted their position and hoped that she would not have to return.

She struggled on, repeating the same phrase, as if it were mantra of divine protection. 'Drew. I must find Drew.'

'Are you going to the top?' The papergirl was blonde haired and young, with sharp eyes and piercings through each eyebrow.

'I'm looking for Drew. Drew Drummond?' Irene hid in the shadows to try and hide her appearance.

'Aye, top floor. That's what I said.' The girl sighed, as if she was granting a major favour in speaking to Irene. She handed her a small pile of newspapers. 'You can take this with you. Save me the bother, ken?'

Irene accepted the newspapers, thankful that she had at last found Drew's apartment. She climbed slowly, with every muscle in her body screaming. Working in a penthouse office with a brass-mirrored elevator and a smart commissionaire to push the buttons had not prepared her for this type of exertion.

The name was bold and plain across the door. Andrew Drummond. Irene nearly sobbed with relief as she knocked. When the door opened she fell inside, sobbing.

'Drew. Drew, you must help me.'

Chapter Seventeen: Edinburgh: July 13

Meigle held up his hand for silence. 'Thank you all for coming to my house at such short notice,' he said. 'I won't keep you long, but I want to keep you abreast of events. As you will be aware from the news, there was an attempted robbery in Edinburgh yesterday. A group attacked the convoy carrying the Queen and various heads of state to the Scottish Parliament. They specifically targeted the Honours.' He waited until the gasps of shock and murmurs of sympathy died down before he continued. 'The army managed to recover the Sword of State, but the crown and sceptre are still missing. That means that the Clach-bhuai has gone.'

There was a few minutes' pandemonium as people shouted their comments. It was Drummond who stood up, looking every one of his sixty – odd years. 'We had a man closely monitoring this group, Sandy. Is he still with them?'

'Stefan Gregovich was killed.' Meigle said the words softly. 'As yet we have no more details for the police have imposed a total security blackout on all information.'

Drummond shook his head. 'That's a bugger. He was a good man.'

'Indeed.' Meigle allowed the news to sink in before he continued. 'So our original plan of following them cannot be followed. However, we are not entirely without clues. For instance, we know that Stefan was working within a small group of people, and we have a picture that we believe shows the woman who masterminded the robbery.' He raised his voice. 'Could you douse the lights, somebody, and show the film?'

The group settled down with only a little grumbling as Meigle adjusted the television. 'This piece was on the television news last night. We copied it and have tried to enhance it as best we can. Now watch closely.'

The members of the Society leaned forward as a slightly fuzzed picture of the Royal Mile was displayed, with crowds of people jostling together. 'Now. Here is a side view of Stefan. He is waiting in the mouth of this close.' Meigle paused the tape to allow the members time to focus on Stefan. He restarted it, and the camera panned onto the crowd. 'And here we have Desmond Nolan. That is his real name, although he travelled here under an alibi. Stefan named him as one of the prime movers in this little escapade. We can see him quite clearly talking with a blonde woman. See?'

Again Meigle paused the tape, allowing the society members time to scribble down notes. 'Does anybody recognise her?'

Most of the members shook their head; some looked puzzled, but nobody came forward with a name. Somebody mentioned that she looked familiar, but was not sure from where.

'I do not recognize her either, but Colonel Drummond is on to her. He has resources that most other people lack.' Meigle forced a smile. 'Is that not correct, James?' He had always admired Drummond's efficiency, but now wondered about replacing him. Drummond had not saved the Clach-bhuai when it mattered.

'I was seconded to the Intelligence Corps for a while,' Drummond sounded just as calm as ever. 'I have retained my contacts.' He stepped out in front of the gathering. 'If this woman is known to any of the intelligence services of the Western World, then we will be able to have her name within a day. After that we will trace her known movements and her likely whereabouts.'

'Good. So all is not lost.' Meigle tried to prevent any panic from the members.

'Hardly.' Drummond languidly returned to his seat. 'You see, Sandy, it is relatively easy to steal an art treasure, even the Clach-bhuai. That sort of thing happens all the time. It's disposing of it that really causes problems. Think about this; trade in stolen artefacts is at least 4000 years old. Looters were digging up the tombs of the pharaohs days after the last royal servant marched away. Put it another way, art historians estimate that around 98% of the antiquities on display in the world's museums have been stolen at some time.'

A woman in a smart denim skirt lifted her hand. 'Surely that makes it easier then? To dispose of things?'

'You'd think so, wouldn't you?' Drummond was using specialist knowledge to regain control of his position. 'However, every known antiquity and every artistic artefact is now known, catalogued and easily recognisable. That means that it would be very difficult to sell the Clach-bhuai, the entire sceptre or the Crown on the open market. As soon as they appear for sale, we will be aware of them.'

'So we just have to wait?' The woman seemed pleased with the simplicity of the plan.

'Not quite.' Producing his pipe, Drummond looked to Meigle, received a quiet nod of permission and began to stuff tobacco into the bowl. 'It is unlikely that the Honours were stolen for a speculative sale. There are two other possibilities.' He held up his left hand and raised a finger. 'One: they may have been stolen to make some political point. We know that this fellow Desmond Nolan has a strong Irish Republican connection, so it is possible that his colleagues are similarly involved. Unfortunately, Stefan did not send us all their names. Perhaps they intend to ransom the Honours for some political advantage. In that case we will eventually hear from them and will act accordingly.'

'So that's hopeful,' the woman said.

'As far as we are concerned, that is extremely hopeful.' Drummond lit his pipe and puffed aromatic smoke toward the members. 'The government may not be so happy.'

'And the other possibility?' The woman was looking quite optimistic.

'Not so good. The Honours may have been stolen to order. We suspect that some master criminal has ordered them stolen, so he can offer them for sale on the underground market. If we are correct, then they will be far more difficult to trace. There are quite a number of crooked dealers out there.'

As the denim-skirted woman nodded cautiously, Drummond shook his head. 'Even worse, the Honours may have been stolen for the personal enjoyment of just such a Mr Big. The last few decades have seen an upsurge in the theft of cultural heritage. The Taliban destroyed everything they could in Afghanistan, but there was still a strong trickle of artefacts that left the country, and the Iraq War saw massive looting. You will remember that the Iraqi National Museum in Baghdad was virtually stripped bare? Some of the oldest and most famous artefacts in the world disappeared, such as the Uruk Vase, which is the world's oldest narrative work of art.' He shook his head. 'It's probably older than our Clach-bhuai, if not as important to us. The stolen art trade is the second largest traffic in the world, after drugs.'

'So what can we do?' The woman's confidence had evaporated as quickly as it had risen, but Drummond replaced his pipe in his mouth and smiled around the stem.

'We are creating a database of the known collectors of rare artefacts, legal and illegal. Obviously an organisation so old as ours has a number of assets; Sandy Meigle is a financial wizard and manages our finances with great aplomb, so we are offering incentives for any information that will lead to the recovery of the artefacts, but without actually revealing the provenance of the Clach-bhuai.'

'Will that work? Will that be enough?'

'It's early days yet. Dealers in artefacts prize their reputations for honesty. If they lose that, they lose quite a lot, so some, at least, will be pleased to help.' He smiled again, with the stem of his pipe clicking cheerfully against his teeth. 'I have forwarded full particulars to the collectors within the Society.'

'You said that Stefan had not sent us the full names of the thieves,' the woman did not seem reassured. 'Could you tell us what you do know?'

'There were five of them. Desmond Nolan, a man named Bryan, a woman he knew as Mary and a young marine named Patrick.' Drummond glanced toward Meigle. 'There was also another woman, but Stefan was not sure of her. Her name was Irene or Amanda; he was not sure which.' He gestured toward the television with the stem of his pipe. 'It is possible that the young lady on the video recording is this person, but it may also be Mary.'

'It's like a detective story, isn't it?' a tall man with a weathered face said.

'Indeed.' Meigle stood up. 'Obviously if any of you hear of anything at all, you will contact Colonel Drummond or myself. There has been some sort of news blackout imposed, which may mean that the police are pursuing some positive line of enquiry, or that they do not wish the public to know exactly what is happening.'

'Bad PR to lose your crown jewels,' the weathered man said.

'Indeed. And bad for us to lose the Clach-bhuai, particularly as we were warned about the impending attempt.' Meigle glanced at Drummond, 'would you like to draw this meeting to a close, James? You are the security officer.'

Drummond did not show any offence at the implied slight. Instead he again showed the picture of the blonde woman. 'This woman, Amanda, Irene or Mary, may be the key to the whole thing. If we can find her, or find out who she is, I think we will unravel the rest. I have people making prints of her face even as we talk, and they will be delivered to your address first thing tomorrow morning. From this time onward, our Society has one objective. Locate this woman, ladies and gentleman, and bring news of her to me.'

Just for a second Meigle saw the urbane mask drop from Drummond's face, revealing the stark severity of a lifetime in the British Army. He was suddenly very glad that he was not the young woman whose face smiled from the television. He also thought it would be a good idea to retain James Drummond in his present position.

Chapter Eighteen: Edinburgh: July 13

'Amanda?' Drew stood in the doorway for a long second, then threw the door wide open and held out a hand. 'Man, you look terrible! Come away in.'

Even as she collapsed over the threshold, Irene's analytical mind noted that the flat was different to anything she had expected, with rugs scattered over the sanded wooden floors and walls devoid of pictures. Suddenly she could not restrain her sobbing and Drew guided her to a rope-and-canvas chair. 'You're hurt, Amanda. There's blood on your face.' He eased her down. 'What happened? Your phone went dead yesterday. I kept mine on in case you phoned back, but my batteries ran out.'

Irene shook her head. She had not prepared a lie, so spoke as much of the truth as seemed sensible. 'I was watching for the Queen when the explosions went off, and I was caught in the panic. I don't know where I ran, or why, but I got trampled.' The tears were genuine.

'Your hand is hurt too.' Drew narrowed his eyes as he studied her. 'And you're favouring your left side. You've had a rough time, I think.' Irene thought that he hesitated. 'Do you trust me?'

'Of course,' she looked up.

'Then let's have a look.' He knelt at her side. 'Where does it hurt?'

'Everywhere.' Irene spoke through her sobs. She looked up. 'Will you help me?'

'Of course I will.'

Drew's hands were gentle as he stripped off her outer clothing, exclaiming at the extensive bruising and deep scrapes across her ribs and side. 'It's all right, Amanda,' he said as she placed a protective hand on her breasts. 'You're safe with me. You've been in the wars, haven't you? Maybe we'd best take you to the hospital.' He sounded concerned.

'No,' Irene shook her head. 'No. It looks worse than it is. Just let me sleep for a while and I'll be OK.'

'Aye. Maybe.' He knelt at her side. 'A bath first, I think, then into bed. We'll discuss this later, but I think you'd better see a doctor. I think you have at least one broken finger there.'

The throbbing in her fingers was so constant that Irene could almost ignore it. She glanced at her hand, seeing the mud and congealed blood. 'Maybe.' She heard Drew draw the bath and allowed him to carry her into the bathroom.

'Can you manage to climb in yourself?' his voice was quiet.

Irene nearly laughed. During the last eighteen hours she had taken part in an armed robbery, witnessed at least three killings, endured a car chase, been stamped on by a woman, fallen from a helicopter and dodged the Edinburgh police, to say nothing of stealing and concealing a priceless national treasure. Now this kind, naïve man was asking if she needed help to step inside a bath.

She considered the problem.

'I don't think so.' The lip of the bath seemed immensely high as her injuries stiffened. 'Could you lift me in?' She looked down at herself, seeing the bruises that stretched from just under her left arm to her thigh and the shallow scrapes that the sceptre had caused across her ribs. As Drew reached down, sudden embarrassment caused her to cover herself with her hands. 'I'll take off my things in the bath. Once you've gone.'

'Of course.' Drew did not press the issue. She was no lightweight but he lifted her without effort and lowered her tenderly into the warm water.

Irene gasped at the initial sting, and then smiled. 'Thank you. I hate to be a pain, but could you unhook my bra?' She leaned forward, her left arm covering her breasts as he complied. 'Thank you again.'

'Call me if you need anything.' Drew kept his back turned as he left the room, 'and don't worry. You're safe with me.'

Given her situation, the words sounded ironic. Irene wondered if Drew would be so helpful if he knew that he was harbouring a fugitive. She waited until he had left the room before wriggling off her pants and lying back, allowing the warm water to soothe away some of her aches. Her hand was throbbing, but it was not the pain that caused tears to seep from her eyes. She could still see people retching in the street and could hear Desmond's scream as the bayonet plunged in. Why had it all gone wrong? She shook her head, forcing herself to concentrate on something else. She checked out her surroundings.

The bathroom was decidedly masculine in its lack of frills, but it was also scrupulously clean, with stark white tiles, a small circular mirror and a simple shower unit in the corner. Deciding that the room desperately needed a woman's touch, Irene smiled and began to gently soap the most tender of her injuries. Even the soap was plain white, with hardly a scent.

There was a tap on the door, and as Irene covered herself and invited him to enter, Drew poked in his hand. 'Towels,' he said, 'and some clean clothes. Not quite your size but better than nothing. I'll just drop them.' He paused for a second. 'I've no lady's underclothing, I'm afraid, so you'll have to go commando for a while.'

Irene looked round and smiled her thanks, until she realised that he could not see her. 'Thank you, Drew.'

'Just take your time.'

The door closed again and Irene lay back. She closed her eyes, listening to Drew moving around the flat. She heard a slight click, followed by the drone of the television. She had not considered Drew as an avid television watcher, and wondered about his taste in programmes. He would be watching something intellectual, no doubt, but certainly nothing about interior decoration.

Only when the water began to cool did Irene ease herself out of the bath. 'Is it all right if I borrow your shower to wash my hair?'

'Of course it is.'

The power jet took her by surprise, but she luxuriated in the tingle of hot water against her scalp. Only when she opened her eyes and saw the black rivulets trickling down her body did Irene realise that she was washing away her hair dye. The combination of CS gas and sweaty exertion must have created some reaction to loosen the chemicals.

'Oh fuck!' She jerked back from the nozzle and wiped the condensation from the mirror. A black and red badger stared back. 'Oh God, Oh Lord help me.' For a second Irene panicked; Drew would know at once that she had something to hide. He would put two and two together; he would work out that she had stolen the Honours and would hand her in to the police.

A deep breath calmed her nerves. Why should he think anything of the sort? Many women dyed their hair; it was not suspicious.

'Are you all right in there?' Drew's voice managed to combine cheerfulness with concern.

'Just washing the dye from my hair,' Irene tried to sound as natural as possible. It seemed strange to clean up in a strange bathroom, but she did not want Drew to think of her as a slob this early in their relationship.

What relationship?

The towels were clean but hard, and Drew's choice of clothing was utilitarian. Irene was not sure what she had expected, tweeds perhaps, but instead there was a pair of jeans that flapped loosely past her feet, a voluminous blue rugby shirt with a small white thistle and a pair of brown slippers that were at least five sizes too large.

With her trouser legs rolled up, Irene shuffled into the living room and plumped herself onto the practical, wood-and-fabric three-piece suite. There was a small television opposite, with a round table and two chairs, while the books seemed to be colour-coded into the plain bookcase. Everything was functionally neat. Drew was standing looking out of the window, but turned when he heard her enter. 'That's the rain on,' he said, inconsequentially, and then grinned across to her. 'How's the hand?'

'Sore,' Irene held up her fingers. 'But I don't think that it's broken. Soaking it in the bath helped.'

'Can you move it?' Drew moved closer. 'Give a wee wiggle.'

Irene tried and winced. 'Maybe not yet.'

'Maybe not at all.' He took her hand very gently. 'I think that we'll take you to the outpatients and have a doctor look at these.'

Feeling better after her bath, Irene nodded. 'If you think so.'

'I do.' He stepped back, head to one as he examined her. 'Red hair, eh? Do you have the temper to go with the colouring?'

'Oh yes.' Irene nodded. 'I can have a vile temper when I choose.'

'Excellent,' Drew approved. 'Then we can have some fine arguments. There's nothing better than a good shouting match to sweeten the air.'

Irene looked away. Her father had been the last man to raise his voice at her. Since leaving home, she had always chosen men whom she could dominate. She did not know how she would react to a man who shouted back.

'That was a joke,' Drew told her. 'There's no need to look worried.' He stepped back. 'You have been through a bad time, haven't you?'

Irene shook her head. 'I'm sorry,' she said, and stopped. She could not remember when she had last apologised to anybody. She must concentrate; she had to use Drew to escape from this mess that she was in. 'I hate to ask this, Drew, but do you have anything to eat in the house?'

'Of course. Stupid of me.' Drew tapped his head. 'Some host me, eh? You must be starving. Sit down and I'll see what's in the fridge.'

Used to Patrick's invariable diet of pizzas and coke, Irene was surprised when Drew served her a cooked, if not particularly healthy, meal of sausage, egg and bacon. She ate heartily, wincing only when she had occasion to use her left hand, and did not complain when Drew leaned over to cut her food.

She was even more impressed when Drew carried her sodden clothes through to the kitchen and placed them in the washing machine. 'I'll give these a quick run-through' he said, as nonchalantly as if he had known her for years. 'You don't mind, do you?'

'No, no.' Irene shook her head. 'Thank you.' She felt herself colour as she thought of the underwear that she had left in the bathroom, but Drew forestalled her.

'I collected your bits and pieces. I'll do them too.'

Irene listened to the sudden hum and rattle of the washing machine and smiled as Drew appeared with a mug in each hand. 'Is that coffee?'

'You're American, aren't you? Then you prefer coffee to tea. I've seen the films.'

They laughed together.

'Coffee's good,' Irene approved.

They sat in companionable silence for a few minutes, until Drew asked Irene to tell her story. He listened as she related how she had been waiting for the Queen, and then had been caught up in the panic after the bombs had gone off.

'They were only smoke canisters and thunder-flashes, apparently,' Drew told her, 'mingled with CS gas to cause the maximum panic. Most of the security was drawn to the Queen and other heads of state while the terrorists hit the crown jewels.'

'Was it terrorists?'

Drew shrugged. 'So they say on the News. They have identified one of them as an American IRA man, and they've published pictures of some woman that they think was involved. The BBC seems to think that she financed the operation.'

'Oh?' Irene felt the sudden hammering of her heart. She measured the distance to the door, wondering if she could make it out before Drew caught her. 'A woman? What's she like?'

'No idea.' Drew shook his head. 'The picture on my telly went days ago and I haven't got round to getting it repaired, so I can only listen to the news.'

Irene grinned as relief replaced the tension. It may be only a temporary reprieve, but she would take the opportunity to recover her strength. 'God, but I'm tired.'

'You will be,' Drew looked over to her. 'How's your hand?'

'Much better,' Irene stifled a yawn.

'OK. You get some sleep now, Amanda, and we'll see how it looks later.'

She hesitated for only a minute. 'Irene. My name's Irene. I wasn't sure of you then, so I used a false name.' She waited, bracing herself for his anger.

'Irene?' He surveyed her again, head to one side. 'Aye, it suits you better. Amanda is for dark haired women, Irene's right for a red head. My name's still Drew, though.' He nodded to a door across the tiny corridor. 'The bedroom's through there. Off you go.'

Irene rose obediently. She hesitated. If she fell asleep and Drew saw the news or read a newspaper, she would be trapped. She might waken to a room full of police.

'It's all right,' Drew mistook her indecision. 'I won't jump in beside you. You're perfectly safe here.'

'No, I didn't think you would.' Irene shook her head. 'I just don't like to abuse your hospitality. I can't pay you back or anything.'

Drew shrugged again. 'Pay me back for what? What man would not like a beautiful redhead to descend upon their house on a Sunday morning?' He grinned. 'This is all like a fairy story for me. And you haven't slapped my face yet.'

'Nor will I,' Irene promised. Extending a hand, she touched his shoulder. 'Thank you, Drew.'

The bedroom was as Spartan as the rest of the house, with a simple bed that could either have been a small double or a wide single. The sheets were crisp and white, with a plain blue coverlet. A single blue runner adorned the varnished floorboards and the only piece of furniture was a plain pine wardrobe. With no mirror, Irene could not even inspect her appearance, but despite Drew's words, she still closed the door tightly before sliding into bed. The last thing she heard was the drumbeat of rain on the window.

* * * *

The outpatients department of the Western General was busy with a host of minor casualties, from an elderly woman who had burned her hand to a boy who had fallen from his bike. Drew remained at Irene's side, flicking through the pile of magazines that the management provided. Irene stepped forward when she heard her name called, explained that she had lost her passport and was surprised when the young Asian doctor waved away her excuses.

'I'm a doctor, not a bureaucrat,' he said. 'We don't care about that sort of thing in Scotland.'

He examined her fingers with gentle care, pressed into the knuckle and nodded. 'Not broken, but badly bruised. Don't use them for a few weeks and they'll be fine, but I would certainly see your own doctor when you get back home.' He looked at her through tired eyes. 'Is there anything else?'

'No,' the bath and sleep had eased away Irene's other injuries. 'But thank you,' she felt relief that there would be no more official probing. When she stepped out of the consultancy room, Drew was waiting for her.

'There's the News,' Drew said, when she had relayed the doctor's advice. 'We'll see what's happened with the Crown jewels robbery.'

Irene felt a sickening slide of despair. She thought quickly. 'Oh, I don't really care,' she said, and began to pull him toward the exit. 'Come on, it's not fair expecting you to spend your Sunday in a hospital.'

Where Patrick would have done exactly as she ordered, Drew proved more stubborn. 'Just a minute,' he said. 'I'm interested in this.' He remained behind as Irene hovered at the door. She prepared to run the second her face flashed onto the screen.

The first image was on the procession, with the Queen waving to the crowd. Then the camera panned onto the glass-topped Rolls Royce, concentrating on the glittering jewellery of the Honours. The voice-over mentioned the great age of the jewels and their long previous history, before focussing on the sudden jets of smoke and ensuing panic.

'It is believed that a hitherto unknown splinter group of Irish terrorists are behind the attack. Security forces recovered the Sword of State, while one of the terrorists was killed at the scene. Police have identified the body as Desmond Nolan, who was known to have been active in Northern Ireland.'

Irene shuddered as a picture of a younger-looking Desmond flicked onto the screen.

'A second man died when the attackers apparently fought before boarding a helicopter.' The newsreader's urbane tones altered as he put a hand to his ear. 'We have breaking news on this report. The police have lifted a news blanket on various aspects of the story, but we can now send you live to the island of Islay, off the west coast of Scotland, where significant events have occurred.'

Irene watched with sick fascination as a picture of a ragged bay with smooth sand appeared. There was a grey-painted naval vessel offshore, beside a long white yacht, from which smoke drifted.

'We are now in a position to inform you that in a joint operation between the army, Royal Navy and various Scottish police forces, the Scottish Crown has been recovered. Security reasons have not allowed us to show this footage until now.'

The picture changed again, showing a small helicopter hovering above Edinburgh, before it disappeared into the distance. A detached voice gave a running commentary, explaining how radar and a police helicopter tailed the machine right across Scotland, but could not intercept for fear of risking damage to the crown, or causing casualties among people living below.

'The helicopter descended on the west coast of Islay and two men and one woman ran into this boat.' The picture showed the yacht that Irene had chartered. 'The Royal Navy patrol boat, *Somerled,* intercepted the yacht before it left Scottish waters.'

There was a picture of a confused chase, white water around the bows of *Somerled* and the sharp crack of gunfire.

'When the yacht refused to heave to when ordered, *Somerled* fired a warning shot across her bows and sent a boarding party of Royal Marines.'

The picture snapped to a library shot of a group of tough looking men speeding across a stretch of water that certainly was not off Scotland, and then changed back to the yacht. 'Unfortunately there was resistance and one of the Royal Marines was slightly wounded. Three people on board the yacht were killed, and one wounded.'

Irene closed her eyes, unsure what to think. After all her planning, the British authorities had ended her robbery attempt within a day. Was Patrick one of the three dead? And Bryan? Or had the Royal Marines killed three members of the yacht's crew? She staggered as she realised that only Patrick's betrayal had saved her from death or capture, but Drew was there to support her.

'Easy now Irene. That's reaction to the doctor.' His voice was calm and gentle as he lowered her gently onto a seat. Nobody in the waiting room looked at her, for every eye was on the television.

'Police have not yet released pictures of those killed in the yacht, but say there were two men and one woman. As yet, the police do not know the names of the deceased. One of the bodies was badly burned when an explosion set fire to the yacht, but police have stated that he had a tattoo with the name 'Linda.' However, the woman the police believe masterminded the operation is still loose. They have released a picture of this woman, and ask anybody who may recognise her to contact them as soon as possible. They also stress that she may be highly dangerous and advise that nobody approaches her.'

Irene looked toward the door. Somebody was bound to recognize her now. Her dreams would end here, in this crowded out-patients department of the British National Health Service.

'Now there's a tough looking girl.' Drew commented quietly. 'Did you see her yesterday?'

Irene looked up, fighting the fear that drained the strength from her legs. The woman stared out from the television screen, her face slightly blurred and her mouth open as she spoke to Desmond. She was blonde and fairly attractive, but the television definition had imposed a hard line along her jaw.

Irene recognized her at once. She had been with the protesters calling for a Scottish Republic.

'Oh sweet Jesus Lord,' Irene could not prevent the tears. 'She stood right beside me.' Hysteria returned with the sudden release of tension and she leaned her face against Drew's arm, sobbing. She was safe; Patrick was dead and the police did not have her picture.

Chapter Nineteen: Edinburgh: July

The relief was so strong that Irene had to prevent herself from giggling. She was in the clear. She had a forged passport and had given a false name at the hotel. She had given a different name again when she chartered the yacht, and with Patrick and the others dead, there was nobody who could recognize her.

'Suck an elf,' she breathed out loud as the strain of the last few days evaporated. A few seconds ago she had looked failure in the face, but now she contemplated success. She had done it. The police would search for this Scottish Republican woman, no doubt question her for days and either frame her, or release her, but every hour now was valuable. All she had to do was remain calm, retrieve the sceptre and get it back home. After that, her future was secure. Once again Irene visualised the immense riches of the Manning Corporation, the power to hire and fire and build, and all the prestige that she had never known.

'Are you all right?' Drew was at her side, immediately solicitous as he knelt down.

'Oh yes. Oh yes, I am.' Irene stalled her smile in time. 'I just realized how close I came to being killed.'

'It was that bad, eh?' Drew nodded his sympathy. 'Well, you're safe enough now.' When he held out his hand it seemed only natural that she should take it. 'Where to? My place, or back to your hotel.'

The implications were so obvious that Irene smiled. 'You're not the most subtle of men, are you?'

'That's not one of my faults,' he agreed.

'So what exactly are you offering?' Irene knew that she should feel grief, or at least remorse, for the death of Patrick and the others, but compared to the fact that she was alive, safe and on course for success, they just did not matter.

'My flat and my company,' Drew said bluntly.

'In return for what?'

'Your company and conversation.'

'Nothing else?' Irene enjoyed this flirting game, when she could tease a man to test his limits, but Drew seemed immune.

'What else could I possibly want?'

Irene was unsure whether to slap him, laugh or feel grateful. 'A patient to nurse?' she suggested, and patted his arm, smiling. 'Honestly, Drew, I don't know what I would have done without you.' She thought quickly. She had arrived under an assumed name, and if she checked out of her room, there would be no record of her at all. About to ask him for a lift to her hotel, Irene quickly changed her mind. Perhaps it would be better if he did not know from where she had come.

'Could you take me to the railroad station?' She felt satisfaction as disappointment flickered in Drew's face.

'If that's what you want. Are you leaving then?'

'No, but my hotel is near there, and I must pick up my bags.' She leaned closer, allowing him to experience the warmth of her body. 'You don't expect a gal to come to your apartment without her stuff, do you? After all, I have no change of clothes with me, and I can't wear your old jeans for ever!' She put her mouth against his ear. 'Denim is a fine material, but it can be a mite rough with nothing beneath.'

'There once was a fairy…' Drew began, but Irene stopped him with a laugh.

'And she was called Nough. I've heard that one. Could you take me to the station?'

'Of course. But there is one stipulation.'

'Oh?' Irene waited for the axe to fall.

'I'd like you to wear this.' Drew produced the box from his inside pocket and snapped it open. The Luckenbooth brooch was inside, simple, silver and insidiously serene.

'That would be my pleasure.' Lifting the brooch, Irene pinned it onto her tee shirt just beneath her left breast. 'Although nobody wears brooches nowadays and it does not quite fit in with the rest of my present wardrobe.' She had given no commitment, so there was no reason why she should feel such a charlatan.

Drew stepped back and examined her critically. 'I've no complaints,' he said. 'It looks fine just where it is.' His grin seemed impulsive. 'Come on then, what are you hanging about there for?'

Irene felt nervous as she checked out of the hotel, but the receptionist only commented on the heavy rain as she accepted Irene's cash payment. Lifting her single travelling bag, Irene headed for the teeming shops of Princes Street before she returned to Drew's flat.

Drew was smiling as he opened the door to her. He had changed into a checked shirt and a pair of neatly pressed, if slightly faded, corduroy trousers. 'I've got the wine ready,' he said.

She held up the bottle of champagne that she had purchased. 'So have I.'

Unable to function properly without her daily dose of drivel, Irene persuaded Drew to buy a new television and they spent the entire evening watching DVDs, with breaks for the news. The first time she heard the theme music for the News, Irene felt her mouth go dry, but the police were still jubilant that they had recovered the Crown and were getting closer to the arrest of the blonde woman.

'Nasty business, that,' Drew said casually. 'Six killed, a policeman wounded and scores of people hospitalised with smoke inhalation and minor injuries.' He stretched out on the chair, 'I hope that woman is feeling guilty.'

She was, Irene thought, but feigned nonchalance. 'She's probably living in the South of France by now, on the proceeds of her robbery.'

Drew nodded. 'Could be. That sceptre thing must be worth a few quid. Don't know who'd buy it though.' He shrugged. 'Maybe she'll melt it down for gold.'

Irene killed the impulse to tell him that it was silver-gilt. 'Maybe she will. She spoiled my day anyway. I never did get to see the Queen.'

'Neither you did.' Drew grinned across to her. 'I'd write to her, if I were you, and demand a private audience.'

They both laughed and Drew opened the wine. When he pulled two glasses from a presentation box, Irene wondered briefly if they had been a Christmas present or if he had bought them specially, decided that she did not care much either way and watched him pour.

'Nice glasses,' she said.

'Edinburgh Crystal,' he told her. 'I had to buy them specifically for you, so I hope you feel privileged. My previous female guests would be more likely to drink lager straight from the can.'

Irene smiled at this straightforward admission. 'Classy gals, eh?'

'Nothing but the best for me.' He lifted his glass in salute and for a second Irene saw his face distorted by the deep red wine. He looked thoughtful, perhaps slightly worried and on an impulse she leaned across and kissed him.

'What was that for?' He touched his cheek, surprised.

'For everything,' she said. 'And just for being there.'

'Don't be silly,' Drew smiled across to her. 'It's a real pleasure to have you.'

Irene smiled back. 'You haven't had me,' she reminded. 'Not yet anyway.' She was surprised when he looked almost shocked. 'I'm sorry,' she said at once. 'I didn't mean to embarrass you.'

'Quite the reverse,' Drew shook his head slowly. 'I'm just not used to drop-dead-gorgeous women saying things like that to me. I thought that it only happened in films.'

Irene waited for a moment or two, and then spoke softly and slowly. 'Oh no, Drew. It happens in real life too, and thanks for the drop-dead compliment.' She lifted her glass and sipped, allowing the wine to moisten her lips. She could feel Drew watching her. 'Do you have work tomorrow?'

'Nor the next day,' he said quietly.

'Good.' Irene stood up and stretched slowly. 'Then there's no need to rush.'

'Absolutely none,' he agreed.

* * * *

Irene felt a sense of déjà vu when she rose early and slipped out of the bed. She glanced behind her, watched Drew shift slightly to claim more space on the cramped bed and then closed the door. Her bag lay outside the bedroom. Long and leather, it was battered from hard usage and plastered with stickers from her travels. Removing every document that might possibly be used to identify her, Irene stuffed them inside her spare coat, turned the bag upside down and emptied the contents onto the floor. Taking only the coat and the empty bag, she left the remainder for Drew to wonder over and slipped outside. The papergirl stared as she ran down the stairs.

Rain had cleansed the Dean Village of its summer dust, leaving it baby-bright in the early sun. Save for the diligent blackbirds, the streets were quiet, so Irene headed toward the riverbank where she had left the sceptre. Already she felt the familiar stimulation of anticipation, mingled with sick dread at the prospect of being caught. She wondered if risk was inherent to every success; perhaps businesswomen and criminals shared the buzz of high-stake gamblers.

It took only a few minutes to reach the iron railing at the waterside. She stopped abruptly, staring at the river. Only two days ago it had been a gentle brown drift, but the heavy rain since then had raised the level far higher than she had imagined. It surged across the bank, completely submerging the bed of nettles where she had hidden the sceptre, and leaping against the wall in which the railings were set.

Irene looked downward as the torrent washed the optimism from her world. The downside of the gambling buzz was the speed in which hope malformed into catastrophe. She could not have calculated the relationship between Patrick and Mary, nor could she have foreseen the downpour of the last two days. Once again fate had intervened with her dreams, and she would have to innovate.

The current looked viciously swift and the river dangerous. Without the nettles as a guide, she could only guess where she had placed the sceptre. Swallowing, Irene glanced counted her options. She could give up and fly home as a failure, she could wade into the water, or she could wait until the river subsided, which, given the fickle Scottish weather, might be days. The longer she waited, the greater the chance of discovery and arrest.

Irene closed her eyes. She was wrong; there was only one possible option. Swearing, she leaned her bag against the wall, climbed over the iron railings and lowered herself into the water. It was neither as cold nor as deep as she had feared, but the current tugged unpleasantly at her legs as she felt her way along the banking. She stumbled over something hard, and gasped as her foot sank deep into a hole.

'Shitting hell!'

For the first time Irene wondered if the holes were natural, or had some sort of animal made them? Irene flinched; rats were a pet hate; they symbolised the dirt and disorder that she despised so much. Swearing to combat her fear, she thrust her uninjured left hand under the water, groping cautiously.

At first she felt only the tangle of weeds and grass, then the softness of earth and finally she made contact with something substantial and cloth covered.

'Got you,' Irene said, softly, and knelt down for a better grip. The river swirled around her waist, splashing upward as she struggled under the surface. She swore, spat out a mouthful of dirty water, took a deep breath and plunged her arm under again, reaching deep into the hole.

Once she obtained a hold on the cloth it was the work of a moment to haul the bundle free. With her hands trembling, Irene dragged off the sodden coat and stared at the sceptre. Filtered by overhanging trees, the sun gleamed along the length of the gilded silver shaft and reflected a thousand shards of light from the crystal orb on top.

Irene breathed deeply. She held her destiny in her hands; nobody knew where she was and the future was bright. All she had to do was reach the United States for her life to reach an entirely new level.

'Hey you! What's that?'

Irene looked up. Five youths leaned over the railing, one grinning, the others staring at her. One of the two girls smiled slowly and pointed. Her accent was broad and ugly.

'Are you deaf? I said, what the fuck's that?'

'Nothing for you.' Hastily re-wrapping the sceptre, Irene glanced to her left, where the river suddenly descended in the waterfall that she had admired earlier. Then it had been something to enhance the scenery, now it was a brawling barrier that blocked her retreat. The banking rose steeply to her right, disappearing under the tall arches of the Dean Bridge. There was no escape in either direction.

'Come here.' The girl obviously spoke for the rest of the youths, who clustered against the railing. One lifted her bag, rummaged inside and swore.

'Just shite.'

'Nae money?' Grabbing the bag, the spokeswoman glanced inside. 'Gie's that thing.'

'Come and get it,' Irene invited. She knew that she would have no chance if they all came at once, but gambled that they would be reluctant to enter the river.

'You bring it here,' the spokeswoman ordered. 'And I'll have that too.' She pointed to the Luckenbooth brooch that was pinned to Irene's breast.

Irene looked at them for a long minute. Each face crammed fifty years of cynical experience into its sixteen years of life. The boys wore hooded tops and baggy trousers while both girls sported long-peaked baseball caps. The spokeswoman had her hands deep in the pockets of her fringed white jacket.

Swearing loudly, the taller of the boys swung himself over the railings and plunged into the water. He landed clumsily, slipping on the uneven ground, and Irene swung the sceptre in a frantic round-arm blow that caught him across the head. She thrilled at the contact and as he stumbled, shouting, 'that was sair.' Irene hit him again, venomously, so he fell face first into the river. Dirty water cascaded, droplets hanging for a second, glittering in the sunlight before dropping to the disturbed surface.

'You bitch!' Lifting a stone, the first girl threw it at Irene. 'We'll kill you for that!' She vaulted the rail with ease, landing lightly in the water. 'Get her!'

The other youths followed, splashing onto the flooded riverbank in a flurry of spray and a volley of language more foul than Irene had ever heard. She hit at one, and then stepped backward, stumbling as her feet left the bank and thrust into the deeper water of the river.

Now it was Irene's turn to swear. She staggered, nearly falling as the spokeswoman aimed a punch for her throat. Irene jerked back, further into the river, and glanced sideways. She could see the lip of the waterfall, swollen by the rain into an ear-battering deluge.

'Oh Jesus Lord!'

The second girl pulled something from her pocket, fingered a switch and a three-inch long blade flicked out. She circled her wrist, feinted for Irene's face then slashed sideways at her stomach. One of the boys giggled high-pitched and jumped to her side. 'Cut her! Rip her open!'

Irene did not see Drew arrive until the furthest youth yelled and fell suddenly quiet. The second boy turned around, swearing. Drew blocked his kick with a sweep of his foot, scraped the edge of his shoe down the youth's shin and stamped down hard. When the boy roared, Drew rammed straight fingers into his throat.

'Oh Jesus Lord,' Irene repeated.

Thrusting the sceptre back inside its dripping cover, she stepped back into deeper water, turned and ran. She had noticed that there was a slight lip along the very edge of the waterfall, a smoother ledge of shallower water. Either she chanced the lip, or she tried to explain to Drew exactly what she was doing. Irene knew that she could not cope with discovery and imprisonment; she must escape.

The first steps were terrifying, with the current thrusting against her legs and the shocking drop tugging her down, but Irene pushed on, sobbing her fear. She could hear the noise behind her, the constant curses from the youths and the sound of blows, but she dared not turn back.

'I've not finished with you yet.' The knife girl had followed, lifting her legs high as she traced the lip of the fall.

Irene turned just as the girl lunged forward with her face contorted and knife slashing wickedly. Irene ducked, swayed and nearly fell as the current smashed against her thighs. The roar of the waterfall increased, white water cascading smoothly down to explode in a welter of froth and spray. She saw a bus passing over the bridge above and for one surreal moment she wondered what the passengers would think about two females fighting on the lip of a waterfall in the early morning.

'Come here you cow!' The girl jumped at Irene, screaming to her friends to help her. Irene cowered under the ferocity of the attack, jerked back to avoid the knife and yelled as the girl swung a roundhouse punch that smacked against her cheekbone. She reeled and swayed sideways, facing the drop as the current surged around and between her legs. She watched, horrified, as a tree branch hurtled end-over-end downward before it was trapped in a mini-whirlpool, circling for eternity at the base of the fall.

'You little bitch.' Irene was not sure if it was the sting of the punch or the horror of that drop that shocked her into retaliation. She turned around, flinched as the girl spat at her, and instinctively pushed outward. The girl lost her balance, and sat heavily in the foaming brown water, screeching profanities.

'I'll kill you!' The girl kicked out with one foot, raising a cloud of water and spray but not making any connection.

Irene ducked back, slipped, and looked down. Again she saw the swoop of brown and white water and the suck and surge fifteen feet below.

'Come on! Get her!' The second girl hauled her friend upright and pushed her toward Irene, a pair of sodden, baseball-hatted youths that screamed obscene hatred as they tottered along the lip of the waterfall. Turning, Irene fled.

There was a stone ledge at the opposite side of the river, and above that the cliff-like face of an old mill building, since converted into flats. Wincing at the re-awakened pain in her ribs, Irene dragged herself onto the ledge, kicked backward at the nearest of her pursuers and felt the satisfaction of solid contact. She plunged ahead, into a patch of tangled shrubbery that clawed at her face and body. Swearing, she swung the sceptre in a desperate effort to escape, squealed as something wrapped around her ankle and plunged on, sobbing.

'Irene!'

She heard Drew's voice behind her but did not turn around, scrabbled up a wall by her fingertips and nearly fell into a neatly groomed garden complete with a line of washing. Scrambling over a low railing with a locked gate, she flinched when the sceptre caught between the rails. Tugging frantically, she jerked it free and emerged into the street opposite Drew's flat. Ignoring the familiar dog-walker, she turned right and ran uphill and onward until she was stumbling down a steep hill of terraced Victorian houses. After a few minutes she turned round but there was nobody following her, and little traffic. She leaned against a lamp-post, gasping to catch the breath that burned in her chest.

Keeping the coat secure around the sceptre, Irene walked solidly downhill, knowing that people were staring at this sodden creature plodding through Edinburgh's conventional morning. When a group of business-suited women at a bus stop deliberately stared, Irene knew that she must find somewhere to hide and collect her thoughts. She stopped at the top of a street that swooped downward to a gothic palace of spires and turrets. Trees lined the road, stretching backward into what Irene decided must be a public park, somewhere that promised concealment from the inquisitive.

Hugging the sceptre to her side, she passed through the park's empty space and entered the adjoining Royal Botanic Garden. After the last hectic hour, she felt as if she had entered an oasis of calm, with copses of seclusion and shaded corners for sanctuary.

A fine group of greenhouses offered a combined asylum of warmth and shelter, so Irene paid the entrance fee, forced a smile when the attendant asked if she had fallen in the pond, and moved to the warmest of the environments. Almost immediately steam began to rise from her clothes. Golden fish swam languidly among placid water lilies.

'Sweet Lord, how did I get into this situation?' Irene leaned against the bole of a palm tree and took deep breaths to control the racing of her heart. She looked down at her dripping denims and sodden sneakers. What had happened to the woman who shopped at Herald Square, who treated Macy's like her neighbourhood store and was on first name terms with the manager of Gucci on Fifth Avenue?

It seemed forever since she had walked in the shadow of the Empire State Building or dodged the Times Square traffic. She missed the Manhattan skyline and the cosmopolitan bustle of Queens, the look of an Armani suit on a downtown city trader and the nasal sting of a New York accent. Even more, she hated this running, wondering whom she could trust and where she could go.

For one moment Irene pondered sending the sceptre back to the castle and returning, tail between her legs, to relative obscurity. Surely as a runner up in *The Neophyte* she could land a well-paid job at home, something that would provide security and a comfortable life style. She touched the jacket, feeling the hard shaft of the sceptre, the smoothness of the crystal ball and sensing the latent power. No; Irene shook her head; she had come too far to give up now, she must continue.

She thought of Ms Manning's expression when she saw the sceptre. There would be surprise, astonishment, delight and finally admiration. Ms Manning would extend her hand in congratulations and open wide the door of opportunity. Ms Manning would eject Kendrick from his position and install her as the new neophyte, with all the honours and advantages that the position held. Within ten years, perhaps within five, she would be installed as the new owner of the Manning Corporation, with more power than most people could ever comprehend.

Again Irene ran her fingers over the sceptre. This was her ticket to security; all she had to do was transport it over to the United States. It was only then that the next horror struck her. She had recovered her true passport from the secure locker at the railroad station, and thrown it casually in her bag, but now that bag, and all its incriminating contents, was lost. The youths at the waterfall would have it.

'Oh shit,' Irene felt the familiar slide of despair. 'Oh dear God!'

Hearing footsteps, she hastily replaced the cover on the sceptre and looked up, but the short man in the black jacket was far too busy stealing samples from a plant to pay her any attention. Holding the sceptre close, she fought to control the trembling of her body. Where could she go from here? Sensing somebody beside her, she glanced upward.

Drew adjusted his sleeve so it covered his watch. He was smiling as he looked at her, his head tilted to one side. 'You're a hard woman to keep tabs on.'

'Drew!' Hugging the covered sceptre close, Irene struggled to her feet. 'What are you doing here?'

'Following you.' Drew said quietly. 'It looks like you're in trouble.'

She shook her head instinctively. 'No, no. I'm fine. I just panicked, that's all.' Reaching out with her left hand, she touched his arm. 'Look, thanks for your help back there. I…' she forced a stutter, 'I didn't know what to do.'

'I think that there's more than that.' Drew's look was as level as any Irene had seen in her life. Ignoring the curious glance of the man in the black jacket, he knelt down beside her and spoke quietly. 'Half the world is searching for the object you are holding so tightly.'

'What?' Irene pulled the jacket closer to her side.

'The sceptre,' Drew said quietly, 'from the Honours of Scotland.' His sudden grin put her off balance. 'It's all right, Irene. I'm not going to tell anybody. It's nothing to do with me.'

Holding the sceptre so tight that her hand ached, Irene dragged herself to her feet.

'Come on. Let's go home and we can discuss all this.' Although Drew only placed the tip of one finger on her shoulder, she squirmed at the touch. 'You need some dry clothes anyway. And your passport.' Opening his very-conservative jacket, Drew allowed her to see the bulge of documents in the inside pocket. 'It's quite safe.'

Irene nodded, feeling a fresh surge of relief. Drew always seemed to be available when she needed him, like some guardian angel. She looked up. 'Could I have it, please?'

The passport was in the front of the bundle of documents that Drew placed in her outstretched hand. 'But now you're wondering if you can trust me,' he voiced her thoughts.

Irene nodded; the shaft of the sceptre was hard beneath the coat.

'Can you afford not to?' He held the stare of a uniformed attendant until the man dropped his eyes. 'Come on, Irene, and I'll tell you all about me. My favourite subject.'

Irene nearly smiled as she allowed him to guide her out of the greenhouse. She still held the sceptre close but did not complain when Drew's arm wrapped around her shoulder.

Changed and dry again, Irene was uncertain whether to feel defeated or glad when she placed the sceptre on top of the kitchen table. They both looked at it without speaking, and eventually Drew ran his finger up the shaft onto the crystal ball near the tip. 'That's some machine,' he said.

'Beautiful, isn't it?' Irene agreed.

'Were you part of the robbery? Or did you just happen to find this lying in the street.'

'I was part of the robbery,' Irene confirmed. She waited for the condemnation.

Instead, Drew sat opposite her, his face concerned. 'Do you want to talk about it?' When Irene shook her head, he smiled. 'As you wish.'

'I don't know what to do, Drew.'

He nodded. 'Aye, so I can see. Running through Edinburgh in wet jeans with this little beauty bundled under your arm is not the answer. Neither is hiding in the Botanics, waiting for better days. I take it that you had intended to escape in that yacht the Navy caught?'

'Yes, but it all went wrong.' Irene fought the tears that threatened to overwhelm her. She wanted desperately to tell Drew everything, but knew that she should not. 'I don't know what happened, but I ended up with the sceptre and all the rest were killed.'

'I see.' Drew leaned back. 'So what is your plan now? Do you have a plan now?'

Irene shook her head. 'No. Not really.'

'So why not just dump this thing and get home? As far as I can see, the police do not know about you. They are chasing a completely different woman.' Drew placed his hand on the sceptre. 'It all depends on how badly you want to keep this.'

Irene put her hand beside his and gripped tightly. 'I have to have it.' She was surprised at the determination in her own voice. 'It means everything to me.'

'Everything?' Drew did not relinquish his grip. 'Think about what you really want before you make a decision. People have already died because of this bit stick. Does it mean enough for you to risk your life too?'

Irene considered. What were her alternatives? She had come so far and actually had the sceptre in her hand. If she returned it to Ms Manning, her future would be assured. If she gave up now, what would the remainder of her life hold? She would always be seen as *The Neophyte* loser. At best she would be offered a position in middle management in some mediocre organisation. If she were lucky she would be in New York or Chicago; if unlucky she would be in Nowheresville, some hick town at the back of beyond. But people had died because of her; that realisation made her sick. She straightened her back, knowing that she could not bring them back.

'Yes,' Irene answered slowly. She had cleared her mind of doubt. She needed this sceptre to create the life that she wanted. 'Yes, I am prepared to risk my life for this artefact.'

'Right then.' Drew nodded. 'That's the first point. Second point: what do you intend doing with it? I take it that you don't want to keep it as a souvenir of Scotland.'

'I intend to sell it.' Irene felt her chin rise.

'Very good. It will not be easy to sell on the open market as its image has been transmitted across the world. I doubt that there is anybody, anywhere who is not aware of the theft.'

'I know that,' Irene said quietly.

'So either you are very optimistic, or you already know where you'll sell it.' Drew looked directly at her. 'Despite your recent antics, you do not strike me as the overly-stupid type, so I think you will have a buyer all lined up.'

Irene said nothing.

'But you are not going to tell me, which is probably very wise.' Standing up, Drew made coffee and placed one cup on either side of the sceptre. 'But I would like to know if you intend the sceptre to remain in this country, or if it will be transported abroad?'

Again Irene kept quiet. She sipped her coffee and shook her head.

'OK. As you wish. Now listen. I think you realise that I like you.' He waited until Irene nodded before continuing. 'I also think that you are a rogue, searching for something, perhaps an anchor to keep you secure.'

Irene could not stop her smile. 'I've never been called a rogue before.'

'No? Well, you have now. Am I correct?'

'Am I a rogue?' Irene rolled the syllables around her tongue. She had thought of herself as a businesswoman, making her way as best she could, or a high-flier, but this new description was interesting, and not unpleasing. The name conjured up images of loveable characters from her childhood, people who danced on the edge of the law, rather than died-in-the-wool criminals, Johnnie Armstrong as opposed to Al Capone. 'Perhaps I am.'

'Well then, now that we have both admitted the fact, we can move on. I would like to get to know you even better.'

Irene glanced toward the open bedroom door, where the sheets remained rumpled from the previous night. 'You knew me quite well last night, I thought.'

Drew smiled. 'Parts of you, but that's only physical; the real you is buried much deeper inside. As I said, I would like to know you better, but this thing is a barrier between us.'

Shrugging, Irene shifted the position of the sceptre so it no longer bisected the table.

'Exactly. If we can push it aside permanently, then the problem will disappear. So it is in my best interests to help you get rid of it.'

'But you called me a rogue,' Irene said. 'Does it not concern you that I am a thief? And that I was involved in the death of six people?'

Drew shook his head. 'Not really. Did you kill any of them?'

'No, of course not.' Irene shook her head.

248

'And, just as important, did you arrange for any of their deaths?'

Again Irene shook her head.

'So then, why should a few stray deaths concern me? One man was a soldier; he died performing his duty. That was regrettable but every soldier knows that he might be killed. Death is part of a soldier's contract. The others were all bad men and women. Your fellow thieves, I believe, although I suspect that they were less roguish and more pure bad than you.'

Irene looked away. She thought of Patrick in happier times, and of Mary driving with great skill, of Desmond's joy when he produced the false documents and of Bryan laughing over some foolish practical joke. She had never got to know Stefan, but he had not done her any harm.

'I don't know about that.'

'I do. Trust me.' Drew sipped at his coffee. 'In a way their deaths give you a decided advantage, because they were the only people who could identify you.'

'Except you,' Irene pointed out.

'Except me,' Drew agreed. 'But I am no threat to you, so long as you are no threat to me. And I know that you do not carry a gun.'

'How do you know that?'

'I've been through your possessions,' he told her frankly. 'And I've seen you in action with these kids this morning. You were not particularly impressive, so I doubt you are a black belt in karate or anything. So, we are back to the first point. If we can get rid of the sceptre, we can get to know each other better.'

'What if I don't want to know you?' Irene asked.

'Then I have spent a few days of my life in the company of a beautiful woman.' Drew smiled. 'So can we agree to trust each other a little bit more?'

Irene drew a deep breath. She glanced at the sceptre and thought of all that it represented to her life, then at Drew sitting opposite. She did not have many options. 'I would love to trust you,' she told him, truthfully. 'But I am not very good at trust.'

'That's settled then.' Drew took the coffee cups to the sink and washed them out. 'If you do your best, I'm sure it will be enough. So, let's get rid of this thing and take it from there.'

Sunlight from the window glittered on the silver-gilt shaft of the sceptre and cast short shadows across the table. Irene looked closer, examining for the first time the beautiful figurines that decorated the filial. The Virgin and Child reminded her of the sceptre's papal origins, while Gothic canopies sheltered Scotland's Saint Andrew and a sombre looking Saint James. She shook her head, wondering at the small dolphins that frolicked in seeming mockery on either side of the saints.

'It is very beautiful,' Irene said.

'And very dangerous. If it is to remain inside the UK there will not be too much of a problem,' Drew returned with fresh coffee. 'We can bundle it into the boot of the car and drive to wherever your destination may be. We'll be home and dry within 24 hours, unless it's going to one of the islands?'

Irene shook her head. 'I want to deliver it out of the country.'

'More difficult,' Drew mused. 'The Customs are searching every bag and piece of baggage at every airport and ferry terminal. There are huge delays now, with planes held up and ferries running around 10 hours late. You've caused a great deal of trouble, Miss Rogue.'

Irene nodded. 'I realise that.' She was not proud of the impact she had made.

'Good. Had you thought how to take it abroad?'

'When the yacht idea failed, I was going to wrap it up and post it.'

Drew shook his head. The Royal Mail is checking every parcel over a certain size, as are the private courier firms. So you are delaying the mail too; which is a criminal offence, by the way.' He looked stern for a minute. 'You rogue.'

Irene met his smile. 'The States,' she said. 'I want the sceptre to go to the States.'

'Ah.' Drew nodded. 'I wondered about that, what with you being an American. Any particular part?'

'Yes, but I'm not saying.'

'OK.' Drew did not press the point. He lifted the sceptre. 'Heavy little bugger, isn't it? Imagine; I'm holding part of the heritage of Scotland in my grubby little paws.'

'Yes,' Irene said. 'And if you help me, you will be taking that heritage out of Scotland. Don't you feel bad about that?'

Drew shook his head. 'Not even a little bit,' he said. 'You see, I've done my bit for my country. I was in the Guards. An officer, no less, and there was an incident in Iraq. The usual; there was a roadside bomb and one of my men was injured. He lost a leg. The next minute a mob of Iraqis gathered around and tried to drag him away. We rescued him and sent out a snatch squad that pulled in the ringleader, but another of my men went a bit far and kicked the bastard. He was captured by the TV cameras and hung out to dry.'

'What do you mean?'

'Court martialled and sent to the Glasshouse, and that's a living hell. I was defending officer, but they ordered me not to defend too vigorously. All PR you see, the British government bowing to international public opinion and let the poor squaddies suffer. As always.'

Irene nodded. 'And did you defend him?'

'As best I could. Too well in fact, so I was told not to expect any promotion. Queen and country eh?' For the first time in Irene's experience, Drew dropped his expression of urbane civility.

'I see.' Irene shifted uncomfortably in her seat. 'So what did you do?'

'Sent in my papers. Resigned. I was an officer, following the orders of the government, which is fair enough, but not at the expense of my own men. So if that government loses some of its treasure, why should I care?' His smile was as infectious as that of Patrick, but with more depth. 'Anyway, I fancy you more than I fancy the Prime Minister.'

Irene nodded. 'Well, that's reassuring.' Now that she had a handle on Drew, she could understand him a whole lot better; he would be easier to manage. 'So you're not just helping me because of my pretty face?'

Drew smiled again. 'Well, that is one factor, but there is more,' he said, 'but this is neither the time nor place. Let's work out how to get this thing to wherever you want it to go.'

'I've told you. America,' Irene repeated, 'and I'm not saying more than that.'

Drew looked at her. 'There's no need. We can do America.'

They both looked around when somebody knocked loudly at the door.

Chapter Twenty: Edinburgh & E. Lothian: July

'Oh Lord,' Irene stared at Drew. 'Who's that?'

'No idea,' Drew shook his head. Lifting the sceptre, he thrust it behind the television. 'Probably the man to read the electric meter.' His grin was reassuring as he opened the door.

'Andrew. Just thought I would pop by to see how things were.' James Drummond walked in as if he owned the flat. He removed his cap as he spoke to Irene. 'Good morning, my dear, I did not realise my son had company.' He held out his hand. 'How do you do?'

Glancing toward the television, Irene rose and shook hands. She felt sick. 'Very well, thank you, sir.'

'Sir?' Drummond raised his eyebrows as he studied Irene, taking in everything. 'I haven't been called that for a while.' Indicating that Irene should sit, he nodded to Drew. 'She's far too good for you, Andrew. Put the kettle on for an old man, won't you?'

They sat around the table, with father and son drinking Earl Grey tea and Irene boosting her nerves with Kenyan coffee.

'Are you not going to introduce us?' Drummond asked, and Drew grinned.

'Irene, this is my father, Dad, this is Irene Armstrong from America.'

'South Carolina?' Drummond asked, and nodded when Irene corrected him.

'Not far off, one state north.' She smiled, immediately liking this genial old man.

'My apologies. So what brings you to Scotland?' Drummond held her eyes. 'And don't tell me that you came solely to see this reprobate.'

'She's on holiday,' Drew replied for her. 'But she was caught up in that nonsense in the High Street.'

'Ah yes,' Drummond nodded. 'Nasty business, yon. You weren't hurt, were you?'

'Only shaken up a bit,' Irene could see the end of the sceptre protruding from behind the television and shifted slightly to block Drummond's view.

'Not the best introduction to Scotland,' Drummond said. 'Well, I won't keep you two apart for long. I just wanted to ask Andrew if he has considered my offer.'

Drew shook his head. 'No, Dad, regretfully, I must decline.'

Finishing his tea, Drummond rose quickly from the chair. 'As you wish. But if you reconsider…'

'You'll be the first to know.' Drew assured him. He escorted his father to the door, watched him descend the stairs and blew a sigh of relief.

'That could have been nasty,' Irene said.

'It could have been much worse than you realise,' Drew told her. 'The sooner we have your sceptre away the better.'

* * *

'How are things?' Drummond swung his driver, eying the fairway to check for any unexpected folds of ground.

'Going steadily.' Meigle sounded more confident than he looked. 'We have narrowed the possible buyers down to two; an Indian financial wizard and an American tycoon. I have people checking them out even as we speak.' He enjoyed bringing Drummond to unfamiliar courses just to see him fret. Drummond was a man who hated to be defeated in anything,

254

even a game of golf. Maybe that was the secret of his constant success.

Drummond thrust the tee into the ground and placed the ball on top. He looked to his left, where Firth of Forth provided a beautiful backdrop to the course. 'I hate playing on East Lothian links. There's always that damned wind.'

'That's why I took you here,' Meigle told him. 'Think of it as a challenge.' He watched as Drummond swung. There was a neat click and the ball travelled dead straight for two hundred yards, before kicking onto the rough. 'Nasty little eddy there. I should have warned you.' He swung in turn; aiming to the left so the wind carried his ball directly to the edge of the green.

Both men walked along the fairway in silence. Not until Drummond had found his ball and prepared for his second shot did Meigle speak again. 'It's a pity that Andrew declined to join us. A man like him would have been a major asset.'

'Indeed.' Drummond selected a four iron and addressed the ball.

'I'm not sure what to do about him.'

'I think it will be all right.' Drummond hit the ball neatly so it rose high and dropped onto the green, but rather than stop, it continued to roll, finding sanctuary in an ugly sand bunker.

'I hope so. Oh, bad luck with that lie. I meant to warn you about the camber of this green.' Meigle strolled casually to his own ball. Kneeling beside it, he measured the distance to the hole. 'How was he when he told you?'

'Busy with his new girlfriend. Irene Armstrong, her name.' Drummond said.

Meigle stood up and gripped his putter. 'Armstrong, eh? Is that *the* Irene Armstrong?'

'That's the one.'

'That's interesting.' Meigle swung smoothly and the ball eased across the smooth grass, to stop at the very lip of the hole.

They walked to the bunker and contemplated Drummond's ball, which was wedged under the near lip.

'Awkward shot,' Meigle said. 'You could take it out and drop a stroke.'

'Rather not.' Drummond contemplated his ball, stepped into the bunker to the bunker and selected a sand wedge. 'I'll try my best.' He met Meigle's eye. 'They have the sceptre there.'

'Good show.' Meigle watched as Drummond hacked at the ball. It flew straight up into the air, hovered for a second and returned, further back in the bunker. 'Pity. It was a nice try.' Walking forward, he removed the pin, stood over his ball and tapped it into the hole. 'Are you sure about the sceptre?' He looked up suddenly. 'Is the Powerstone safe?'

'I saw the sceptre myself, but I didn't see the stone. They tried to hide the thing behind the television. Shall I get it back?' Drummond's next shot chipped the ball out of the bunker. It hovered in the air for a second and fell right beside the hole. 'Your decision, but I don't want Andrew hurt.'

Meigle nodded. 'Afraid we can't guarantee that,' he said. 'What with the situation being what it is.'

'I understand.' Drummond prepared to lift the ball. 'Will you take it that I can't miss from here?'

'Take your shot,' Meigle insisted. 'Try your best.'

Drummond straddled the ball and pushed it into the hole. 'I won't help you with Andrew, you know.'

'Didn't think that you would,' Meigle said, replacing the pin. 'I quite understand, of course.'

'I'd prefer to keep the Clach-bhuai under observation. Make sure it's safe, and see where it's headed.'

'That might be possible,' Meigle agreed.

They walked to the edge of the second fairway and dropped their balls. Meigle smiled as Drummond tested the wind. The graceful cone of Berwick Law rose behind them. Two people stood at the summit, gazing at the view. 'I could send somebody to follow them.'

'You'll need a good man.' Drummond teed up and cracked a shot that slewed into the worst of the rough.

Meigle shook his head in sympathy. 'Two good men. Iain Hardy and young Kenny Mossman.' He drove his shot a straight two hundred yards down the fairway. 'You know, ten years ago I could beat three hundred yards. Now I'm pleased if I top two-fifty.'

'That's just old age, Sandy,' Drummond said, 'Iain Hardy I can understand; handy enough, but only a foot soldier. I'm not sure that I would send Mossman. Is he not a bit valuable to lose? Andrew was a guardsman, remember.'

'Mossman's not irreplaceable.' Meigle said.

Drummond nodded. 'Nobody is.'

Meigle began the long walk up the fairway. Suddenly he felt very old. 'I wouldn't like us to fall out over this, Jamie. Not after so long.'

Drummond nodded. 'No. We shouldn't fall out.'

'No. So we'll just watch and follow. But if the Clach-bhuai is in danger, then I'm afraid it could get nasty.'

'I appreciate that, Sandy.' He scanned the rough for his ball. 'Next time that I'm on this blasted course I will hire a caddy.'

'Maybe you should; the wind is a bit tricky, coming straight off the sea here.' Meigle waited until Drummond located his ball. 'Bad lie, I'm afraid.'

'Bad lie altogether, Sandy. I won't be pleased if Andrew gets hurt.' Drummond lined up his shot and chipped onto the fairway.

'The Society is more important than any of us.' Meigle said. 'You know how it is.'

Drummond nodded, watching as Meigle knocked his ball into the centre of the green. 'We could be opposed then.'

'I'm afraid so.'

Drummond hit the ball too hard, so it overshot the green by ten yards, bounced and rolled off to the side. 'Damn. Can't get the feel of this course at all.'

'You have to watch for the wind, Jamie.' Meigle shook his head. 'You can't go against it, you see.'

'Maybe I have to.' Drummond waited until Meigle removed the pin and holed his shot. 'Two up already, eh? Good playing; it's awkward when family and duty clash.'

'We might still get Andrew back.' Meigle glanced over to Drummond and smiled. 'That American woman's not that damned attractive.'

When Drummond looked up there was no humour at all in his face. 'I don't think he's only involved for tits and bits, Sandy. Young Andrew's smitten this time.'

'Ah,' Meigle measured the length of the next fairway before dropping his ball. 'I'd better warn Kenny and Iain then. Maybe they'd better leave Andrew and get rid of the girl.'

Drummond teed up and addressed the ball. 'That might be best.' He hit his drive straight onto the green.

Chapter Twenty-One: Sutherland: August

Irene did not immediately feel secure among the granite hills and sudden sea lochs of Sutherland. Even at the height of summer, with scores of visitors thronging even the smallest of the villages, she was aware of an atmosphere of watchfulness, as if these dark mountains were suspicious of her presence.

'Where are we?' They had been driving for hours across the body of Scotland. At first Irene had enjoyed the novelty of changing scenery, but now the procession of rugged hills, lonely lochs and one-horse villages wearied her.

'Coigach,' Drew said. The name sounded like an ancient curse. He pulled the Audi into one of the passing places in the single-track road and opened the window. Only the distant bleat of a sheep and the hush of breaking waves shivered the silence. To their right, gaunt mountains rose like the bones of a prehistoric giant. Wild, untamed, unreachable, they looked older than anything Irene could have imagined.

'How much further?' She felt like a child again, completely under the control of somebody. Then it had been her parents, now it was Drew. He seemed different since he had told her something of himself, much more serious.

'Not far, my little rogue.' He allowed the silence to seep into the car. 'But I want to stop for a few minutes.'

'Why?' Irene heard the faint piping of a curlew. It sounded eerie, perfect for this place of rock and water and pre-history. Something flew past, its beak down-curving ahead of scimitar wings.

'There's been a car behind us since we left Inverness. Not many people use this road, so I'll let it overtake.' Drew glanced in his mirror. 'It might be an idea if you ducked down for a minute. Hide your face.'

'What?' Irene looked at him in some alarm. 'Nobody knows my face.'

'Let's keep it that way, shall we?'

Irene slid down the leather seat. She heard the hum of an approaching vehicle, felt the passage of wind as it passed, and bobbed back up. Drew had his mobile phone in his hand.

'I got his photograph,' he said calmly, and showed the slightly blurred image. 'Do you know him?'

Irene shook her head.

'I do. He is an associate of my father. '

'So why is he here?' Irene felt panic claw at her stomach as her voice raised an octave.

'Could be perfectly innocent business. He is some sort of lawyer, I believe. On the other hand my father could have sent him, which is bad news.'

'Bad news? Why?'

Drew shrugged. He waited until the road was empty in both directions before pulling out. 'My father belongs to some ancient society dedicated to protecting that sceptre of yours. Or at least that wee crystal ball on top. It seems to be a sort of powerstone.'

'What? What are you saying? Secret society? What sort of secret society? ' The panic was greater now as Irene realised that she was in one of the most deserted parts of Europe in the company of a man she hardly knew. 'Let me out. Stop the car and let me out.' She heard the pitch of her voice rising.

Drew pulled to a halt beside a group of sheep. Beyond a slender verge of grass, the sea shushed onto a beach of rounded stones. There were small islands offshore, and a scattering of seabirds floating on the swell. 'You're not a prisoner,' he told her. 'You are free to go any time you like, but I have told you before that you're in no danger from me.' When he killed the engine the silence pressed upon them.

'Your say that your father is in some society to protect the sceptre?' Irene found it difficult to control her voice.

'That's right.' Drew's sudden grin took her by surprise. 'Ironic isn't it? That's why he came down the other day. He wanted me to join. It seems that it's been a family tradition for hundreds of years.'

Irene opened the door. One of the sheep bleated noisily. 'Sweet Lord, what have I got myself into?'

'The presence of terrorists and murderers, thieves and vagabonds,' Drew told her cheerfully. 'But what did you expect, mixing with royalty? They were the biggest cut-throats going. The man with the longest sword was king; the woman who could manipulate best was queen. Welcome to Scotland.'

Swinging her legs outside the car, Irene sat on the seat and remembered the tale of Johnnie Armstrong. 'This is not what I expected.'

'Life never is,' Drew's voice hardened.

'It all seemed so easy once.' Irene sighed. 'What did I do wrong?'

'Nothing.' Drew sounded more sympathetic. 'We're all the same, Irene. We are all trying to live the best way we can. It's just that the dice of life are loaded in favour of the wrong people; don't ask me why. If you want to succeed, you have to get your hands on the right dice.'

'How do I do that?' She looked around.

'I think that's what you're trying to do now. Come back inside. I've got to see a man about a boat.' When Drew's phone rang he lifted it, but killed the signal. 'That's my father phoning now. Talk of the devil eh?' He waited for a few minutes and punched in a text message, but waited until Irene had returned to her position before restarting the car. 'Aye, they don't make rogues like they used to.' He glanced across to her. 'Or perhaps they do. Who says that your namesake Johnnie Armstrong was always brave? I'll bet he found life a complete bugger from time to time.'

'Johnnie Armstrong?' Irene forced a smile. 'My father used to tell me about him.'

Irene relapsed into silence for a few minutes as she watched the vista of mountains and water slide past. 'If it's a family tradition to join this society, Drew, why are you helping me?'

He glanced at her and shrugged. 'I've already told you one reason. I quite like you. But after serving in Iraq and Afghanistan, I also dislike societies that protect their secrets by casual murder.' He waited until she reacted before continuing. 'The Society had a meeting not long back; the same day I met our friend out there,' he nodded in the direction of the road in front, 'and one of the new members refused to co-operate. My father and another equally charming old buffer left the meeting early, and next day I heard that the new member had died in a car crash.'

'Shit!' Irene stared at him. 'They murdered him?'

'Her,' Drew corrected. 'They murdered her.'

Irene looked out to sea. Three thousand miles of Atlantic stretched between here and home. 'And now this society is after us?'

'So it seems.' Drew's grin reappeared. 'Exciting, isn't it?'

'Are you not afraid?' Irene asked, still curious despite the now familiar sick slide of fear.

Drew shrugged. 'Probably.' He faced her, driving one-handed on the twisting road. 'If you want to end this, I can contact the old man. The second we hand back the trinket, the

Society will lose interest, although they might want to know for whom it's destined.'

'That is only my business, I'm afraid,' Irene felt her back stiffen as she waited for Drew's reaction. When he only shrugged, she reached over and switched on the radio. The educated tones of a Highland broadcaster filled the car.

'…terrorist attack in the Middle East. Back here in Scotland the police have finished interviewing a woman over the theft of the Crown Jewels. The woman was caught on CCTV camera speaking with one of the thieves, but police are now satisfied that she was not involved with the July 12 attack. The Scottish Crown and Sword of State have since been recovered, but the sceptre, a gift from the Pope in 1496, is still missing.' 'Detective Chief Inspector Murdoch, leading the investigation, said yesterday that he was vigorously pursuing a number of lines of enquiry and expected further developments to occur shortly.'

'A number of lines of enquiry?' Irene turned the radio off. 'What does that mean?'

'It means that they have not got a clue what to do next.' Drew grinned to her. 'Anyway, you'll be out of the country within a few hours and then you'll have nothing to worry about.'

Irene nodded, but when she closed her eyes, she could see Desmond fall as the soldier lunged with his bayonet. With every member of her team dead except her, it seemed that the Scottish authorities were not interested in arresting those who stole their Honours. Like King James V, they were more intent on vengeance than justice. 'Put your foot down, Drew, and get me out of this country.'

They passed over a hump-backed bridge and stopped at a black and white road sign that said Alltgobhlach. Only the sea broke the silence when Drew switched off the engine, and Irene studied the village. It did not take long. A single medium sized building with two petrol pumps stood beside a small terrace of cottages, and then came a small church, another bridge and then a final road sign.

'Highland metropolis, eh?'

'Alltgobhlach. The forked burn.' Drew had parked in a small area of grass beside the beach, where a single child's swing creaked slightly in the breeze and a herring gull watched from the back of a green wooden bench. 'We'll have a wee breather here, a bite to eat and it will be time for a spot of fishing.'

Irene was still dazed at the thought of a secret society chasing her across Scotland. 'The sceptre?'

'Leave it where it is.' Drew had repacked the sceptre in a stout canvas bag, which he had placed beside the spare tyre in the boot. 'You can hardly carry that around with you.'

The larger building boasted a sign proclaiming that it was the Alltgobhlach Hotel and claimed to have the last petrol for forty miles. It also extended a hundred thousand welcomes in Gaelic, but the woman behind the tiny reception desk spoke with the sharp accent of London. She signed them in without interest.

'We're here for the fishing,' Drew told her breezily. 'So I'll want to hire a boat for the night.'

'That will be great,' the woman said. 'I'll get my husband to see you.'

After they had eaten a poor meal of overcooked chicken and vegetables straight from the freezer, Irene followed Drew outside. Ignoring the distant shrill of what she took to be bagpipes, she looked out to the bay, seeing a group of humped islets and the faint line of a larger island on the far horizon.

'The big one's Lewis,' Drew told her. 'The largest of the Outer Hebrides.'

There was one large boat afloat in the water and five smaller hire boats lying bottom up on the shingle beach. Drew chose one at random, and the hotel owner helped him turn it the right way up for a proper inspection.

'Not bad,' Drew probed the wooden planks of the clinker built hull. 'Sound as a pound.' Eighteen feet long, the boat came equipped with a Yamaha outboard motor and a set of oars. 'I'll take it out tonight,' he said. 'Could you put it on my bill?'

'Of course.' The owner smiled. Irene guessed that he would add everything possible to the bill, on any pretext. 'We can hire our rods too.'

'We have rods in the car,' Drew said. 'I like to use my own. I know the balance better.

Irene had been with Drew when he walked into the sports shop in Edinburgh and asked for a sea fishing rod. 'Do you do a lot of fishing, sir?' the assistant had asked, and had provided a free crash course on the basics when Drew admitted that he had never fished in his life.

'Of course, sir. Well, I'll leave you to get acquainted with the boat, if you will excuse me? Best to take it for a short trip in the bay here before nightfall, to make sure you know how she handles.' The hotel owner walked briskly away, red tartan trousers bulging around his hips.

'I still don't understand exactly what we're doing.' Irene disliked the small-girl complaint in her own voice.

'Trust me.' Drew looked up as the piping sound began again. 'But we'll be moving under cover of darkness.' He tossed the car keys over to her. 'Get the fishing gear from the boot, could you? Just carry the whole bundle over and dump it into the boat.'

Irene opened the boot and hauled out the three long rods that Drew had bought, together with the large bag that held the wriggling live bait and the various reels. After checking to ensure that the canvas bag that held the sceptre was secure, she carefully locked the boot and carried the fishing gear to the boat. 'What now?'

Drew looked at his watch. 'Seven o'clock. Now we'll go fishing. Get changed into your warmest clothes, Irene, as it can get damned cold out there, even in summer.'

'Why are we going fishing?' The long drive had wearied Irene more than she knew, so her words sounded slurred even to her own ears.

'To get your sceptre to America, of course.' Drew grinned across to her. 'Now go and get changed. And bring your passport, and anything else that might be used to identify you.'

'Why?'

'In case anybody goes through our stuff when we've gone.' Drew grinned. 'It's all right, Irene. I do know what I'm doing.'

Despite the light sky, the air was cool when they pushed away from the shore, leaving behind the inevitable host of midges. Irene leaned closer to Drew. 'The sceptre!' she hissed. 'It's still in the car!'

'The sceptre is safe enough,' Drew told her. 'Trust me!' He hauled powerfully on the oars until they were into deeper water, and then tilted the outboard motor so the propeller was submerged. The engine sounded loud in the Highland quiet. 'We'll go between these two wee islands,' he said, pointing to a narrow channel of sombre sea.

Seabirds screamed overhead, and a large marine creature surfaced nearby. Unsure what it was, Irene edged closer to Drew.

'Just a seal,' he told her. 'It's perfectly harmless.'

Birdlime smeared the bare rock of the nearest islet, with the swell rhythmically swaying its fringe of seaweed. 'That's Eilean Beg,' Drew told her, 'and a good place for sea bass, so I'm told, so if you'd like to get the rods out now?'

'Is this necessary?' Irene stared at the collection of long rods and fishing equipment with incomprehension. 'I've no idea what to do with all these.'

'You don't have to. You only have to look as though we're fishing.' Settling down, Drew produced a small pair of binoculars from inside his waxed Barbour jacket. He examined the shore for a few minutes, grunted, and handed the binoculars to Irene. 'Look at the car.'

It took a few moments for Irene to adjust the focus, and then she swore. 'They're in the boot! Who are they? They'll find the sceptre!' Dropping the binoculars, she glared at Drew, her voice rising to a scream. 'You did this on purpose! You bastard, you sick, dirty bastard! You came out there to give them the sceptre.'

'Hardly.' He ignored her insults. 'Keep looking.'

'Turn round! Get back to the car!' Furious that she had trusted him, Irene grabbed at Drew's jacket. 'You meant this! You're working for your father.' Only the rocking of the boat and the lingering pain in her right hand prevented her from slapping him.

Drew picked up the binoculars and handed them back to her. 'Keep looking.'

'You bastard!' Irene sat heavily on the centre thwart. She glowered at Drew, then lifted the binoculars and watched all her dreams disappear. There were two men examining their hired car, and although both seemed familiar, she could not say exactly where she had seen them.

'Who are they?' I know them!'

'The small, stocky one is Iain Hardy. He followed us here from Inverness, remember? The other is Kenny Mossman, the jeweller that made your Luckenbooth brooch. They are both Society men.'

Aware that she was shaking with fury, Irene watched the two men remove the spare wheel from the boot and rummage around with the tools. After a few minutes they lifted the long canvas bag in which she had placed the sceptre.

'They've got it,' Irene said quietly. 'They've got it. You've won.' She lowered the binoculars as the realisation of defeat came to her. Her anger dissipated, leaving only numbness. She guessed that bitter despair would come soon, as it had when she lost *The Neophyte* final.' Very clever, Drew, very, very clever. Lure me up here with the promise of help, and then hand everything over to your father's goons.'

'They might be many things,' Drew said, 'but never dragoons.' He sounded as calm as ever. 'And if I had intended taking the sceptre, why should I come away up here? I could have done that at any time. Look again.'

By now the boat was quarter of a mile out to sea, with the waves hissing and bubbling around the wooden hull. They had penetrated deep into the channel between the two islets and were within casting distance of Eilean Mor. Irene could see a host of seabirds among the grass, as well as the ubiquitous black-faced sheep.

'Go on,' Drew encouraged. 'It's all right. We're a dark shape against dark rock. Damned near invisible, indeed. So they can't see us watching them.' She raised the binoculars just as Iain unzipped the canvas bag and plunged his hand inside. Irene watched his expression change from triumph to shock. He withdrew his hand very quickly, and jumped back, his mouth working frantically as he shook his hand as if to rid it of something very unpleasant.

'What? What's happened?' Irene half stood, trying to improve her vision. She sat back as the boat rocked unpleasantly.

'Maggots,' Drew said. 'I made a few alterations at our last comfort stop. I took out the sceptre, put in an old length of wood and poured some of the bait on top. Just a wee message for the boys.'

Irene stared at him, and then began to smile. 'So where is the sceptre?'

'At your feet. In the real bait bag. I can't imagine anybody poking in there for long.' Drew winked at her. 'So let's get you over to America, shall we? Once they've recovered, they'll be after us like a shot.'

'You could have told me,' Irene stared at him, her initial relief fading to irritation, then fury. 'You made me believe that they had the sceptre.'

He grinned at her, obviously enjoying her anger. 'Yes. And it serves you right, Miss Rogue. I told you to trust me, so when you don't, you deserve all the torment that you bring on yourself.'

'You truly are a bastard,' Irene said. 'It's no wonder that all your previous girl friends left you!'

Drew nodded, his face more serious. 'I'm sure that I warned you. It would take a special kind of girl to stay with me, Irene. But I'll enjoy your company as long as I can. Now, let's get you home.' Sparing only once glance behind him,

Drew pushed the throttle and the boat began to speed up. Spray rose from the bows, spattering over Irene.

'We can't go all the way to America in this,' she shouted. 'It's thousands of miles!'

Drew grinned again. 'Have you still not learned to trust your Uncle Drew? Hold on, now.'

Irene shuddered as she eyed the small islet to which Drew steered. A fury of frothed sea and spindrift shrouded the rocky shore, but there was a small bay on the north side, with deep grooves in a rocky beach and a copse of wind stunted rowan trees clustered around the ruins of an ancient building. Hardly slowing down, Drew guided the boat straight toward the moss-furred walls. 'Duck!'

Irene did so, and Drew eased through a dripping archway into the dark interior. 'That was the sea gate,' he said, 'and this is an old stronghold of the Macraes,' he said. 'They were the local hard men, the body guard of the Mackenzies, and they used this castle as an outlying fort to guard Coigach.'

The walls were of blocks of stone, streaked with birdlime and moss, with vegetation spouting from the upper courses. Irene ducked as a wave splashed against the wall, slopping cold water onto her coat. 'So this was a castle then?' She tried to imagine the romantic old clansmen here, with their claymores and targes, but instead saw only piracy, poverty and pain. 'In America, we would have preserved this as a national monument, with an interpretation centre and a shop.'

'I know. But we've got so many crumbling ruins in Scotland that we can neglect most of them. Anyway, it's handy for people like us.'

'Why are we here?' Irene swatted at the first of the midges that searched them out. Smaller than the summer mosquitoes of the States, they were even more persistent.

'We're hiding from Kenny Mossman; he's a tenacious wee bugger, he saw us in the boat, so he'll be on the water directly. And we're waiting for a lift.'

As the light dipped, the number of midges increased, so Irene spent more time slapping at them than worrying about the possibility of discovery. Twice she saw Drew busy texting on his mobile, but she said nothing. Once she heard the drone of an outboard motor, but nobody probed into their refuge.

'The locals know about this place,' Drew told her quietly, 'but they won't tell the outsiders. Kenny's fine in Edinburgh, but he's lost out here.'

'Does he not have a map?'

'Probably,' Drew said, 'but this castle is only marked as a ruin. There are no details.'

'So how do you know?' Irene clawed a score of voracious black insects from her face.

'One of my lads came from here. You'll meet him later. Now keep still and keep quiet.'

Covering her head with her jacket, Irene endured the swarms for two hours as the light slowly faded. At length, when she felt as though the voracious insects were crawling through her hair and exploring every part of her body, Drew nudged her. 'Irene. Go right into the bows and look forward. Tell me if you see anything.'

Irene crept forward, staring into what seemed the most evocative ocean sunset that she had ever experienced as Drew extended the oars and eased the boat out of the sea gate.

'The Macraes used to bring their birlinns in here,' Drew murmured. 'They were good seamen in those days, using only oar and sail power.' He grinned to her. 'Now we have to emulate them, but with the Society after us.'

Irene blinked as they passed through a tangle of vegetation, until she realised that a falling tide had enlarged the opening so there was more headroom but less water under the keel. She peered out to sea.

'Don't look at the sun,' Drew warned. 'It'll kill your vision. Look toward the land; can you see any other boats?'

At first Irene could not make anything out save the sombre shape of Scotland, and then she saw the pricking lights from Alltgobhlach reflected on the sea. There was a definite black dot near Eilean Mor.

'I think that there's something there.' She pointed.

'Fine. That'll be Kenny.' Still using the oars, Drew eased the boat round, keeping close to the island despite the surge and crash of waves shattering against the rocks. Only when he was in the lee of the island did he start the motor, steering out to sea.

'Keep alert,' Drew ordered, 'but look toward the land. Tell me the moment that you see anything.'

Irene scrambled astern. For years, Central Park was all the Great Outdoors she experienced, but here she was playing pirates in the back of nowhere, with her future and freedom in the care of an enigmatic Scotsman. She peered into the mustering dark, searching for the elusive speck of Kenny's boat. 'They're moving!' She grasped for the binoculars but found it hard to focus. 'I think I can see white water under the bows.'

'Are they coming this way?'

'I don't know.'

'Concentrate! Is there a white wake?' Although Drew kept his voice low, there was no mistaking his intensity.

'No,' Irene swallowed away the fear that blocked her throat. 'No. There's only a white splurge!'

'Damn. He's coming this way then. He's better than I thought.'

Irene recognised affection behind the insults but said nothing. She could clearly hear the drone of motor now, and looked at Drew. He nodded. 'Aye, that's our Kenny. Sound like a powerful beast he's got, so he'll be with us shortly.'

'What can I do?' Irene recognised the plea in her voice. She could never have asked that of Patrick.

'Ignore Kenny now,' Drew sounded as calm as ever. 'Go into the bows and look seaward. Look for anything that should not be there.'

'What are you going to do?' Scrambling forward, Irene positioned herself as far forward as she could, leaning over the prow with the binoculars pressed to her eyes.

'Keep the engine going and row,' Drew said. 'If I row like hell, we might outdistance Kenny.'

Irene felt the boat rock as he moved, then she heard the kiss of oars in the sea. She stared forward as the brilliant red sky gradually fading to the colour of watered pink silk, tinged with grey. When the sun slithered behind the distant gloom of Lewis, the sea took on a more sinister aspect. Oily waves rose around them, bubbled beneath their keel and surged astern in a swathe of frothy white. She started when something large splashed nearby.

'Just a basking shark,' Drew soothed her. 'Nothing to worry about.'

'Where are we going? That island over there?' She pointed with the binoculars. 'Are we going to Lewis?'

'I've told you already. We're going to America,' Drew said. 'I hope you have your passport. And your toothbrush.' He glanced astern and swore again. 'I can't see Kenny now, but I hear his motor.'

Irene was aware that the growl of the diesel engine was steadily increasing. Irene tried to find Kenny with the binoculars but with could make out nothing against the dark loom of the land. 'At least he won't see us either.'

'No. He'll go for the sound. Noise travels for miles out here.' Leaning forward, Drew cut the engine, and then eased himself back onto the central thwart. He grabbed the oars, sighing. 'I'll have to row like a galley slave.' There was silence for a few minutes, save for the creak of the oarlocks and the swish of water.

'He's still coming.' For the first time since she realised that the sceptre was safe, Irene began to panic. 'He's coming right for us!'

Drew rested on the oars for a few seconds, listening. 'I think that you are right,' he said. 'He must be using night glasses. Clever man, our Kenny.' Swiftly shipping the oars, he restarted the engine. 'No point in silence then. Hold on, Irene.'

As Drew gunned the engine, a powerful light gleamed from the other boat. Irene watched as it reflected from the now dark water, gradually creeping closer. She blinked in the sudden glare, and ducked her head.

'They've seen us!'

'Grab an oar,' Drew ordered. He pointed to a forward thwart. 'Sit there and row like buggery!'

Irene looked at him. 'I don't know how.'

'Then learn quickly, girl.' Reaching out, he sat her ungently down on the unforgiving wood. 'Grab one oar in each hand; dip them in the water and pull.' He swore as the light returned, highlighting the shape of his cheekbone and jaw. 'It's your freedom, rogue-woman, so work for it.'

Irene felt for the oars. They felt cold and very heavy, the length clumsy as she dipped them in the water.

'Row!' Drew commanded. 'Dip!'

She obeyed, copying his movements.

'Pull!'

She leaned into the stroke, feeling the drag of water against the concave blades of the oars.

'Now out and back, and don't splash too much!'

Gasping with the effort, Irene obeyed, following Drew's instructions as best she could, until her muscles ached with the strain and her hands seemed to turn to claws, but still Kenny's harsh light glared on to her.

'Andrew Drummond!' The voice was metallic, obviously carried by a megaphone. 'Stop where you are. There is nowhere that you can go!'

'No!' Irene tried to stand, to shield her eyes from that relentless light, but in doing so one of the oars slipped free and arrowed into the water. She watched it float away as despair took her hopes.

Chapter Twenty-Two: North Atlantic: August

When Drew looked up, squinting into the light, Irene saw his chin out-thrust in determination. 'Bugger you, Kenny Mossman! If you want me, come and get me!'

The roar of engines increased and as the searchlight shifted its angle, Irene saw the other craft. It was twice as large as their boat, with double inboard motors and a tripod to hold the searchlight. Silhouetted against the light, she could clearly see a man standing. He held an AK-47, which he swivelled toward her.

'Iain has you covered, Drew,' the metallic voice sounded urgent. 'So don't be foolish. It's not you we want; it's the Clach-bhuai, and the girl.'

There was the sharp crack of a shot, and something smashed against the gunwale, shaking the boat and showering splinters over Irene.

She screamed.

Drew pulled her close. 'You hurt?'

Irene shook her head.

'Fine.' Still holding her, Drew lifted his voice. 'You're too late, Kenny, son,' he said. 'Look ahead.'

The unlit vessel seemed to loom out of the water, dominating their boat like some powered island, but Drew manoeuvred skilfully to the opposite side.

'We're safe now, Irene,' he said softly. 'Even a Borderer would not be reckless enough to shoot us in front of witnesses.'

A man appeared on the gunwale, 'in you come, darling.' He hauled Irene over the handrail and inboard. She collapsed on the deck, her legs trembling.

'Oh thank God. Drew?'

'Coming!' Drew grinned up at her and tossed in his fishing gear and the bait bag with scent regard to the priceless contents. He vaulted the rail. 'All right, Irene?'

She nodded, allowing her head to rest on his shoulder for a long second as she relished being on a deck that still swooped and tossed but felt far more stable than the open boat she had just left. 'How about Kenny?'

'How about him?' Drew hugged her briefly and kissed her forehead. 'Behave now, little rogue.' He looked up as somebody approached. 'All right, Willie?'

'All right.' The man was as tall as Drew, but with the subtly different Highland accent. He smelled of diesel oil and fish. 'Is this your girl?'

'This is Irene. She's helping me leave Scotland for a while.'

The man's hand encircled Irene's like a clamp. 'Willie MacRae.' Used to the flabby grip of office workers, Irene winced involuntarily. Willie immediately opened his hand and apologised.

'Not at all,' Irene said. 'You caught me by surprise.'

'You're Canadian,' Willie accused.

'American.'

When Willie apologised for any offence, Irene immediately liked him.

'See that boat there?' Drew pointed to Kenny's craft. 'There's a man with a gun on board. He doesn't like me very much. Shall we get under way?'

'Aye, aye sir,' somebody said, with more than a touch of sarcasm.

'Are you absconding with his wife?' Willie looked Irene up and down and nodded approvingly. 'Good choice. Better class than the tarts you used to pick up.'

Unsure whether to feel complimented or insulted, Irene contented herself with a whispered comment to Drew that they would discuss his previous women later. She started as a powerful engine suddenly roared beneath her feet.

'Where are we going?'

'Straight over to Portsmouth, New Hampshire,' Drew told her, 'non stop, so you had better get some rest.'

Irene looked up, realising that she had not slept for over twenty-four hours. As the adrenalin drained from her system, the rush of tiredness took her by surprise, but she still gathered up the bag containing the sceptre before following Willie MacRae down below.

Irene had never seen anything quite like the vessel that carried her across the Atlantic. It was a millionaire's plaything, a yacht of such power that it made light of the three thousand miles of Atlantic waterway. She spent most of her time on deck, watching the long bows smash through the waves, but made occasional visits to a galley so modern it made her New York kitchen looked antique. Even Ms Manning would have been proud to own such a yacht.

'Is this yours, Drew?' Irene wondered, and felt slightly disappointed when he shook his head.

'Not on your life. I just know the skipper. Willie's what you call a ferryman. He picks up yachts for paying clients and delivers them wherever they are wanted. Some American billionaire bought this one and I hitched a ride.'

'It's beautiful.' Irene said. When she ran the Manning Corporation, she would buy a boat like this and call it *Johnnie Armstrong's Revenge*. The thought was cheering.

The fog came unexpectedly and Irene huddled into her coat when they nosed toward the North American coastline. However luxurious the boat, it did not run to a wardrobe of warm clothing for any female passengers that they happened to pick up, and even a July fog was chilling at this latitude.

'You all right?' Drew slid an arm around her as she stood on the greasy foredeck, staring into the amorphous mass ahead.

'Fine.' Irene suppressed a shiver. 'Typical, isn't it? We cross all those miles of sea and sail into this stuff just off America.'

'Shocking,' Drew agreed. 'I'm sure that the Pilgrim Fathers never had this trouble.' He gestured back to the cabin. 'Would you not be better inside? It's a hell of a lot warmer.'

'I'm fine,' Irene said. 'Besides, if we hit something, I can get off easier out here.'

Drew shook his head. 'We won't hit anything. Not with all the electronic equipment that she carries. According to Willie, she has integrated Simrad Radar, GPS, Chart plotter and echo sounder. It's like the starship *Enterprise* in there,' he nodded to the bridge.

'Thanks, but I'm not keen on boldly trekking.' Irene looked around her. She could see a yellowing glow ahead, as if America was calling to her through the fog, but even the powerful lights of the yacht could not penetrate the murk. On an impulse, she yelled out, only to hear her own words bounced back, distorted and unintelligible.

'Don't get too cold,' Drew advised, and returned back below.

With her radar circling steadily, the yacht crept on, engine hushed by the fog, her two-man crew quietly efficient and only Irene on deck. She shivered and pulled her coat closer to her throat, wondering how efficient the United States Customs would be, and how Ms Manning would greet her.

The yellow glow increased, shone bright for a second and vanished. America lay over there, just beyond that light. That was her home, her land of opportunity. For a long moment Irene stared into the fog, and then she fingered the Luckenbooth brooch and glanced upward at the bridge. She could see Drew, bowed over the controls, his face frowning in concentration, and she smiled. He was a good man, and whatever had motivated him into helping her, he deserved a reward.

'Drew.' Irene crept up behind him as he examined the fluorescent green dials that gave their position and bearing. 'Are you driving this boat?'

He turned around, shaking his head. 'Just being nosey.'

'Then leave that to Willie. I'm sure he knows what he's doing.' She crooked an enticing finger and he followed, with that slightly puzzled look on his face that meant he did not trust her.

Reaching out, Irene took hold of the front of his jacket and pulled him down the short ladder to the accommodation below. 'A toast to America,' she said, opening the door to her cabin.

The bunk was only a little narrower than Drew's bed in Edinburgh, and the steady motion of the boat had an almost aphrodisiac effect as she slipped off her clothes and stood naked before him.

'Well now,' Drew began to unbutton his shirt, his hands slow and easy.

Irene positioned herself directly in front of him, staring unsmiling into his eyes as she completed his undressing and ran her hands down his flanks and up the curve of his hips, where she stopped, running her thumb over her nails.

'This is a nice surprise,' he began, but she put a finger to his mouth.

'Shhh. Don't spoil the mood,' she said, straightened her fingers and patted the warm bulge of his buttocks. With Drew, there was no desire to hurt. 'Come on, now.' Lying slowly on top of the bed, she guided him on top of her.

The lighthouse at the entrance of Portsmouth harbour glimmered briefly through the porthole, illuminating the play of muscles on his body as he responded to her requests, and then Irene grinned, cupped his face and asked exactly what he wanted.

'A present from America,' she said, smiling, 'I promise not to be shocked.'

Drew shook his head, 'don't make promises that you cannot keep,' but his response pleased her and they made gentle love in the cabin until he dozed to sleep and she could slip away in the quiet light of morning.

Irene had never been in New Hampshire before, but she liked the brightly painted wooden houses of Portsmouth and the yellow-suited fishermen busy on the State Fishing Pier. She liked the bright American flag that hung limp from its pole and the long, measured accents of the men on the quay. She liked the pick-up trucks with their nautical contents and the women in tight denims who exchanged calm words over steaming mugs of coffee.

Stepping ashore as soon as the yacht tied up, Irene waved a fast farewell to Willie and vanished among the harbour side streets before anybody could ask where she was going.

She felt the brisk beating of her heart as she located an ATM and withdrew the first American money that she had seen in weeks, boarded a bus at random and sat back as it roared into the wooded countryside. It was good to see the familiar road signs and shops, but better to know that she was free in her own land and her future lay before her. Irene fingered the Luckenbooth brooch.

'Good-bye, Drew Drummond,' she said softly. 'I liked you a lot, but you helped me of your own free will. I never made any commitment.' She knew that she spoke only the truth, but still wondered why she had to justify herself. She hugged the canvas bag to her side. With the wriggling fish bait removed, the bag held only the sceptre and her destiny.

Chapter Twenty-Three: New York & Mannadu: August

Luxuriating in her own identity, Irene returned to her Manhattan apartment, greeting Mark with a friendly smile and an uncharacteristic kiss.

'Well now Miss Armstrong,' Mark stepped back slightly, one hand to his cheek. 'It's good to have you back. And will Mr McKim be joining you?'

'Never again, Mark,' Irene told him nothing but the truth. 'I am afraid he preferred the company of another woman.'

When Mark murmured something both embarrassed and incoherent, Irene allowed her hand to drift over his arm. 'I'm sure that I will soon find a suitable replacement,' she teased, and spent a bittersweet hour removing all traces of Patrick from her apartment. The sceptre looked good sitting on top of her kitchen table, and for one longing moment she wondered about keeping it. However, the rival temptation of power and prestige disposed of that frivolity.

Although Ms Manning had been at pains to hide the location of her hideaway, Irene knew that it was in the northern United States. It took her only half an hour with an atlas to work out that it was in South Dakota, and a few extra minutes with the Google Earth website helped her find the general area, although Ms Manning's influence had no doubt ensured that the building had been erased from any images.

With all the terrorist security constraints in operation, Irene travelled by train across America, lying back in comfort as she enjoyed the unified diversity of Americans and sipped strong coffee. She watched her own country unfolding on either side. 'Excuse me, but were you not on the television recently?' The speaker was male, quite presentable and under forty. Irene charmed him with an easy smile.

'I was,' she admitted. 'I was defeated in the final of *The Neophyte.*'

The return smile was genuine. 'So you were. Well, well done for reaching that far! I thought that you should have won, after fighting your way to the top.' Producing a business card, the man hesitated a little before handing it to her. 'I don't like to ask, but if you are ever looking for a position, I own a fairly successful chain of companies…'

Irene accepted the card. 'That is so kind of you!' She increased the intensity of her smile. 'I will certainly keep you in mind, Mr…' she checked the name on the card, 'Mr Johansson. I may well be in touch.'

She waited until Mr Johansson withdrew to his own seat, sat back and basked in the warm glow of recognition. Not long now and Ms Manning would also be offering her congratulations.

Irene rolled along Highway 29 in her hired Ford 4X4 pickup, enjoying the feeling of power of the massive engine. The Sioux Falls were well behind her, with their quota of excited children and baseball-hatted men from Eastern cities; the air was crisp, dry and clear, the land huge and open with none of the dampness that she had always felt in Scotland.

Once she past Beresford Irene headed west, into the vast plain that she remembered so well. With the radio tuned into a Country and Western station, she checked the map that she had drawn herself, crossed the Vermillion River and left the road for an unmarked track that hopefully led toward Ms Manning's property. There was a fence that stretched from horizon to horizon, and she drove alongside, jolting on the rough ground as she listened to the swish of grass beneath her wheels.

When Irene saw the speck far in the distance, she stopped her vehicle and raised the binoculars she had bought in Sioux Falls. Dull green, low and broad, it could only be a Jeep, and she grinned. No doubt the occupant was a member of Ms Manning's private army, come to check her out. Well, he was welcome.

Irene drove on, searching for the gate that she knew was here, somewhere. Everything had appeared so simple on the computer screen in her apartment, but this land was so vast that scale was deceptive. She drove on, very aware that the Jeep was closing fast. Far overhead, clouds gathered, promising a storm.

The sound of the shot shocked her and she stared at the rear-view mirror. A man was leaning out of the passenger window of the Jeep, pointing a rifle in the air. He shouted something, the words lost in the distance, and fired again. She heard the ripping whistle of a bullet passing close to the Ford.

'Welcome to the Manning Corporation,' Irene said, ducked down and pressed her foot hard on the gas. She masked the familiar apprehension with flippancy. 'Pedal to the metal, as they say.'

The Ford jumped ahead, bouncing on the rough ground, tossing Irene high up in the air and banging her painfully down. She gasped involuntarily and glanced in the mirror. The man had slid back inside the Jeep, which seemed to diminish in size as she accelerated.

'Come on boys!' Irene yelled. 'I must be getting close!' Strangely she was more excited than worried, for she knew that she was not yet trespassing, and could not imagine that any employee of Ms Manning would engage in casual murder. That shot had surely been only a warning.

Irene saw the gate in the distance. It was high, tubular steel and rigged with cameras. There was no mistaking the mark of Ms Manning. 'I'm home, boys, Irene Armstrong is coming to claim her life.'

The bullet sliced across the bonnet of the Ford, raising a thin sliver of metal in its passage.

Irene could not suppress her scream. She could see the Jeep, much closer now, with the rifle thrust through the side window. She saw the barrel of the rifle jerk, heard the report of another shot, but did not see what happened to the bullet.

'Fuck!' Irene ducked, trying to make herself as small a target as possible, peering over the steering wheel as she negotiated the rough terrain. Glancing in her mirror, she saw the Jeep power forward, cutting the angle between her and the gate. What was he trying to do? Surely Ms Manning had not demanded that every visitor to her property should be killed?

Swearing, Irene swung the wheel, hoping to arrive at the gate first, but the other driver was good. Anticipating her move, he sent his vehicle into a hand brake turn that sent the Jeep directly in front of her. She had no option but to pull aside, but screamed again as the Ford slammed sideways, its offside front wheel crashing into a hidden hole. She swore again, pushed the automatic gear into reverse and yelled, shouting every obscene word that she knew as the wheels spun, carving a useless groove in the prairie. Dust rose, but the Ford was immobile, its nose tilted at a frightening angle and one of its back wheels off the ground.

The sound of the engine mirrored Irene's own frustrated scream. She had come so far, only to end up in a hole a few short yards from success.

She swore again and banged her fists on the dashboard, but the Ford did not respond. Sliding free of the Ford, she looked up, seeing the fence a mere ten yards away, with the Manning property stretching beyond, the prize for which she had striven for so long just outside her reach. No! She would not give up. If she could not drive, then she would walk to Mannadu, however far it was.

'I am Irene Armstrong! There is nothing I cannot do!'

When she looked back, the Jeep had stopped directly in front of the gate. Dust drifted slowly upwards, clearing far above the height of the fence.

The passenger door opened and a man stepped out. Irene gasped as she recognised the sallow face and wiry red hair of Kenny Mossman.

'Kenny! It's me!' Irene pointed to the Luckenbooth brooch that she still wore. 'Irene! You remember me? You made this!'

Kenny nodded. Kneeling, he aimed the rifle directly at the brooch. 'You stole the Clach-bhuai,' he said, quietly. 'There is neither excuse nor reprieve.' As he spoke, the driver's door opened and the squat, bald man emerged. He walked slowly toward Irene, unsmiling. She remembered that his name was Iain.

'You have one choice,' Iain said. 'Hand over the sceptre, or we will shoot you and take it.'

Irene glanced toward Kenny. She remembered him as a quiet man with gentle humour, but when he levelled his rifle there was nothing in his eyes but determination.

Iain had left the Jeep and was walking toward her, his right hand extended, as if expecting her to tamely hand over the sceptre. She had thought of him as small and fat, but now he looked stocky and powerful, with a chin that thrust forward and forearms that filled the sleeve of his dark suit.

'You won't take it!' Irene backed away. She could see the fence arrowing into the distance, a barricade between the

Manning Corporation and the outside world, a barrier between the mediocre and the sublime. She knew on which side she belonged, and after so much effort, she would never give up. Swooping into the Ford, Irene snatched up her bag. 'Here it is! Here's your damned sceptre!' She saw Kenny's attention falter slightly as his eyes switched from the brooch on her breast to the bag. 'Come and get it boys, but be careful. If you shoot me you might hit the jewels!'

'Don't be stupid, Irene!' Kenny sounded hoarse. 'We don't want to hurt you. We just want the Clach-bhuai!'

'Come get it!' Turning, Irene began to run. She had no doubt that she could outdistance the stocky Iain, but Kenny would pose more of a problem. He was about her age and looked wiry, rather than thin, although his city pallor hinted that he was not much of an athlete.

She heard the crack of the rifle at the same time as she saw the little fountain of dust leap up five yards in front of her.

'Irene! Stop!'

Glancing over her shoulder, Irene saw Iain lumbering over the ground, but Kenny was on one knee, with the rifle pulled hard into his shoulder. At that range he could not miss, but she was determined not to surrender. It would be better to die here than to live in relative poverty, haunted always by the knowledge that things could have been so much better.

'Shoot then!' Thrusting the bag over her shoulder, so it would bounce across her back, Irene ran on. If Kenny's aim was out, he would damage the damned sceptre, and they would both have lost. If his aim were true, then all her troubles would be over. She ran on, hopelessly, stumbling over the long grass as her breath burned in her throat.

She heard Kenny curse, and then he was running too, so they both raced for the gate. Irene was the faster, but Kenny caught her as she struggled with the simple lock.

He was a lightweight, but so determined that his initial rush knocked her back. The bag skiffed across the waving grass and she swore again, frantic with fear. Kenny seemed to be all over her, all effort but no skill. Irene ducked a wild slap, thrust her knee hard into his groin and heard his agonised gasp. Kenny fell back and Irene wriggled free and scrabbled for the bag.

There was a man reaching it and for a shocking instant she recognised James Drummond, tall and elderly with eyes as hard as anthracite. Instinctively ducking low, Irene pushed the bag away, rolled across the ground and held it close to her body.

'Leave that!' Drummond's voice was sharp, but before he could move the gate opened and a small convoy erupted from beyond the barrier. The largest vehicle sped between her and Drummond.

'I've won!' Irene held up her bag, 'Armstrong's revenge!'

She watched as two of the Manning vehicles hustled around the Jeep, which backed away and roared toward the highway. She saw Drummond watching her, his face looking old and defeated through the Jeep's rear windscreen

Irene recognised the largest vehicle as the Ford Expedition King Ranch, with the Manning logo on its doors and same laconic driver who had brought her here so many months ago. The passenger door opened.

'You'd have been a lot quicker if you had trusted me!' Drew grinned at her across three yards of prairie. 'Running off like that, I was so disappointed in you!' Stepping out of the vehicle, he held the door open for her. 'Come on then, you little rogue. Ms Manning is waiting for you.'

'Oh, sweet Lord in heaven.' Irene felt the strength seep from her legs as Drew strode toward her, arms extended. She felt him catch her as she fell.

They sat under a shaded bower looking over the courtyard, with the playful splash of the fountain a backdrop to their conversation.

'So you made it then, Irene.' Ms Manning was as direct and calm as ever.' 'You found an amazingly historic artefact, obtained it and brought it here against many odds.'

Irene nodded. 'Yes, but I don't understand. How does Drew Drummond fit into this?' She leaned back in her seat, allowing the high sun to warm her face.

'I work for Ms Manning,' Drew told her. 'She paid me good money to look after you. Which was an enjoyable job in itself, mind you.'

'So you knew all the time? About the Honours, I mean?'

Drew shrugged. 'I had a fair idea when I watched you sniffing about Edinburgh Castle, then my father mentioned something about a threat to the Clach-bhuai and I put two and two together. It was not hard, really.'

'What's the Clach-bhuai? Another name for this?' Irene lifted the sceptre that she had carried from the Old World to the New. Although she had brought it specifically for Ms Manning, she could not bear to let it go.

'Just the top part, that wee bit of crystal,' Drew pointed out the orb. 'There is religious significance. It was used by the Druids it seems, and maybe by Pontius Pilate.'

'Is that so? I met his bodyguard in Edinburgh.' Irene examined the crystal. 'It doesn't look very special.'

'Oh, it's special enough.' Drew grinned. 'And you fought off the Society out there. That was something.'

'So it was,' Ms Manning agreed. 'And what was just as important, you did not reveal for whom you stole it, not even to your lover.'

Irene could not stop the blood from flushing to her face. 'You know about that?'

'I asked Drew to test you. If you had revealed my name, or even hinted who I was, you would have lost the final challenge and Drew would have taken the sceptre back the same day.'

Irene glanced at Drew, who shrugged and nodded. 'Nothing personal, Irene. All in a day's work, you understand.'

'So you were playing with me all along,' Irene shook her head, 'you cold blooded bastard.'

'Thank you. I notice you slipped the leash as soon as you thought I could no longer help you. Greyhound bus to New York, railroad to South Dakota, hired car from Sioux Falls; nice itinerary.'

'Were you following me all the way?' Irene felt anger battling with the smug satisfaction of achievement.

'Look.' Drew slipped off the battered silver watch that Irene had admired. He flicked back the face and she saw a map of the area, with a constant red light in the centre. 'That's you. My watch is connected to the Manning satellites, so I can follow you wherever you go. That's how I could help you in Edinburgh, when these neds attacked you, remember? And I traced you to the Botanic Garden after?'

Irene felt small as she stared at the watch. 'So you've known where I was all along? I still don't understand.'

Leaning forward, Drew allowed the back of his hand to smooth against her breast as he unclipped the Luckenbooth brooch. 'There is a tiny transmitter in the back of this jewellery. I like the irony, with a member of the Society providing so much help.' His grin revealed that he enjoyed the

291

humour of the situation. 'When I first gave you the brooch, it was just that, one of Kenny's Luckenbooth brooches. But when you rejected it – and hurt me dreadfully, of course – I added the transmitter.'

'So it was never a love token then,' Irene said.

'Love token?' Drew shook his head. 'Hardly that, Irene; you were part of the job; nothing more.'

Irene looked up quickly and caught the lie in his eyes. 'I thought the same about you,' she said, carelessly. She prised the transmitter from the back of the Luckenbooth and replaced the brooch back on her breast. 'As Ms Manning told me once, it's a tough life at the top, and there is no place for a partner.' She looked at Drew with new respect. 'I will wear this forever, as a reminder that even the best of men could be a fraudulent bastard. In future I will fly alone, Drew, but better that than a life on the streets.' In her head she heard the mocking chorus of the crowd.

'On the streets! On the streets!'

Laughing, Irene touched the crystal of the Clach-bhuai. She could sense the approval of her father and Johnnie Armstrong.

* * * *

'Damned shame really,' Meigle said.

'What was that?' Drummond held a hand to his ear. 'I can't hear you for the noise in this place.' He looked around at the crowd who had come in to the bar. 'It's always the same when there's a medal competition. The place fills up with all these youngsters who don't understand the traditions of the game. Shouting and drinking and getting above themselves.'

Meigle nodded. 'It's a damned disgrace, Jamie. Mind you, I remember a young couple riding a tandem around here for a bet. Stark naked too, the pair of them.'

Drummond grunted. 'She was a good-looking girl too, in those days. That's why I married her.'

'I know. But it's still a damned shame,' Meigle flapped a hand toward the television screen that occupied one corner of the room. 'Look at that fellow. Well set up, good looking in an American sort of way, nice wife, and he loses his job just like that.'

'What fellow?' Drummond

'That fellow on the television,' Meigle said.

'Kendrick Dontell,' the announcer said, 'who won *The Neophyte* last year, has been sensationally sacked. Ms Rhondda Manning of the Manning Corporation refused to give details, but has revealed that the runner up, Irene Armstrong, is to take Kendrick's place. That means that Armstrong will fall heir to the power and wealth of Ms Manning, who has a reputed 20 billion dollar fortune.'

'That's the girl that your Andrew was running around with,' Meigle said. 'Twenty billion dollars, eh? That's nice money.'

'Nice enough, but he dumped her.' Drummond glanced at the clock above the bar and stood up. 'Time for another round, I think?'

'Why not indeed.' Meigle reached for his clubs. He followed Drummond outside the clubhouse and took a deep breath of the East Lothian air. There was a haar creeping in from the Forth, hazing the white cliffs of the Bass Rock.

'So we've got the Clach-bhuai back and all is right with the world.' Meigle dropped the ball at his feet and addressed it, hardly glancing up the length of the fairway that he knew so well.

'It's only a pity that we can't put the sceptre where it belongs,' Drummond looked out to sea. 'Spoils the set without it.'

'Can't be helped.' Meigle took a practise shot, then cracked the ball a full three hundred yards. 'That beats your average, Sandy.' He watched Drummond tee up. 'Bit of a near run thing, though, with you switching the thing when Kenny was diverting the Armstrong woman.'

'She damned near killed him too.' Drummond sent his ball in the wake of Meigle's, grunting when it bounced a yard short, and then rolled past. 'We'll let the Manning people bask in their triumph for a few years yet, and then sensationally find the genuine article hidden in the castle of some old Border reiver.' He gave an ironic smile. 'Maybe Hollows Tower, Johnnie Armstrong's keep. That would be fitting.'

Meigle nodded. 'Did that woman really think that we would let the Clach-bhuai go so easily? We've been guarding it for near three thousand years.'

Drummond laughed as he strode beside Meigle. 'How many copies of the Honours have the Mossman family made since the sixteenth century? About eight? Well, now that Andrew is back on this side of the Pond, we'll soon bring him into the fold again. All he needs is a good woman.'

Meigle smiled. 'Maybe so, but that last shot of yours has rolled into the rough.'

'Damn it,' Drummond said. 'I never did understand this game.'